MY COMMANDER

BEWITCHED AND BEWILDERED

ALANEA ALDER

AWARD-WINNING AUTHOR

www.sacredforestpublishing.com
P.O.Box 280
Moyock, NC, 27958
ISBN:
Digital ISBN-13: 978-1-941315-00-2
Print ISBN-13: 978-1-941315-01-9
Sacred Forest Publishing

Cover Design and Interior format by The Killion Group
http://thekilliongroupinc.com

DEDICATION

To my street team, I couldn't have done this without you! You really are my Angels!

Also, a huge thank you to my family for giving me the space to get this one written, hope you enjoy the new world of Lycaonia and discovering it with Meryn.

~ *Amor Vincit Omnia* —
Love Conquers All ~

PROLOGUE

"Aiden, come find me!" the soft voice teased. Aiden looked around; he was in the forest between the Alpha and Beta estates. Stumbling blindly, he couldn't see where she was hiding. A growing sense of dread had his heart beating out of control.

"Quit playing and come out," he yelled.

"Sourpuss!" Her feminine laughter echoed off the trees.

"Come on now, no more playing," he called out. There was nothing but silence.

"That's not funny, come out!"

"Aiden!" Her scream shattered the silence. He ran toward her voice. When he got to the clearing, he bellowed out his rage. She was lying in a growing pool of blood. Her long, brown hair framed her petite body on either side. She wore a delicate white lace summer dress and was the most beautiful woman he had ever seen. She was his mate, and she was dying. He raced over and dropped to his knees, lifting her small body into his arms.

"Stay with me, baby, please!" he begged.

"Why didn't you look for me?" Her large green eyes held so much pain.

"I didn't know." He choked on the words.

"I would have loved you forever." And then her eyes closed.

Aiden sat up in bed clutching his chest. He had been dreaming of this woman for the past two weeks, with her long, soft brown hair, expressive green eyes and pale skin. She looked so innocent and fragile. Most nights the dreams were wonderful, but the nightmares had started three nights ago and he was scared to death that his mate was out there and he had no idea where to find her.

He swung his legs over the bed and leaned forward, elbows on his knees, face in his hands. He tried to shake off the feeling that something was terribly wrong. Sighing, he sat up and scrubbed his hands over his face. He stood and decided against taking a shower; they were doing drills today and he would be sweaty and rank in less than an hour anyway.

He put on his training gear and went downstairs. Gavriel was at the table frowning into his coffee mug.

"You too?" Aiden asked. Gavriel looked up and nodded.

So far, they were the only two in their unit who had started dreaming of their mates. In theory he understood the elders' concerns for the next generation. At first, casting a spell to bring their mates to them had seemed extreme, but with his nightmares came a growing sense of urgency. Maybe they had been right after all. Damn.

"Bad?" Aiden asked turning his attention back to his second in command.

"I think my mate may be mentally retarded, either that or she has a severe inner ear imbalance. Every night it's as if I watch her from afar, I have never seen a more accident-prone person in my life. I fear she will get herself killed before I can find her," Gavriel scowled. Aiden winced. Gavriel was one of the most elegant and graceful men he knew. What could Fate be thinking, pairing him with a woman like that?

"You?" Gavriel asked.

"She was murdered again. I didn't get there in time," Aiden whispered. Gavriel set his cup down.

"Aiden, you say the word, and we will begin looking for her."

"Thank you. I would accept, but I have no idea where to start."

"You two look especially gloomy this morning." Colton breezed in and immediately went to the coffee pot.

"Had trouble sleeping," Gavriel said smoothly, nodding at Aiden with a knowing look. Aiden smiled back; he was grateful that he didn't have to discuss his nightmare further.

"So what's on the agenda for today?" Colton turned, holding his favorite mug. It was a caricature of a busty beer maiden holding two beer steins; the caption read "I like big jugs and I cannot lie." Aiden felt himself begin to smile. Only Colton could pull him out of his bad moods so easily.

"We're doing drills." Aiden sipped his coffee.

"Which ones?"

"All of them."

Colton choked on his coffee. "All of them?"

"All of them. Every mother's son of you. We go until we drop." Aiden figured that if he had to push himself to exhaustion to avoid dreaming, he was dragging the men along for the miserable ride.

"Can I call in sick?" Colton faked a cough.

"No. Call Lorcan and Sascha; we're training with Beta and Gamma today. Let them know we'll be using our facilities." Aiden drained his coffee cup as Gavriel stood and finished what was left of his. They headed out to the unit's training grounds, leaving Colton to moan and groan behind them. Aiden began calling out drill exercises to the early arrivals. He turned to stare at the woods.

It was just a dream. She isn't real. Aiden exhaled and concentrated on the men. He didn't need a woman cluttering up his life, and he sure as hell didn't need the distraction.

CHAPTER ONE

"I love rock and roll, so put another coin in the jukebox, baby." Meryn turned up the volume on her iPod and jammed along with Joan Jett. She had woken up to an overwhelming need to go exploring, so she had shoved her laptop into her backpack and jumped in her car. Thirty minutes later, she parked on the side of an old country road and headed out on foot. She was now staring at a high, very official-looking chain link fence. Her inborn sense of curiosity, which had gotten her into more than one scrape in the past, coupled with the strange feeling to go forward, was pushing her to scale the fence and see what lay beyond. Shrugging, she started to climb. She quickly came to the conclusion that climbing fences was much harder than it looked on TV. She cleared the top, climbed down a few feet and then jumped the rest of the way down. Bopping her head to the music, she looked around and began to walk forward.

It was October and the crisp autumn air that smelled of leaves and earth made it a perfect day for hiking and exploring. She zipped her hoodie closed as a cloud passed over the sun, lowering the afternoon temperature. She always wore her hoodies three sizes too large, which made them comfortable and snuggly like a blanket. She had been waiting for fall weather all summer so she could begin wearing her hoodies again.

The only thing she didn't like about wearing them was that they usually covered up her favorite t-shirts. Today she was sporting a vintage *Teenage Mutant Ninja Turtles* tee she had found at the thrift store. She had layered that over a white thermal and was happy with the result. Graphic tees were her weakness.

As the wind picked up, she started to second-guess cutting her hair. She ran a hand over the short pixie cut and grinned. She loved how easy it was to take care of, and it was a fun, sassy look. But damn if the back of her neck wasn't getting cold. *Note to self. Buy more scarves!* She was about to continue with her walk when movement out of the corner of her eye had her freezing mid-step. She turned to see a tall, blond man with green eyes staring at her with an amused look as he leaned against a... was that an assault rifle? She pulled her earbuds out of her ears.

"Um, hello."

"Hello, little one. Did you know you're on private property?"

"Really? I had no idea," Meryn fudged.

He raised an eyebrow. "The ten foot fence right behind you didn't give it away?"

Meryn turned to look at the fence.

"How'd that get there?" She pretended to be shocked.

"You're funny. But not funny enough to avoid trouble." He took a step forward and she took a step back.

"I was just curious about what was back here."

More men began to pour out of the woods on all sides. Panicked, she turned and ran for the fence. Large hands grabbed at her and pulled her backward.

“Put me down, you asshole!” She screamed as the men looked at each other in shock.

“Quit squirming. Ow! Stop trying to kick me in the balls!” the blond man yelled as Meryn flailed uselessly.

“This is assault and battery!”

“You're the one assaulting me, you crazy female! I think you broke my nose!” Finally, he gained control and held her out in front of him, grasping her upper arms.

Meryn looked around helplessly as she dangled in his grasp. Her hopes for escape plummeted when she saw that they were now completely surrounded by no less than twelve huge men, all carrying weapons.

“Okay, I saw this movie and I didn't like it. Can I just go home now?” She took in their military gear and closed her eyes. “I didn't see anything, I swear.”

“Who sent you?” Meryn opened her eyes to see another blond man stepping forward. At first she thought he might be related to the guy holding her, but this man had amber-colored eyes, not green. He also had higher cheekbones and fuller lips. It was a gorgeous combination.

“No one.”

“So you just decided to climb a random fence, just to see what was on the other side?” There was no hiding the sarcasm in that question.

She nodded frantically. “Actually, yeah. I just moved to town and today when I woke up, I had this overwhelming urge to go exploring. It pushed me here.” She noticed how the men gave each other meaningful looks.

“So are you guys like paramilitary? Secret CIA training base? That would be cool,” Meryn asked.

All eyes turned back to her. She flinched and closed her eyes again.

"I mean, I see nothing, I hear nothing and I most definitely won't say shit."

The man behind her snorted as the sound of men approaching had her opening her eyes again. Out of the woods, two more men appeared. One looked like he glided over the fallen leaves; the other trampled through them recklessly, his deep blue eyes hard. He looked like he was the type of man who wore a perpetual scowl.

The angry one looked her over. "What's your name?"

"These are not the droids you are looking for," she said. The smaller, auburn-haired man to her left cracked up. The hulking man glared at him.

"Quiet, Keelan." He turned his gaze back to her.

"Come on, that's *Star Wars*," Keelan explained.

"She fights star type wars?" he asked concerned.

She looked up at him. "Seriously?"

He opened his mouth to answer and froze. He closed his eyes and dropped his head back. His muscled chest expanded as he took a deep breath. His entire body shuddered. His head snapped back and when he looked her up and down he had a stunned expression on his face.

"You cut your hair," he whispered.

She nodded, then froze. How in the hell did he know that? Meryn began to struggle to get down. Something freaky was going on and she had to get out of there.

"So, what do we do with her?" her captor asked, shaking her small frame as if she were a rag doll. The large man's eyes turned solid black and a low rumble emanated from his throat. Growling he stepped forward and pulled her from the blond man's hands and into the curve of his body. He snapped and snarled at the other men.

"Get back! That woman is his mate! Back off, that's an order, Colton!" a dark-haired man yelled. Meryn felt the huge man rub his cheek on the top of her head almost as if he were trying to get his scent on her. She felt a rush of panic when the men began to move away. They looked normal. They weren't snarling and growling. She reached a hand out to the blond man.

"Please! Don't let him take me!"

The blond man looked torn. "Aiden, she's scared! Calm down!" he yelled.

A roar from the man holding her nearly burst her eardrums. He slung her over his shoulder and ran from the clearing. She thrashed to get down. Her stomach was killing her from where his shoulder kept squashing her insides as he ran. Grabbing his waist she bit his back over his kidney. Roaring, he flipped her around and cradled her in his arms. His pace quickened as he turned and darted through the trees.

"Neanderthal! Put me down! Put me down, now!" Her tiny fists beat on his chest and head. He ignored her efforts. When a large house came into view, she struggled more, knowing that if he got her inside, she would never be able to leave. It had zero effect on the man. He kicked the door in.

The downstairs became a blur as he moved through the house. He ran up the stairs and down a long hallway. Too soon, he was opening a door. He quickly closed it behind him before setting her down. He stood back, smiling down at her. He was still smiling when she jumped and her fist connected with his nose. He shook his head looking like he was trying to focus.

"Let me go!" Her foot slammed into his shin and he let out an undignified yelp.

"Woman, quit hitting me!" he bellowed.

"This is kidnapping and false imprisonment!" She slung her backpack forward and pulled out her phone. He plucked it from her hand. He grabbed her backpack to take it from her, but she held on tight with both hands.

Frustrated, he lifted it over her head but she still didn't let go; she simply dangled from the straps. He shook it and finally she lost her grip and fell to the floor. She scowled up at him from a sitting position.

"You're the soft, feminine woman from my dreams? My delicate innocent? You, with your short hair, dirty sneakers and preadolescent male clothing?" He sounded confused. He leaned forward and inhaled again.

"Why are you sniffing me?" She scooted away, crab-walking backward on her hands and feet.

"Oh, God, is this like *Silence of the Lambs*?" Tears flowed down her face. "I don't want to go down the hole! I won't put lotion on the skin! Look at me, you won't be able to wear my skin, I won't cover your huge ass!" she wailed.

He took a careful step backward.

"I'll be back." He turned and fled from the room. She heard a small metallic *click* as the door was locked. She then heard something that had her brain working overtime.

"My mate is fucking nuts!"

Meryn jumped up when the door shut, and tried to open it. Dammit, she *was* locked in. Mate? What did he mean by *mate*? She ran to the window and looked down. She was at least three stories up, so jumping out was impossible. She was about to turn back to the room when she saw the man who had grabbed her from the fence run into the backyard. The huge, snarly man. Aiden had called the blond man Colton. She watched as Colton began to strip out of his clothing. She tilted her head to admire the view. He had a great ass. A moment later she started to think that one of the military guys had slipped her some hallucinogens, because one second Colton was a man with a fine ass, the next he was a huge dog running into the woods.

She stumbled back from the window, tripped over an expensive-looking rug and fell flat on her butt. She was in a world of shit now. Fact one: the big guy that growled and brought her back here had to be one of the sexiest men she had ever seen in her life. Actually, all of the men were gorgeous, but there was something about that hulking brute that just made her want to snuggle up and take a nap...after a long afternoon of hot sex. Fact two: at least one guy here turned into a dog. Fact three: no one seemed all that concerned that she had been taken, so help was probably not on its way. She was on her own. Why did all the crazy stuff happen to her? Did she just attract crazy shit?

She heard the door open and the big guy walked in slowly before shutting the door behind him. She stood and backed up until she hit the wall. He held up his hands.

"Your name is Aiden, right?" she asked. Somehow, giving him a name made him slightly less scary and more likely to be reasoned with.

He nodded. "I'm not going to hurt you."

His deep, sexy voice should be outlawed.

"I'm sure that's what all the serial killers say to their victims." She eyed the lamp on the nightstand.

"I just want to talk." His words were careful and he spoke in gentle tones.

"I suppose you want to talk about your dog people." She edged closer to the nightstand.

"Dog people? Oh, you saw Colton. Right. How do I explain this?" He rubbed the back of his neck, his face taking on a sheepish expression. If he weren't her abductor, she would say he looked adorable.

"Start with the dog thing." she suggested.

"Colton is one of the men in the unit that I serve with. Each man in the unit is a little... *different* than most people. Colton happens to be a shifter. He can turn into a wolf."

Meryn blinked. Then blinked again. Without looking away from him, she ran her fingers over the heavy looking lamp base.

"So you're a wolf?" she asked, not really wanting to know the answer.

He looked offended. "Of course not."

She let out a relieved breath.

"I'm a bear."

She closed her eyes. "Why me? Why does this shit always happen to me?" When she opened her eyes he had moved a little closer. She tensed. He leaned in and sniffed her hair.

"Are you sniffing me?" she asked incredulously.

"I want to be sure. Let me ask you something, are you drawn to me?" His eyebrows were bunched together as he frowned down at her.

"Do you mean do I want to have hot, sweaty sex with you?" she asked.

"No! Wait. Do you?" he asked hopefully.

"Not answering that."

"Right." Aiden thought for a second before asking. "Do you know about animals?"

"I guess I know what most people know."

"Do you know that wolves mate for life?"

"So do swans." She had seen that on *National Geographic*. He looked surprised.

"They do? Really?"

"Yup," she nodded.

"I never knew that."

"What was your point?"

"Sorry, got distracted. The point is that people like me, and the 'dog people' like Colton, we only get one mate in life, like wolves in the wild. You are my mate." He smiled down at her.

Oh God, he wanted to mate with her!

She grabbed the lamp and pulled the wire from the socket.

"Is this some freaky-ass cult?" She threw the lamp as hard as she could at him. She smiled in satisfaction when it bounced off his head. The satisfaction was short lived when he turned his irritated gaze her way. She jumped on the bed and kept going until she backed into the corner with the second nightstand at her back and the king size mattress between them.

"I won't become part of the collective. I refuse to have your babies. Resistance isn't futile!" she screamed and picked up the second lamp. He turned and fled the room. Breathing hard, she put the lamp down with shaking hands. He seemed to run from objects thrown at him. She decided she needed to search the room and bathroom for more projectile objects. Feeling better now that she had even a small plan she got to work.

Aiden sat downstairs with his men around him. He let Lorcan's unit set up patrols in case any other women decided to scale their perimeter fences. How could one tiny woman cause so much damn trouble?

"She's lively," Darian said consolingly.

"I have no idea what she is saying half the time," Aiden groaned.

"She's female; of course you don't," Keelan said.

"Let her calm down. She's been up there for the past couple of hours, she should be getting hungry. Maybe by providing food, you can show her that you mean to take care of her and be a good mate," Gavriel suggested.

"That's not a bad idea. I know food always makes me feel better." Aiden nodded. Maybe a nice quiet dinner where they could get to know one another was just the thing they needed.

"Do we have any food here?"

"Leftovers from that Italian place we went to the other day, it should still be good," Keelan reminded him.

"Okay. I'm going to try to feed her and get her to listen." Aiden stood with a renewed sense of purpose. His men on the other hand, looked worried.

"I'm sure everything will be okay." He smiled, feeling more and more confident. He could, after all, handle one small human female.

She heard him at the door and jumped up. Grabbing the heavy porcelain toilet back, she ran over and climbed up on the long dresser next to the door. She held her breath when the door inched open. He had only taken a single step inside the room when she brought the toilet back down on his head as hard as she could. He fell to his knees with a loud crash. Two Styrofoam containers dropped out of his hands and landed on the floor. He floundered around on all fours before falling forward. Shaking, she dropped the toilet back, hopped down and ran out of the room. Just outside the door she spotted her backpack on the floor. She grabbed it and sprinted through the hallway and down the stairs. If she could just get outside, she could make her way back to the fence and find her car. She was about to open the front door when she was grabbed from behind. The blond man, Colton, held her again.

"Let me go!"

"No way, small fry." A pain-filled roar echoed from upstairs.

"Okay, I know I pissed him off, please let me go."

"What did you do?"

"Hit him over the head with the back of the toilet," she whispered.

"Seriously?" Colton began to shake with laughter, never loosening his grip. She twisted and turned in an effort to get away. Loud footsteps had her looking up. Aiden, looking furious, stomped down the stairs cursing and rubbing the back of his head. Not stopping, he grabbed her by the arm, swung open the front door and dragged her outside.

"What are you doing, Aiden?" Colton asked, jogging behind them.

Aiden was taking such large strides he was literally dragging her along. They didn't stop until they came to a car. He opened the back and threw her in. He got in the driver's seat and she began to kick at the back of his head. When her sneaker bounced off for the second time, he got out, opened the door and grabbed her again. When she saw where he was about to put her she began crying.

"Please, don't!" He tossed her in the trunk and slammed it shut. Darkness began to close in on all sides.

"Dammit! She's human, Aiden, you can't drive around with her in the trunk," she heard Colton yell.

"I'm not going far."

"Where are we going?" The voices were getting further away.

"My parents' house." The two car doors shutting vibrated the frame of the car. Seconds later, the engine started and she could feel them moving. She reached into her backpack and fished around for her phone. She turned it on and her heart sank. No service. Crying softly in fear and frustration, she prayed he wouldn't kill her.

CHAPTER TWO

When the car stopped, Meryn was exhausted. She had been kicking the roof of the trunk the entire trip. She heard the doors open and shut, then male laughter.

"You're going to have to get that hammered out," she heard Colton say.

"Goddamn, woman!" The trunk flew open and she scowled up at the men. Their bodies were black silhouettes blocking out the brightness of the sun. Aiden reached in and pulled her from the trunk. He half dragged, half carried her up the path to a very expensive-looking mansion. The front door opened and a man in butler attire, without batting an eye, stepped aside for Aiden to enter.

"Shall I inform your parents of your arrival, sir?" Meryn stared; he was the quintessential butler. Perfectly combed gray hair. Clean shaven. Crisp collar and well knotted tie. She looked down. Yup. Even his shoes were polished to a glossy black.

"Is your name Alfred?" she asked, unable to help herself. He winked at her, his eyes kind.

"My name is Marius Steward, and you are?" he asked, eyeing Aiden, who held her upper arm nearly over her head, which had her lurching around on tiptoe.

"My name is Meryn Evans. I've been kidnapped by this crazy asshole who wants me to join his cult, have his babies and wear my skin. Can you call the police, please?" Bushy gray eyebrows shot up, though the man's facial expression never changed. Aiden snarled down at her.

"He *what*?" a female voice exclaimed. Meryn looked up the grand staircase as the most elegant couple she had ever seen descended toward them. The woman wore her honey blonde hair up in a Victorian style bun. Her light brown eyes flashed as she moved forward. Her lavender dress was layers of lace and satin, cinched around a tiny waist. The man at her side wore a dark suit and cravat. They looked like they had just walked out of a scene from *Pride and Prejudice*. Meryn couldn't help the tiny sigh of envy. Never in a million years could she look like that.

"Aiden, what have you told this poor child? And let go of her arm; you'll pull it out of the socket like that," the woman admonished. Aiden immediately released her arm. Meryn eyed the woman with new respect. If she had Aiden hopping to, then maybe she could help her get out of here.

"She is a menace! She gave Colton a bloody lip, threw a lamp at me, knocked me unconscious with the back of my toilet, kicked me in the back of the head... twice, and dented the roof of my trunk!" Meryn noticed that he roared the last grievance. Trust a man to be more worried about his car than his possible concussion.

"And *how* did she dent the roof of your trunk?" Meryn heard the edge to the woman's voice and answered quickly, hoping to garner sympathy for her situation.

"He threw me in the trunk of his car. I was kicking it from the inside trying to escape." She sniffed dramatically and glared at Aiden. She noticed that he had suddenly paled.

"Oh, son." The handsome older man covered his face with his hand and the woman stared at them in shock.

"You locked her in the trunk?"

"She was kicking me," Aiden protested.

"She is human and half your size!"

"You don't understand--she is a terrorist!"

"She is your mate, isn't she?" the woman asked. Meryn started to feel uneasy. There was that *mate* word again.

"Maybe," Aiden muttered under his breath. He stuck his hands in his pockets and stared at the floor. Meryn looked over to see Colton grinning like an idiot taking the whole thing in. She frowned at him. He winked at her.

Yup, an idiot.

"You couldn't explain things to her in a normal way? You had to kidnap and assault her?" the woman demanded, her hands on her hips accentuating her small waist. Meryn looked down at the puffy layers of her extra-large hoodie, worn jeans and dirty sneakers. Yeah, there was no comparison.

"I tried to serve her dinner and that was when she hit me over the head."

"I was trying to escape. You had me locked up for hours," Meryn clarified.

"That's because you threw the lamp at me and were screaming about cults. I was letting you calm down." Aiden glared down at her; she glared right back. The sound of hands clapping together had them both looking at the woman.

"This is what we're going to do. We're going to go to the kitchen and let Marius make us a nice pot of tea. We'll sit down and I'll try to answer your questions. Please know that you are not in any danger. In fact every single person in this room would gladly defend you against any possible threat. You're in the safest place you could be." The woman stepped forward and looped an arm through hers. They walked toward the back of the house. Meryn hoped that after their explanation maybe they would just let her go. The woman leaned forward and whispered.

"His bark is worse than his bite. He's a good man. He has dedicated his life to protecting our people." The woman patted her arm.

"He doesn't like me," Meryn whispered.

"Why do you say that?" The woman asked.

"Because I don't look like you. He knew I had cut my hair, I don't think he likes how I look with it short. He said I look like a boy." Meryn ran a hand over her short-cropped curls and the woman laughed.

"Trust me, dear, he wouldn't want a mate that looked like his mother." Meryn stopped and stared.

There was no way this woman was his mother!

The woman pulled her along until they were in the kitchen. Meryn momentarily forgot about the woman's age and gawked at the room in front of her. The magazine-cover-worthy kitchen had warm, light brown stone countertops, industrial stainless steel appliances and even a brick oven. This was every chef's or baker's dream kitchen. They all sat down around a large, dark wood table. The woman's words started to sink in.

"You're his mother? No way! You're not old enough to be his mother."

"Thank you for that, darling, but I'm older than I look."

Meryn edged away in her chair. "You're dog people too, aren't you?"

The woman looked at her, confused.

"She means shifters. She saw Colton shift in the yard," Aiden explained to his mother.

"Sweetheart, Aiden is a bear; we're his parents, that makes us bears as well. My name is Adelaide McKenzie and this is my mate, Byron McKenzie. You of course have met Aiden. The blond man, who looks entirely too amused at my son's discomfort, is his childhood best friend Colton Albright, and the delightful man who is making our tea for us is my squire, Marius Steward." Adelaide made the introductions and Meryn nodded and kept her mouth shut. The less they knew about her the better.

"I hope you like Earl Grey, little miss." Marius set a fragile looking china cup and saucer in front of her. As he poured the dark liquid in her cup the floral scent of bergamot filled the air. She inhaled deeply. Earl Grey had always been a favorite. He held up a sugar bowl filled with tiny white cubes and a pair of tongs.

"Four, please." He nodded, and with practiced ease dropped four of the sugar cubes in her cup. She picked up a tiny silver spoon and began to stir.

"Four?" Aiden stared.

"I like it sweet."

"So do I." Byron smiled at her kindly and took three cubes.

"Now, in all the ruckus, did my son explain that you were his mate?" Adelaide asked sipping her tea.

"He said we were mates, but I kinda freaked out after that."

"That's understandable, considering the situation." Byron shot an amused look at his son.

"How could he know that we are mates? We've just met," Meryn asked. She still didn't quite believe this was happening, but seeing Colton shift had definitely swayed things in her mind. Either they were telling the truth, or her genius mind had finally cracked. She personally didn't think that she was that weak, so that only left the explanation that they weren't lying and really were bear people.

"Being shifters, we know by scent," Adelaide explained.

"So that's why he kept sniffing me," Meryn mused out loud, and Byron laughed.

"A mate's scent to a male is like catnip to a cat; we can't get enough of it." Aiden's father leaned over and buried his nose in Adelaide's neck, breathing deeply. He smiled at his mate as if to make the point.

"So, Colton with the great ass, is a dog shifter?" Meryn asked. Aiden growled loudly.

"I do have a great ass," Colton admitted, beaming.

Aiden's father ran a hand over his mouth smiling. Aiden stood, sending his chair flying backward.

"You shouldn't be looking at anyone else's ass!" he bellowed, chest heaving. Thirty minutes ago, she would have been terrified, but he had kidnapped her, stuffed her in his trunk and manhandled her. She had met his parents and saw their love for each other and their son, and it had changed her perception of him. She was no longer afraid of him. He was just a grumpy, spoiled-ass bear and she was tired of his growling.

She stood, ready to bellow back when she noticed that he towered over her. Grumbling, she climbed onto the chair. She was still only about chin level. He smirked down at her. Seething in frustration, she climbed on top of the table and put her finger right in his face.

"Don't you *dare* tell me what to do! I am a grown woman, and if I want to look at naked men, I will!" She knew she was screeching but couldn't help it--this man drove her nuts.

"You want to look at naked men, start with me!" Aiden whipped off his shirt and stood in front of her his hands on his hips.

All coherent thought flew from her mind. Meryn felt her IQ dropping along with her eyes as she took in every... single... inch of him. The man was a work of art. Never before had she seen something so perfect. He was built, but not bulky. His muscles had definition and she appreciated every dip and ridge. Her eyes moved down his body and the view only got better. Mentally she traced each rigid valley that made up his eight-pack. Her eyes followed the smattering of dark hairs down until she was looking at where his pants began. She couldn't help her physical reaction to him if she tried. Groaning, he pulled her off of the table and into his arms. His lips found hers and her world changed forever.

She had never felt such need, such urgency as she did when his tongue twined around hers. It was as if he was inhaling her, absorbing every breath and drop of sweat. He fed from her lips as if he was dying and she was his last meal. Vaguely, she was aware of everyone quietly leaving the kitchen, but she didn't care. All she wanted was this man, forever. She had gone her entire life without ever experiencing this drowning need, and now that she had, she would never let it go. It was as if her body was coming alive for the first time under his touch.

She wrapped her legs around his waist and practically climbed up his body. She buried her hands in his hair and allowed him to dominate her mouth. He pulled away and she whimpered. His lips traced her ear and her breath caught; when his soft lips trailed down the slope of her neck, she moaned. He pulled away again and she noticed that his eyes were different now. They were no longer a bright blue, but an unreadable black. She tensed. She had forgotten that he wasn't human. The black eyes were eerie. She was trying not to be afraid, but it wasn't something a person could exactly control.

He must have noticed the change in her ardor because he blinked and closed his eyes. Pulling her close, he buried his face in her neck.

"Please don't be afraid of me. Not me. We may have had a rocky start, but I would never hurt you. Never," he whispered harshly.

It was his desperate request that swayed her. It touched her very soul. It was filled with a raw sense of loneliness that she understood all too well. In that moment she knew that she would never be afraid of him again. Hesitant at first, she wrapped her arms around his head and stroked his hair. A shudder went through his body and his arms tightened.

"I'm sorry I hit you with the toilet," she whispered. He chuckled and she felt a sense of accomplishment. It was the reaction she had been hoping for. She pulled back suddenly, desperate to see his smile.

He looked down at her, his eyes blue again. Laugh lines creased the corner of his eyes and a gentle smile greeted her. There would be no other man after him; how could any other compare? In less than one afternoon he had changed her life forever. Yet, it felt so perfect she was scared to trust it.

"I'm so fucked," she exhaled and glared up at him.

"Not yet." He winked and in that moment he reminded her of his father. Maybe there was something about shifters that meant that they would never grow up and stay little boys forever. Looking up at his smiling face, she couldn't really find anything wrong with that.

She and Aiden joined the others in what Adelaide called her drawing room. She sat next to his mother and he took a seat in one of the many wingback chairs. Aiden kept staring at her as if seeing her for the first time. She felt conflicted. This man was a growly, horrible brute who had manhandled and kidnapped her. But he was also gorgeous, pouted adorably, and lit her body on fire. To call the police or not call the police: that was the question.

"Do you like baking?" Adelaide asked, her eyes alight with enthusiasm.

Meryn shrugged. "I guess, I mean, who doesn't like homemade chocolate chip cookie dough?"

"You eat the dough? You don't bake it?" Adelaide asked, eyes wide.

"Wait, you've never eaten cookie dough before?" Meryn couldn't believe this crazy talk. Poor woman.

"Marius, do we have the ingredients for chocolate chip cookies?" Adelaide turned to her squire.

He nodded. "Of course, my lady."

Smiling she turned back to Meryn.

"I've always dreamed of making cookies with a daughter." Her eyes were shining with unshed tears. Meryn sighed. Yup, so not calling the police. This woman was too sweet. She couldn't have her son arrested. Her stomach chose that moment to growl loudly. She flushed with embarrassment. Marius leaned forward.

"What would little miss like for supper?"

"Anything would be great, I'm not picky."

"Sirs?" Marius turned to Aiden and Colton.

"One of your famous sandwiches would be amazing right now, Marius." Colton licked his lips.

"Yeah, that sounds perfect." Aiden nodded.

"Are they that good?" Meryn asked curious. Both men nodded.

"Can I have one too?"

"Of course. I'll be back presently." Marius gave another half bow and left the room.

"He is so cool!" Meryn smiled at Adelaide.

"That he is. He was a gift from my mother."

Meryn turned. "Huh? Like you own him? Isn't that illegal?"

Adelaide gave a tinkling laugh.

"No, darling, he is my employee, but it goes beyond that. When I mated to Byron, my mother knew I would assume the role of Lady McKenzie since Byron, as Unit Commander, was anticipated to become the Council Elder for shifters and lead our people. She knew I would need an ally, someone to help me run the household. Things were different then," she sighed. "My mother arranged for one of the most highly trained squires to take the position. He has been with me ever since," Adelaide explained.

Byron nodded. "We couldn't do without him. He helped run the house, raise the boys and assist with social functions. I was leery at first--after all, there was another man helping to take care of my mate--but looking back, we never could have made it this far without him. It helped that he soon found his own mate. A lovely woman who took on the role of keeping the other servants organized. It has allowed me to concentrate on council work and Aiden's mother to assist with various charities," Byron explained.

Meryn shot a scared look to Aiden. He looked back at her in concern.

"What is it? What has you looking so terrified?" he asked, leaning forward.

"I can't do the social thing or the charity thing. In fact, I can't do the servant thing, either. I can't be like that." Meryn felt her breathing pick up. She hated being around a lot of people. There was no way in hell she could become like Adelaide.

"It's okay, darling, breathe. It won't happen overnight. You and Aiden have plenty of time before Aiden takes over for his father. By that time, you'll be more comfortable with our society, even the social parties and backbiting." Adelaide rubbed her back soothingly.

"Backbiting?"

"Oh, my, yes. Society here can be very cruel. There is a lot of keeping up appearances, if you know what I mean."

"People are mean to you? Why don't you just punch them in the face?" Meryn asked. Adelaide looked at her, appalled. Colton chuckled.

"We definitely have time before you take over, dear," Byron laughed.

"Have you never had a circle of girlfriends where one friend would deliberately invite another to spite you? That sort of thing?" Adelaide asked.

"Nope. I didn't have friends growing up. I mostly stayed to myself," Meryn shrugged. Adelaide chewed on her lower lip in consternation.

"She'll be fine, darling, a breath of fresh air." Byron nodded at Meryn encouragingly.

"Little miss, sirs, your supper," Marius announced from the door before wheeling in a large cart. He lifted the silver domed lids and Meryn gasped. How had the man thrown together gourmet-looking sandwiches in such a short time? She could already feel her mouth watering. Marius placed a napkin in her lap and handed her a plate. The sandwich looked scrumptious. The vinegar and oil glistened from the lettuce mix, the ham and turkey looked fresh cut, and he had added two different types of cheeses.

"Thank you, Marius." Aiden accepted his plate.

"Thanks, Marius, as always, this is amazing." Colton had already inhaled half of his sandwich. Meryn took a bite and practically moaned.

"Nummy!"

"Glad you think so." Marius smiled down at her.

"Marius, can you arrange for squire interviews for Meryn? I think having someone at her side showing her society would help her acclimate to our world." Adelaide snagged a chip from Meryn's plate.

"Of course, my lady, I'll get word out immediately." Marius bowed again and left, taking the cart with him. Meryn was munching away on her sandwich when she realized what Adelaide said.

"What do you mean, *world*?"

"You're not in Kansas anymore, Dorothy," Colton chimed in. Meryn looked to Aiden, who nodded.

"Where exactly am I, then?" Meryn asked, setting her sandwich down.

"May I be the first to welcome you to Lycaonia, one of four hidden paranormal cities in the United States?" Byron placed a hand over his heart and gave a half bow from his seat.

"One of?" Meryn squeaked.

"There are four major paranormal cities, we call them pillar cities. Lycaonia is the shifter city; Noctem Falls is the vampire city; Éire Danu is the fae city; and Storm Keep is the witches' city. Each city is home to a four-person council that rules our people. The council in each city has one council member from each race represented," Byron began.

"Lycaonia protects the Southeast and Mid-Atlantic region. Éire Danu protects the Northeast and Midwest region. Storm Keep protects the Pacific

Northwest region and Noctem Falls protects the Southwest region," Adelaide continued.

"So four cities, four council members per city. That means you have a sixteen person council that rules your people. What do you do in the instance of a tie?" Meryn was fascinated. This was better than watching the history channel.

"I am the tie-breaking vote as Unit Commander," Aiden said.

"What are units?"

"Colton and I are part of a unit. Units are made up of five men. For Lycaonia, that means a shifter leader, a vampire as second-in-command, a shifter as third-in-command, a fae, and a witch," Aiden explained carefully. Meryn could tell that he was watching for signs of imminent freak out.

"Okay, so shifters, vampires, witches and fae, oh my!" Meryn grinned at Colton, who gave her a mock salute for running with the *Wizard of Oz* reference.

"You're the leader?" She turned to Aiden and he nodded.

"You must be third-in-command, since you shift into a dog," Meryn grinned at Colton.

"I am not a dog! I am a wolf!" Colton protested loudly.

"Mangy mutt." Aiden laughed and punched Colton in the shoulder. Meryn liked this side of Aiden; he seemed almost normal.

"How many units are there?"

"There are six units per city," Adelaide answered. Meryn looked down at her fingers.

"So there are one hundred and twenty unit members? Who's in charge of all of them?" Meryn asked.

"I am." Aiden's smile was somewhat sad. Meryn couldn't tell if he was unhappy with being the Unit

Commander, or if there were just some aspects to the job he didn't like.

"You're doing a fine job, son." Byron clapped a hand on Aiden's shoulder. Aiden nodded and his face cleared. Meryn stared at him thoughtfully.

"And that is why he needs you," Adelaide whispered in her ear. When Meryn looked up she could tell the older woman had caught that sad look too.

"What?" Byron and Aiden asked together.

"Nothing," Meryn and Adelaide answered in response. Meryn looked at Adelaide and they both started giggling.

"So what do you have all of these warriors for? Keeping humans out?" Meryn bit into her sandwich. She chewed and noticed everyone got quiet.

"Wha'?" she asked, her mouth full.

"Unit warriors are needed to protect other paranormals and humans from something we have always called ferals. Ferals are men, and sometimes women, who willingly give up their souls for the rush of the kill. They give in to their dark nature. For shifters, they lose the ability to shift, but retain an unnatural amount of strength and revel in brutality. Vampires lose their great speed and the ability to manipulate minds, and their bloodlust compounds. The fae lose most of their magic except for some illusion spells, which they delight in using to drive people insane. Witches lose all of their magic, but gain something like a demon familiar, but without the religious context. They exist only to kill, to create chaos and to destroy lives." Aiden spoke in soft tones as he tried to break this upsetting news to her gently. She turned to him.

"Is it safe here?" she whispered. He nodded.

"There's no safer place to be, than here in Lycaonia with the Alpha Unit." He winked at her, trying to get her to smile. She immediately frowned.

"You jokers?" She pointed to him and Colton.

"Hey!" Colton protested.

Aiden laughed and nodded. "We are the best of the very best."

"Well, I'm reassured. I knocked your ass out with your own toilet today," she sighed, and resumed eating the rest of her sandwich.

Someone snorted. Meryn thought that it was Colton, but to her surprise Adelaide gave another undignified snort and laughed loudly. This of course set off her mate, with Aiden and Colton following suit.

"Ferals better watch out for you, then," Aiden grinned at her. Meryn grinned back before a yawn escaped her.

"Oh, my, look at the time. Aiden, can you show Meryn up to your old room?" Adelaide asked, winking at her son, who blushed furiously.

"Of course."

Meryn stood when Aiden did and set her empty plate down on the table.

"Colton, your room, as usual, is ready for you. I swear you spend more time here than you do at your parents' house."

"Thank you, Mother." Colton kissed Adelaide on the cheek and left the room.

Meryn turned to Aiden's mother. "Thank you for making this not so crazy." Meryn didn't know how to thank someone for easing her into this freaky life.

"It gets better, dear, you'll see." Adelaide kissed her cheek and picked up the empty plate. Byron kissed her forehead and followed his mate as she headed toward the kitchen.

"Shall we?" Aiden asked offering her his arm. She smiled at him. She could get used to this treatment. It was a damn sight better than being locked in a trunk.

"What do you mean, you're sleeping in here too?" Meryn demanded. She should have known he was being too nice.

"This is my room for when I stay here."

"Fine, take me to a guest room," Meryn fumed.

"We don't have guest rooms," Aiden muttered under his breath. Even Meryn knew that was a lie; this house had to have close to a hundred rooms.

"I call bullshit! Fine, I can sleep on the couch!"

"No way in hell. I'm not letting you out of my sight." He crossed his formidable arms over an even more formidable chest. A girl could really get in trouble with those muscles.

"Fine, but there are rules."

"Rules?"

"Yes, rules. Rule number one: stay on your side of the bed. Rule number two: don't touch me, breathe on me, or do anything weird to me in my sleep. Rule number three: don't cross the Great Wall." She counted off each rule on her fingers.

"Great Wall?" He looked puzzled.

She walked over and pulled the bedding down. She then proceeded to pile every extra pillow in the room down the center of the bed. She pointed to one side, then the other.

"My side, your side. *Capiche*?"

"Fine, let's just get some rest. I didn't get any sleep last night and we did drills today. I'm exhausted. You want the shower first?" he asked. She shook her head. He shrugged.

"Suit yourself." He walked into the bathroom and shut the door. She flung herself on the bed. *Oh, Meryn girl, what are you doing? Breaking and entering, getting kidnapped, assaulting your abductor with a toilet and then sexually assaulting said abductor. What sane person does this?* She rolled over and stared at the ceiling. Funny thing was that this was the first time she had felt calm in months.

She had moved to the nearby town two weeks ago. The sudden desire to live somewhere new had driven her crazy. Finally, she had thrown a dart at a map and ended up here. That's when the strange dreams had started. At first, they had been pleasant. Her Prince Charming would find her in a clearing and they would laugh and chat. Some nights turned downright steamy. She had enjoyed those dreams. But then they started getting scary. Someone stalked her in the shadows, and every night for the past week she had been murdered. She couldn't help noticing how much Aiden resembled her Prince Charming, though he was nicer to her in her dream.

She smiled. Even if he was, evidently, a bear shifter, she felt safe with him. She liked the feeling. She would ride this out and see where it took her. She was still grinning up at the ceiling when Aiden walked out with a towel slung low on his hips.

"Did the ceiling say something funny?" he asked, towel-drying his hair. She was too busy trying not to swallow her tongue to respond. She rolled onto her stomach.

"You okay?" he asked. She nodded, still staring.

"Shower's free."

She nodded again.

"You getting in?" he asked, looking amused. She nodded then shook her head as if to clear it.

"Yup, be right back." She hopped off the bed and as she passed him she couldn't help herself. The devil made her do it. She grabbed the edge of the towel and yanked. He gave a yelp and covered his groin with his hands. Laughing, she flung his towel at him.

"You have a great ass, too." Giggling, she ran into the bathroom. Once inside, she leaned against the door. She took a deep breath--she was in trouble, because that man really *did* have the most perfect ass.

Meryn stared at the ceiling. She could practically feel his body heat radiating from his side of the bed. Was he awake? She turned over on her right. The image of his naked body teased her. Why had she thought she was being clever when she yanked that towel off? She was paying the price now. She turned over to her left.

"Can't sleep?" Aiden sounded amused.

She returned to her back. "No. You?"

"No, it's the first night with my mate. I find that sleep is last thing on my mind," he teased.

Meryn didn't want to think about what he implied; she might jump him. To get her mind off of her wanton thoughts, she changed the subject.

"What was it like growing up here?"

"Fun, there are lots of ways for a little boy to get into trouble, especially a little boy trying to emulate his brothers and father."

"Like what?" Meryn was intrigued.

"One night Colton and I snuck out to watch the unit warriors patrol the perimeter, but got caught. I actually had to hide behind my father to stay out of reach from my mother for that one," Aiden chuckled. "What about you? I know you had to have gotten into trouble as a youngster."

"Not really. I stayed to myself mostly. I was raised by my grandmother and didn't want to make her mad." Meryn sat up in bed and peered over her wall.

"Hey, Aiden."

He turned to her. "Yeah?"

"Can you shift for me? I've never seen a bear up close before."

He sat up. "Sure, but you'll have to cover your eyes, I have to be naked to shift."

Meryn shook her head. "Not on your life."

Aiden hesitated for only a moment, then shrugged. He slipped from the bed and stood. He dropped his pajama bottoms and deliberately turned to face her. Her mouth went dry as she stared at his body. It took every ounce of self-discipline not to tackle the man to the floor. It took her three tries to clear her throat.

"Go on." She tried to sound indifferent but knew she failed when he winked saucily at her.

One second, he was her every fantasy come to life; the next he was an extremely large, dark brown bear. Laughing with excitement, she hopped off the bed and walked over to stand in front of him. She reached out a hand and he head-butted her palm. She pulled his shaggy head to her chest and buried her hands in his fur.

"You're not so scary, just a big ole teddy bear." She kissed the top of his nose. He buried his muzzle between her legs and she gasped--the damn thing was cold! Giggling, she raced back to her side of the bed and climbed in. Seconds later she heard the rustle of clothes and felt the bed dip.

"Do you think you'll be happy here, Meryn?" he asked.

"I think so. I'm not going to lie--everything is strange and scary, but also fun and exciting."

"You know I'll be with you every step of the way, right?"

"Yup, I don't know if that is the scary part or the exciting part." She yelped when a pair of fingers appeared from under the wall to pinch her butt. His deep laugh was contagious and she laughed along with him.

"Ow! Definitely scary." She swatted at his hand as it reached for her again.

"Good night, Meryn."

"Good night, Aiden." Meryn was smiling when she turned back over. It was nice to have someone to say good night to.

CHAPTER THREE

Aiden woke the next morning and found himself smiling. He hadn't slept so soundly in weeks. When he went to turn his head, he felt a hand against his face. He sat up and looked down at the small body in the middle of the bed. Meryn, for all her rules the night before, had sought him out in her sleep. Like a stealthy assassin, she had tunneled under her 'Great Wall'. She lay on her back, sprawled arms and legs akimbo. Her mouth was open, she snored lightly, and a thin line of drool traced down her cheek. His heart swelled in his chest. He had never seen anything more adorable in his life. Grinning from ear to ear, he went into his closet and got dressed. When he saw the towel hanging from the door knob, he chuckled. His mate so far had surprised him at every turn. He quietly opened the door and snuck downstairs.

When he walked into the kitchen, four sets of eyes turned to look at him. With the biggest shit-eating grin he could muster, he swaggered to the coffee pot. His men had decided to visit for breakfast.

"Glad to see you got through the night without being knocked unconscious by your tiny mate again," Colton teased. Keelan chuckled and Darian laughed outright.

"She is a delicate flower; she was scared," Aiden protested.

"Where is the fucking coffee?" a gravelly voice demanded from the doorway. Colton lost his composure and began laughing. Even his second in command looked away trying not to smile. Aiden hesitated at giving his mate coffee. She had been pretty high-strung yesterday.

"How about some juice?" he offered.

"How about you shut the fuck up and give me some coffee?" Meryn stumbled through the doorway and collapsed into a chair.

"Oh, yeah, she's real scared," Colton hooted and pounded the table laughing.

"Why are you being loud? Is it fun being so loud, this early in the morning? Do you know what happens to loud morning people? They die. They die horrible deaths, mutilated in their sleep, and are then buried with their balls in their loud fucking mouths." Meryn glared at him through half-shut eyes. The men gulped.

"Here you go, baby, one extra-large mug of coffee. Here's the sugar and cream. Refills whenever you want." Aiden placed the coffee on the table in front of her and backed away slowly. Colton turned to him, his face pale. He shrugged. He had no idea what to do either. Slowly, as Meryn sipped her coffee, her eyes opened. She yawned and then stretched her arms up over her head. By her second cup, she was looking around the kitchen. By the third cup, she was smiling at everyone.

"What's for breakfast?" she asked brightly.

"Whatever the fuck you want," Keelan said, a look of amazement on his face.

"Really? I'd kill for some pancakes." She sighed wistfully. Colton shot out of his seat like a jack-in-the-box.

"No problem. I know where Marius keeps stuff." He hurried over to the pantry and began pulling out ingredients for pancake batter. Aiden sat back in his chair and sipped his coffee. Served the man right for poking fun at his commander.

"Do y'all have an espresso machine?" Meryn turned to him.

"You know what? We'll head to town and get one, just for you," Aiden offered. He never wanted to see what his mate would be like without caffeine.

"Really? They can be kinda expensive; it's why I haven't gotten one yet." She chewed on her bottom lip. And despite the dismemberment threat she had just made to his best friend, he thought she looked cute with her lip between her teeth.

"We'll all chip in, right, guys?" Darian said. The men all nodded.

"Y'all are so sweet. Thank you." She smiled shyly at them. Gavriel met his eyes over Meryn's head across the table and raised an eyebrow. Aiden grinned back. She may be nuts, but she was all his.

"By the way. Who are you all?" Meryn took another sip of coffee.

"This is my unit. You've already met Colton; this is Gavriel Ambrosios, Keelan Ashwood and Darian Vi'Alina." Aiden pointed to each of his men.

She eyed the other three men. She pointed to Darian. He had delicate features but would never be called beautiful. He was too masculine, but there was something about him that was ethereal. His long blond hair was looped and braided down his back. His eyes were a soft lavender that you just didn't see in humans. He was built, but lean.

"Vampire?" she asked. Darian shook his head and stood to his full height.

"Holy shit! You're taller than Aiden and he's like freakishly huge." The difference between her five foot three height and Darian's was evident.

"I am not!" Aiden protested.

Darian grinned and sat back down. "Fae. We're all between six and seven feet tall."

"I thought fae were the "wee" folk."

"Yeah, not so much," Darian shrugged.

"Vi'Alina?" Meryn spoke it slowing to get the pronunciation correct.

"Yes. The 'Vi' prefix indicates that I am the heir for my family line. 'Alina' is the name of my house. If I had brothers, the second-born would be Ri'Alina and the third-born would be Li'Alina," Darian explained.

"What about the fourth-born?" Meryn asked.

Darian shook his head. "We are so long lived that unless a tragedy occurs, no one after the third born inherits. They do not get a prefix for their name."

"So if I were fae I would be Meryn Vi'Evans?" Darian nodded.

"That's cool." Meryn turned to Gavriel who was less ethereal and more dark and dangerous. Aiden valued him as a great strategist and knew he was not one you would ever want to anger.

"You must be the vampire then." He inclined his head.

Keelan frowned. "Why couldn't it be me?" he demanded.

Meryn smiled and pointed to Keelan. He had a short auburn ponytail and amiable brown eyes.

"Because you look too nice and are nowhere near as elegant. He just exudes dark prince," she sighed. Aiden growled. She punched his thigh.

"Ow!"

"She has violent tendencies, just like you," Colton joked. Aiden flipped him off.

"So that means you're the witch. What can you do? Can you fly?" Meryn leaned forward, eyes shining.

"I get premonitions sometimes and I work best with fire and air. My brother Kendrick is stronger, he can manipulate all four elements, but he decided to be an archivist instead of a warrior." Keelan looked down at the table.

"It's a respectable profession, Keelan. We have a rich history that must be maintained," Aiden gently reminded the young witch. He knew that had been a point of contention between the two brothers.

"I know. It's just frustrating that I'm struggling to learn the spells we need and he can do them without thinking about it." Keelan turned his coffee cup in his hand slowly.

"And he's about three hundred years older than you are. Cut yourself some slack," Colton pointed out. Keelan brightened.

"I guess you're right."

Aiden sipped his coffee and enjoyed the sight before him. He couldn't ask for more than his friends and mate sitting together at the breakfast table. Maybe this mating thing would work out after all.

"Hello, boys, how nice of you to visit for breakfast." Adelaide and Byron entered the kitchen. Marius walked in behind them and immediately got to work preparing breakfast, taking over from Colton. The unit members, including Aiden, stood. Meryn looked around, wondering if she should stand too. Byron walked over and kissed her forehead.

"They are standing out of respect for Aiden's mother. They were raised in a time where a man stood when a lady entered the room." Byron sat next to her and Adelaide next to him.

"They didn't stand when I entered the room, but then again, I guess I'm not a lady." Meryn poured herself another cup of coffee. When she looked up, she noticed that Byron was shooting daggers at the other men at the table who all looked properly chastised. Byron raised her hand and kissed it.

"Forgive them, sweetheart. It speaks to their characters, not yours, that they failed to rise when you entered the room. I'm shocked that my son would fail to do so. It's a basic lesson in etiquette that I know was drilled into him when he was a boy." Byron patted her hand and continued to glare at the men.

"Father, I'm sorry," Aiden immediately apologized.

"It's not *my* forgiveness that you need." Byron nodded his head to Meryn. Aiden turned to her.

"I'm sorry, my mate. I was still floating around from the great night's sleep I had last night and wasn't thinking properly this morning. Please forgive me." Meryn was surprised at how truly sorry he sounded, like he had committed some great offense.

"Considering you kidnapped me, locked me up, threw me in your trunk and dragged me around by my arm yesterday, not standing at the breakfast table doesn't seem so bad." She smiled brightly at him.

"You're not going to let me live that down are you?" Aiden groaned.

"Nope."

"What if I take you out and show you the city? We can go shopping. I know where we can get your espresso machine." Aiden took her other hand and brought it to his lips. Now here was the charming man from her dreams.

"Then of course I'll forgive you, now that you're acting like your dream version. I like you better this way. More charming and less growly."

Aiden's face froze his eyes became haunted. "You dreamt of me before coming here?"

"Yup. For weeks I fought against the urge to move. But it was like something was driving me forward. So I threw a dart at a map and ended up in Madison. After I moved into my apartment, I started having dreams. At first they were nice. You were wonderful and sweet. We would lay under these trees and talk. But then they got scary. Last night was the first night in weeks where I haven't dreamt at all. I hated getting out of bed this morning since I slept so well." Meryn was reaching for her coffee cup when Aiden pulled her onto his lap. He held her so close she could feel his heart beating out of control against her cheek.

"Son, what's the matter?" Byron demanded.

"I thought they were just dreams." Aiden buried his face against her neck.

"You've been having nightmares, too?" she whispered. He nodded.

"Nightmares? I thought you said they were nice dreams," Adelaide asked sounding worried. Aiden lifted his head.

"It's like Meryn said. At first they were nice; we'd meet in a clearing in the woods and talk. But then the dreams turned into nightmares. In the dream I would search for her, but couldn't find her. She would call out to me, teasing me, and then it would get quiet. Then I would hear her scream, but I'm too late, she..." he faltered. Meryn pulled away and looked around the table.

"I'm murdered. A man that isn't Aiden comes out of the woods and stabs me repeatedly, like he enjoys it," Meryn shuddered. In her dreams, she could clearly feel the cold steel in her body.

Gavriel stood, chest heaving. "They cannot be prophetic. You have found your mate. She is safe." Gavriel's normally gray eyes began to glow red. Aiden stood and placed Meryn in his seat. He hurried over to Gavriel.

"Breathe, my friend. Meryn is safe. So is your mate. Fate will find a way to bring her to us and then we'll guard them both." Aiden had his hands on Gavriel's shoulders. Keelan reached up to place a hand on Gavriel's forearm.

"*Conquiescere, frater meus.* Be at ease, my brother," Keelan whispered the phrase over and over again. His hand on Gavriel's arm took on a yellow glow. Gavriel took a deep, ragged breath.

"Thank you Aiden, Keelan. I, too, have been having nightmares. I have to put my faith in Fate and pray my mate is delivered to me in time," Gavriel hung his head.

"She'll make it to Lycaonia and then the Alpha Unit will keep her safe." Aiden stood back and helped to ease Gavriel into his chair.

Meryn stood to return to her seat, but Aiden pulled her back into his arms and sat down, placing her once again in his lap. She was going to protest, but after seeing how affected Gavriel was, she knew that Aiden just needed to hold her. She looked at the elegant vampire and wanted to alleviate his worry.

"Aiden is right, you know. I had no choice in coming here. I thought I had a bad case of wanderlust but now I know what it was. It was a relentless driving force. If something like Fate took the trouble to uproot me and move me here, I doubt she would let anything happen to your mate before getting her here."

Gavriel looked at her his eyes unreadable. "Do you really think so?"

Meryn didn't hesitate before nodding. "Absolutely. Especially considering how many books and DVDs I had to pack. My sci-fi collection alone was like ten boxes. Trust me; you have no idea how hard Fate had to work to keep me focused long enough to pack my shit. I kept wanting to stop and read a book or watch a movie I hadn't seen in years." The strain lifted from the vampire's face.

"Thank you, Meryn. I do feel better knowing what Fate must have gone through to get you here." There was a trace of a faint smile on his lips.

"You're welcome," Meryn smiled, then thought about it. "Wait. Was that a compliment?" She frowned. Colton swallowed a chuckle. Gavriel smiled at her.

"I believe it was a compliment, my dear. Fate, after all, has decided you were worth the effort," Adelaide injected. Gavriel nodded.

"Oh, okay." Meryn turned so that she was facing Aiden. "After we go shopping, can we go get my stuff? I've pretty much accepted the fact that I'm not nuts and y'all aren't lying. So I guess I'm sticking around for a while."

"You mean forever," Aiden said in a gruff voice.

"So the rumors are true. My baby brother has found his mate." A deep voice rumbled from the doorway. Meryn turned, and to her surprise, two men who looked eerily identical to Aiden stood smirking at them.

"Meryn, please ignore the pair of grinning fools that are my older brothers. Adam is the ugly one on the left and Adair is the uglier one on the right."

"There are three of you?" She could tell they were related since they all looked just like Byron. Thick black hair and piercing blue eyes. Adam was just as tall as Aiden at six foot six, but with a much leaner build. Adair was shorter at six foot four but more muscled through the chest. Adam had kind eyes and Adair had a teasing smile. She couldn't help waving at them.

"There are four of us," a voice called out from behind the two brothers. "Move out of the way; she wants to meet the sexy one." The voice was light and sounded younger than the other two.

Adam and Adair stepped into the kitchen to make way for yet another man. Meryn couldn't help staring. The last brother was as tall as Adair at six foot four, but that is where the similarities to his brothers ended. This one clearly took after his mother. He wore his long blond hair back in a ponytail and his brown eyes were warm and inviting. He was like the Greek Adonis come to life. He moved forward until he was able to pluck her hand from Aiden's grasp and kiss her knuckles. Aiden growled at his brother.

"My name is Benjamin. I'm afraid Mother ran out of 'A' names and gifted me with a 'B' name like Father." He winked at her devilishly. She giggled up at him and Aiden pulled her close.

"Mine!" he growled. Benjamin placed a hand over his heart and gave a low bow.

"Of course, brother. I was just admiring your beautiful mate. I can only hope that Fate is as kind to me when picking out my future snuggle muffin." He gave an exaggerated sigh. Adelaide laughed.

"Quit teasing your brother. As you can probably tell, he's the youngest." Adelaide patted Benjamin's cheek when he walked over to kiss her good morning.

"Are you all warriors?" Meryn asked. She felt Aiden tense. Adam shook his head.

"Adair and I are somewhat of a scandal. I turned down becoming father's heir and taking over as Unit Commander and eventually Council Elder. It's still unheard-of to reject your family legacy, but I had no desire to become a warrior. I left Lycaonia and studied medicine. I now operate the clinic that takes care of the unit warriors," Adam explained.

"I didn't want to command either. Until Aiden accepted, I'm sure that Adam and I had been close to giving father a complex. His sons didn't want to take after him." Adair gave a booming laugh.

"I was hoping at least one of you would want to inherit. I knew that you each would have to find your own paths. Well, except for Ben. I fear he is determined to remain a little boy forever." Byron scowled at his youngest, who blew his father a kiss in response.

"I turned down Unit Commander to take over as Head Master at the training academy," Adair explained.

"And I am a warrior with the Gamma Unit, I serve under Sascha Baberiov," Benjamin added.

"I'll phone him later to recommend extra drills for you," Adair teased.

"Sirs, ladies. Breakfast is ready to be served. In light of the large party, I have set the dining room table," Marius announced. Meryn was set down on her feet. She tried to peek over to the stove, but servant after servant was streaming by carrying the food away to be served in the dining room.

"Come on, sweetheart, let's get something to eat and then we can visit the city.

"Sounds good." Meryn's stomach filled with butterflies when Aiden reached down and took her hand. It was a simple gesture, but it felt right. When he looked down, Meryn could tell he was staring at her flushed cheeks. He squeezed her hand tighter and led the way.

Adjusting her backpack, Meryn felt a twinge of guilt when they walked outside and she saw the state of his trunk. When she saw that he was watching her, she grimaced and he blushed.

"Sorry about putting you in the trunk," Aiden paused in opening her car door to apologize. Meryn blinked.

"I was just about to apologize for denting your car." Meryn sat down and waited for him to get in. When he was in, he turned to her.

"I'll have Darian fix it. He's a genius with any type of craft. I think it's the fae blood." He ran his hand over his thigh, wiping his palm. If Meryn didn't know any better she would say he was nervous. How adorable!

"So, what do you do for fun?" Meryn looked out the window and watched the scenery fly by. It was hard to believe there was an entire city beyond the trees that humans didn't know about.

"I work out." Aiden licked his lips.

"Of course you do." Meryn smiled, remembering all of his muscles. She made a mental note to introduce him to her Xbox; maybe they could play together.

"How do you keep humans from knowing about all this?" Meryn pointed to the juncture of the road that opened up to an intersection where they could go left, right or straight.

"The witches and fae renew a glamour spell every year at the winter solstice. After they complete the spell, everyone goes to the Council Manor for the Midwinter Ball."

Meryn felt her stomach knot. "Balls, like with poofy dresses and dancing and tiny sandwiches that don't fill you up?"

Aiden's head turned and he looked at her in surprise. "Yeah, I thought all women loved those things."

"Not this one. Do I have to go?"

"Since I'm Unit Commander and my father's heir, it's expected of me to be there. As my mate, it's expected for you to be there."

"Do I *really* have to go?" Meryn repeated, feeling ill thinking about it. Aiden chuckled.

"I'll make sure you aren't left alone. We have the All Hallows' Eve Ball coming up soon; it will give you an idea of what to expect for Midwinter." Meryn placed a hand over her stomach. She felt woozy.

"I hate people."

"You know with the kicking, screaming and assaulting people with toilet pieces, I would never have guessed," Aiden snarked.

"Har, har. You're so funny. Seriously, can I just send a plate of cookies or something?"

"Sorry, darling, but you're high society now."

"Bugger that!" Aiden glanced at her, then back to the road.

"I better warn my mother about tomorrow," Aiden grimaced.

Meryn turned to face him. "Why?"

"Because she is planning to introduce you to her sewing circle. All the founding family matriarchs will be there." He looked apologetic.

"I think I'm going to be sick." She closed her eyes and leaned back in the seat.

Aiden chuckled. After a few minutes he parked and turned the car off. She heard him turn toward her.

"Just smile and nod tomorrow. My mother will do most of the talking. I have a feeling Daphne Bowers will be monopolizing the afternoon anyway. Her daughter-in-law is pregnant, so she will be milking that for every scrap of attention she can get for a while." Meryn opened her eyes and lifted her head.

"So she's preggers. Big deal. They'll probably do one of those diaper cakes or something. I guess I can smile and nod, but I'm bringing my laptop. I can't sew for shit."

Aiden gave her a funny look.

"Meryn, in the paranormal world, being pregnant is a true blessing. Witches can only conceive during the winter solstice, vampires during the spring equinox, shifters at summer solstice and fae during the fall equinox. It's why each equinox and solstice is a huge celebration for us. As each of the four races can only conceive during these times, their children are usually born during a corresponding holiday. Witches are born around the fall equinox; vampires during the long, dark winter solstice; shifters around the spring equinox when most animals are born; and the fae around the summer solstice, at the height of summer when everything is in full bloom. Each race only has a certain time of the year that they are fertile and even then it's not guaranteed that the couple will conceive. After conception, only about sixty percent of all pregnancies make it to full term. It's kept our numbers pretty low."

There was a sadness in his eyes that she wished she could erase.

"That must be hard. I'll make sure that I properly 'Ooooh' and 'Aaaah' at the appropriate moments," Meryn promised.

"You really are anti-social aren't you?"

"I like the guys and your family. But I don't like being fake or being polite to assholes."

Aiden's mouth twitched. "Tomorrow should be interesting."

"I'll be good. Promise." She looked around. "Where are we?"

"This is the Council Manor. My father let me know that the council wanted to speak to me this morning at breakfast. He left about a half an hour before we did to let them know we were coming."

"Is it okay that I go in?" She gawked up at the imposing building. It looked like the Library of Congress. Meryn watched the people walk by their parked car. The men were wearing official-looking robes that gaped to reveal pressed and perfectly tailored suits and cravats. The women were visions of gentility in fall-colored full-length dresses. She glanced down at her *Teenage Mutant Ninja Turtles* t-shirt with her hoodie tied haphazardly around her waist. She glared at Aiden. He didn't even seem to notice. Damn the man. She hated sticking out. Aiden straightened his tie and pulled a military type hat from the backseat. Of course, *he* fit right in with his uniform. He opened his car door.

"Father said it shouldn't take long; they just want me to look into something. Then we can go explore the city." Aiden took her hand. "Ready?"

"I guess so."

He kissed her hand before letting it go, and then got out of the car. He walked around and scowled down at her as she opened her own door, refusing to wait for him. She stuck her tongue out and he surprised her by laughing. Since he was constantly frowning, it made her feel good that she could make him laugh.

Meryn appreciated that Aiden took her hand and was leading the way; otherwise, she knew she would have run into something. The outside of the building was nothing short of amazing, but the inside took her breath away. The stone architecture peaked in rounded archways. The exterior windows tossed rainbows of color on the floors and walls with their stained glass. Statues and old oil paintings decorated the walls. Aiden literally pulled her along as she looked around in childlike wonder. When they turned the corner Meryn gasped.

"What?" Aiden asked.

Meryn stared at the statue in front of them.

"Don't blink. Don't even blink," she whispered.

"What in the hell are you talking about?" Aiden looked around trying to identify a possible hidden threat.

"You blink and you're dead." Meryn stared unblinking at the two large stone angel statues on either side of a heavy-looking wooden door. Aiden's hand went to his sidearm.

"Meryn, that is just a statue."

"But what if it isn't? I mean up until this week I didn't think paranormals existed and now you're all over the fucking place. I can't take the chance." Meryn continued to stare at the statues.

"Why don't I ever understand a word that comes out of your mouth? It's like you're not even speaking English!"

"Oh, my God, what if the Doctor is real too! That would be awesome!" Meryn felt Aiden pulling her closer to the doors, but she refused to take her eyes off of the statues.

"I give up! There's something wrong with you." Meryn could hear the exasperation in his voice.

"You just don't speak geek. That's okay, I can train you." Meryn closed one eye, then the other, then opened them quickly. The statues remained statues.

"These might not be dangerous." She let out a relieved sigh.

"You think?" Aiden asked acerbically. Meryn turned her attention to the highly polished dark wood doors in front of them.

"Those are some impressive-looking doors. Is it to keep us out, or them in?" Aiden closed his eyes and looked like he was mentally counting to ten.

"Most days, to keep us in. Come in, Aiden, let us meet your clever mate," a voice called from beyond the doors. Meryn covered her mouth with her hands. Did all paranormals have phenomenal hearing? Aiden peered down at her, a smile twitching on his lips. He lifted the large iron ring and pulled the door open. Meryn watched as his biceps flexed under his long-sleeved uniform shirt. *Yum.*

They walked on a soft red carpet up to a long wooden panel. Behind it sat four very powerful looking men, only one of whom she recognized.

"Esteemed council members, may I present my mate, Meryn Evans. Meryn, I have the distinct honor of introducing Lycaonia's council members: Elder Celyn Vi'Ailean, our fae representative; Elder Rowan Airgead, our witch representative; Elder René Evreux, our vampire representative; and of course you have already met my father, the shifter representative."

Aiden bowed at the waist. Not knowing what to do, Meryn just waved. Grinning broadly, the large fae elder waved back. Byron nodded. The witch elder smiled warmly, but the vampire elder sniffed and turned up his nose. Meryn felt herself frown.

Please don't let me say anything to get Aiden into trouble.

"What was it that you wished to see me about?" Aiden asked standing to his full height.

"We would like for you to investigate a set of disappearances. Two paranormal couples living in Madison have vanished. The mother of one of the missing women is frantic. If you could take a few men out there and ask around, we would appreciate it. I know that would ease everyone's worries," Elder Airgead explained.

"Of course, sir. I'll take some men out there later today." Aiden gave a half bow. Meryn debated on asking her question, but she figured that she wouldn't find anything out if she kept her mouth shut. She'd take the chance of putting her foot in it for a chance to help.

"Um, sirs, your excellencies?" Meryn hoped that she didn't sound as nervous as she felt.

"What is it, child?" Elder Vi'Ailean asked, his voice soft and gentle.

"If you have any information about the missing couples, I could try to track their last known movements and whereabouts using my laptop." Meryn stared at the tops of her scuffed up Converse.

"You can do that?" Elder Airgead sounded shocked. She lifted her head and nodded.

"I can track their credit cards, purchases, parking tickets, just about anything electronic," she explained.

"All from your laptop?" Elder Airgead asked.

"Sure, that's child's play."

"Are all humans so well versed with technology?" Byron asked, sounding impressed.

"No, though most can do the basics. I'm just very, very good." She couldn't keep the trace of pride out of her voice. She felt Aiden's warm hand on her lower back. He was showing her that he had her back, literally. Feeling braver, she continued.

"I can also compile both couples' information to look for anything that ties them together, to establish a pattern. If we can find the pattern, we can establish a motive and narrow down the search to find the perpetrators." Meryn clenched and unclenched her hands at her sides. Years of watching *CSI* were starting to pay off.

"Impressive. I had no idea my new little daughter was so talented," Byron bragged.

"We don't interact with humans enough to keep up with their technology," the fae Elder admitted.

"I do not know why we even care what happens outside the city. The paranormals living outside of Lycaonia know the risks of trying to fit in with humans. If they really wanted to stay safe they would be behind the city walls," René said disdainfully. Beside her, Meryn felt Aiden tense.

"With all due respect, Elder Evreux, there are more paranormals now than there were even one hundred years ago, despite our declining birth rate. With fewer and fewer pack and pride wars, and established feeding centers for the vampires, older generations are living longer. It's extremely expensive for the average paranormal to live in one of our cities. It has become necessary for larger families to make their way in the human world," Aiden explained. From his slightly condescending tone, Meryn had a feeling it wasn't the first time Aiden had presented this argument.

"Paranormals do not belong amongst humans. They are nothing but insects," Elder Evreux sneered looking right at Meryn.

"René, you will take back those words about my daughter, before I make you!" Byron stood to his full height as his eyes shifted to black. Meryn's eyes widened. She glanced over at Aiden to see what they should do, to see that his eyes had also shifted and his canines had extended past his lips. In response, Elder Evreux stood hissing baring his fangs.

"Byron! René! Stop this at once." Elder Airgead moved between the two men, both of his hands glowing a faint blue color. Both men stood on either side of the witch, breathing heavily and glaring at each other.

"I meant no insult to your daughter," Elder Evreux bit off each word. Byron gave a curt nod and sat back down.

"Holy shit balls! Papa bear is freaking awesome!" Meryn whispered. Five sets of eyes immediately went to her. She stepped behind Aiden. She heard guffaws and peeked out to see that the fae Elder was laughing and wiping tears.

"Meryn, you are an absolute treasure. First Weeping Angels and now this." He took a deep breath and met her eyes.

"Finally! Someone who's intelligent!" Meryn exploded.

"I'm going to pretend you didn't mean to exclude me." Aiden's voice was flat.

"Sure. If that helps you sleep at night." Meryn bumped his hip with hers. He gazed down at her, affection in his eyes.

Meryn was no longer intimidated by these men. They may be all powerful and could shift into large predator animals and cast spells, but at the end of the day, they were just men. Men, she could handle.

"Aiden, please feel free to bring your mate over for tea one afternoon. I would love to see her reactions to Vivian's garden," Elder Vi'Ailean said standing. He then turned to Meryn.

"My mate is also human, so don't let some people's old-fashioned prejudices get to you, my dear." He turned and walked past Elder Evreux.

"Be thankful I wasn't the one who took exception to your words, René. It would have taken more than Rowan's spells to get me to back down." With a regal nod, he swept past René and left the room.

"I swear you guys will drive me to drink. I should be allowed to sedate you three for meetings." Elder Airgead sat back looking tired.

"Where's the fun in that, Rowan?" Byron joked.

"With your permission? I owe my mate a tour of Lycaonia." Aiden bowed.

"Of course, Commander. Meryn, my dear, I hope that our display hasn't soured you toward the city and our people. I think you will find some of the city's sites to be amazing. Maybe you can blogger it on your laptop," Elder Airgead suggested. Meryn smiled.

"You mean blog. Maybe. Do you have the information on the missing couples?" she asked. Elder Airgead nodded and handed her a stack of papers. Meryn stepped forward and accepted them. She opened the flap to her backpack and shoved them inside.

"I can't wait to get started. I love projects. Thank you."

"You carry your laptop with you? Doesn't it get heavy?" Byron asked.

"Nah, I'm used to it. I can't live without it." Meryn swung her backpack on her shoulder.

"Good luck on your project." The witch Elder sat back in his chair.

As they were walking out of the room Meryn looked up at Aiden.

"Are all vampires douchebags? Because Gavriel wasn't." Aiden grabbed her upper arm and almost began sprinting out into the hallway. Behind her, she could hear Byron's booming laughter fill the council hall. Shit! She kept forgetting that there was no such thing as whispering around paranormals!

CHAPTER FOUR

"I swear you are trying to kill me!" Aiden exploded once they were back in the car.

"I'm sorry! I didn't realize that he could hear me. But seriously, that guy was a jerk."

"I know he is, but he is still an Elder. Try not to insult him again. Unfortunately, it isn't us that has to deal with him on a daily basis, it's my father." Aiden started the car.

"Oh, poor Byron." Meryn felt horrible about what she had said now. Aiden looked over and took mercy on her.

"Don't feel too bad. I've done worse. I grew up here, remember." Aiden took her hand in his and rested them on the center console.

"I bet you and Colton were terrors."

"He was. I just went along to see what would happen. Bears are naturally curious."

"You were pretty badass yourself back there. Thank you for sticking up for me."

"Of course, you're my mate."

"And only you can yell at me?" Meryn teased.

"Exactly." Aiden grinned at her and expertly turned the steering wheel with one hand, maneuvering the car into a large public parking garage. When she looked at him and raised an eyebrow, he explained.

"The original city was built before we had cars. The streets are cobblestone and too narrow for vehicles. We built a parking garage on the outskirts and everyone walks in the city. So, where would you like to go first?"

"Coffee."

"We have some amazing museums."

"Coffee!"

"Or we can--"

"Coffee or I'll cut you!"

Aiden laughed and leaned over the console to kiss the tip of her nose. "Okay, okay. Coffee it is. Come on, Menace." He opened the car door and stepped out. Feeling rebellious, she quickly opened her car door and got out. Aiden glared at her.

"Ha!" Meryn gave a fist pump. Aiden rolled his eyes.

She grabbed her backpack and shut the door. She swung her backpack on her back and adjusted the straps.

"You look like a second grader." Aiden had tilted his head and was looking at her funny.

"Fuck and you. I do not. Lots of adults wear vintage t-shirts. It's an 'in' thing right now." Meryn did have to admit, even if to herself, that she thought she resembled a little kid most days, too.

"I think you look cute." Aiden's smile was gentle.

"I'm not cute, I'm sexy," Meryn protested. Aiden had the gall to laugh in her face.

"You're my mate, and I say this with all sincerity. You are not sexy, at all. You are like a feisty little spitfire and that's okay. You're completely different and half of what you say I don't understand, but I wouldn't have you any other way." Aiden ruffled her hair and took her hand. She was torn between melting into a puddle at his feet and being offended that he didn't think she was sexy. Flabbergasted, she walked beside him, stealing glances up at him to see if he had been poking fun at her. When they crossed the pavement and onto the cobblestones, Meryn felt a jolt run through her. There was something about the cobblestones. She jerked her hand out of Aiden's and knelt to lay her palm flat on the stone's surface.

"There's something weird about the stones." But no matter how she looked at them, they were plain, gray, ordinary stones.

"Very good, mate of mine. The stones are bespelled. They promote feelings of community and goodwill," Aiden explained.

"Cool." Meryn stood and immediately Aiden took her hand again. She was beginning to see a pattern. He had to be touching her when they were together. Holding her hand, touching her back, even putting her on his lap.

They walked until they reached the end of the long alley. Aiden looked down at her.

"Welcome to Lycaonia," he said and let go of her hand to push her forward. Meryn stepped beyond the tall buildings of the alleyway and gazed around. Everywhere she turned, there was something new to see. Vendors laughed and shouted out to people as they walked by, trying to sell their wares. Each store was different. In one store window, she could see stacks and stacks of old books and parchment scrolls; at another, swords and daggers. One large store window held tiers of delicate-looking cakes. She felt her mouth begin to water. When she looked across the street, one swinging wooden sign boasted the best magical ingredients sold on the east coast. Magical ingredients! Just when she thought it couldn't get any better, the smells began to hit her. Jasmine, honeysuckle, frankincense, and myrrh. She looked past the magic shop and saw an apothecary. The delicious fragrance of freshly baked bread and cinnamon rolls spun her around to face a bakery with loaves and loaves of bread on display.

"I... I... Oh... Could we... Oh!" Meryn twirled in circles trying to take it all in. She felt one of her episodes coming on. She froze and let her brain take everything in. She could almost feel the images being downloaded and filed away.

"Meryn, Meryn! Are you okay?" Aiden's worried voice brought her back. He was bent down, peering into her face.

"Sorry about that. Sometimes my brain needs to process stuff quickly and I have a moment." She blushed. She knew she was odd; she just hated that he kept seeing her weird side.

"A moment? A Meryn Moment. Got it. You're okay though, right?" Aiden took her hand again. She was starting to feel naked without his large, steadying hand wrapped around hers.

"Meryn Moment? I like that. Sounds better than 'Psycho Seconds' or 'Freak Meltdown'."

"Who called it that?" Aiden frowned.

"My first boyfriend and my second boyfriend," Meryn sighed. She had stopped dating after that.

"Humpf. Don't mind them, Meryn, they were only human." Aiden swung their hands. Meryn felt her heart soar. That's right! They had only been human; she was swimming in a much bigger, freakier pond now. Aiden accepted her for who she was. It felt amazing. Meryn frowned and stopped dead in her tracks. Aiden glanced back, concerned.

"I think I'm falling in love with you," she said flatly. His eyebrows shot up and he stared at her. People passed them on either side as they stared at one another.

“Well, I think I'm starting to love you too,” Aiden grumbled, his cheeks the color of the red apples for sale in the basket next to them.

“Good. Coffee now?”

Aiden cleared his throat and nodded. Meryn noticed that his hand as it gripped hers had gotten moist and trembled slightly. Her silly bear.

“Why do you have cameras on the roofs?” she asked pointing at the roofline. “The entire city is rocking this cool Victorian Steampunk vibe and then you see those cameras and it kinda ruins the atmosphere.”

“Kids. Last year it became the cool thing to 'tag' locations of the city with a spell or in the shifters' cases, urine. We spent a lot of time chasing teenagers and speaking with parents. With the cameras, we just send the parents the captured video of the delinquent kid and bill for cleanup. The vandalism stopped almost immediately. I think the new thing now is vanishing ink tattoos.”

“I guess kids are kids, no matter where you live.” Meryn took a deep breath and beyond the smells of jasmine, myrrh, freshly baked bread, and cinnamon was the crisp smell of autumn. As they walked, Aiden pointed out the training academy and the local school. He walked her down a narrower street that was lined on both sides with small eateries. She caught a whiff of something familiar and began to smile.

“I hope they have pumpkin-flavored drinks.”

“I'm sure they do.” Aiden stopped and held the door open to a smaller shop. The second the door cracked, she could smell heaven. Freshly ground coffee beans lured her in off the sidewalk.

“Welcome to The Jitterbug! Come on in!” a voice called from behind the counter. Meryn looked at the smaller man and smiled. He was shorter than any of the other men she had met so far. She figured he was about five foot eight. But what he lacked in muscles, he made up for in beauty. He had strawberry blond curls and bright teal-colored eyes. The man at his side, who was gazing at him adoringly, was his antithesis. He was taller at five foot ten, and his dark hair was pulled back in a long braid. His brown eyes had flecks of gold in them.

"Commander McKenzie, this is a surprise. You never come to visit. What brings you in?" The smaller man called.

They walked up to the counter.

"My mate demanded coffee, so I brought her to the best in Lycaonia. Meryn, I would like you to meet Sydney Fairfax and Justice O'Malley. They own The Jitterbug. Gentlemen, my mate Meryn Evans."

"Oh, my goodness, the rumors are true. Elder Airgead's spell worked. The warriors are starting to get their mates!" The smaller man, Sydney, began to laugh. "That will make a lot of the single women in the city very unhappy. You've been voted the Most Eligible Bachelor in Lycaonia for the past five years."

"Thrice welcome to Lycaonia, Meryn! What have you seen so far? What can I get you? It's on the house," Justice offered.

"This is the first shop we've gone into, but everything looks amazing. Do you have anything with pumpkin?"

"Of course! It's fall, isn't it? Now, not to brag, but my Pumpkin Apple latte is to die for." Sydney blew on his fingertips and brushed them on the front of his shirt.

"My man is bragging, but he's right. It is amazing." Justice leaned in and kissed the back of

Sydney's neck before returning to the espresso machine. Sydney sighed happily.

"You two are so cute! How long have you been together?" Meryn leaned on the counter.

"Five years now, but he keeps things fresh. I don't know how I was lucky enough to be mated to a man like that, but Fate knows best, right?"

"I think so. Well, I hope so, evidently she brought me here."

"I think Meryn is doing just fine." Aiden wrapped an arm around her shoulders.

"Awww! I never thought I would see the day that hardcore, military Unit Commander Aiden McKenzie would act so damn cute! Girl, what is your secret?" Sydney asked. Meryn leaned in. Sydney bent down to hear.

"I beat him with his toilet," she whispered. Sydney stood back up and stared at Aiden in shock. Aiden sighed and covered his face with his other hand.

"Oh, my Goddess, you're not lying. Ahhhhhh!" Sydney grabbed his stomach, he was laughing so hard. Meryn couldn't help giggling with him. He had the type of laugh that was contagious.

"Leave him alone, you goof. Commander, what can I get started for you?" Justice pushed his mate out of the way.

"Thank you, Justice. I have a whole new respect for you now that I've met Meryn."

"Hey!" Meryn heard Sydney echo her outrage.

"I understand you perfectly, Commander." Justice nodded sagely, and he and Aiden shared a moment.

Sydney's eyes narrowed and he turned to Meryn, "You know what I've learned after being mated for five years, Meryn? Big, funny men sometimes forget that their smaller mates have access to their unconscious bodies when they go to sleep. Sometimes you have to remind them of that." Sydney crossed his arms over his chest.

"That sounds brilliant to me." Meryn glared at Aiden. Both Aiden and Justice visibly gulped.

"Now, baby, you know I love you to pieces; my life would be absolutely boring without you to make each day worth living." Justice pulled Sydney in his arms and was peppering the man's face and neck with kisses. Meryn could see the love between them. Sydney giggled and threw his arms around his mate.

"Forgiven. Get the brooding Commander his coffee and I'll start the latte for Meryn." Sydney laid a scorching kiss on his mate and then began pulling out bottles from under the counter. Justice, smiling like a goof, walked back over. Meryn turned to Aiden.

"I hope you were taking notes."

"As if it would do any good treating you like a normal person. I'd have to do something different, like buy you an espresso machine, right?" Meryn gasped.

"Really! You weren't kidding at breakfast? Really?" Meryn hopped up and down in excitement.

"Yes, you little menace, I'll buy you an espresso machine. I'd fear for my life each morning if you didn't have one." Meryn jumped up and wrapped her arms around his neck. When Aiden's arms wrapped around her, she began to kiss his face.

"Thank you!" Meryn wiggled until he put her back down.

"Where are they? Are they here? Do we have to order?" Meryn looked around the shop.

"Go around the far side of the counter, I have some of the more popular ones on display. I recommend a one button, super automatic. They are easy to use and can give you anything from an espresso shot to cappuccinos," Sydney advised.

"Of course we can also set you up on an espresso bean delivery schedule as well," Justice added. Aiden sighed.

"Go ahead. I knew that this would be expensive, but she's worth it."

Meryn felt tears fill her eyes. No one had ever done anything like this for her in her entire life. Unable to help herself, she let the tears fall. Instantly, Aiden was at her side.

"Hey, this was supposed to make you happy, not sad." He wiped away her tears with his callused fingers.

"No one has ever done anything so nice for me before. Thank you," Meryn whispered and buried her face in his chest.

"Get used to it. I have a feeling I'm going to enjoy spoiling you." Aiden rubbed his cheek along the top of her head. She suddenly felt more at ease knowing he was trying to mark her.

"You two are so beautiful!" Sydney sniffled behind the counter.

"He's pretty amazing, right?" Meryn asked, stepping away from Aiden wiping her eyes on her shirt.

"You both are. Now. Which machine do you think you would want?" Sydney wiped his eyes on his towel and walked her over to the shelves.

"I like that one. It's the one that has been on my Amazon wish list for months." Meryn pointed to the silver one that boasted ease of use, not only in making drinks but also in the maintenance of the machine.

"Great choice. To set you up on a reoccurring bean order, I need to know how many shots you'll go through. How many drinks do you think you'll have?"

"In a day?"

"Sure." Sydney pulled out a clipboard from beside the register.

"Um. Two to wake up. One for mid morning, one after lunch. One afternoon pick me up and one after dinner. So, six." Meryn held up her fingers. Sydney stared.

"Do humans process caffeine differently than shifters?" Sydney asked. Justice cleared his throat and responded.

"Caffeine affects them more." They all stared at her.

"What?" They continued to stare.

"I need it to live!" She stamped her foot.

"She's scary in the morning before coffee." Aiden shuddered. Both Justice and Sydney looked at her in renewed horror. Evidently, anything bad enough to scare a Unit Commander was pretty bad.

"I'll set up that delivery order immediately. In fact, take some beans from stock for the next few days." Sydney went behind the counter and pulled out a bag of beans.

"I'll get the machine." Justice disappeared, heading to the back.

"Girl, kudos to you. I can't wait to see how those hoity-toity society puppets will react to you," Sydney snickered.

"Don't remind me. She's been invited to participate in mother's sewing circle tomorrow." Aiden groaned.

"The Daughters Lycaonia Sewing Circle? Seriously? Is that wise?" Sydney eyed Meryn.

"Probably not, but my mother wants to show her off."

“She's met Meryn, right?” Sydney asked. Aiden nodded.

“I'm right here, guys!” Meryn whacked Aiden, “I said I would be good and I will.” Meryn's sour mood evaporated when Justice walked back from the stockroom with a brand new espresso machine.

“Okay, girlfriend, here's the beans, a few bottles of syrup, a recipe list, and my phone number. Call me later and I'll give you the scoop on all the proper ladies you'll meet tomorrow.” Sydney handed her a pretty paper shopping bag filled with coffee supplies.

“Thank you, Sydney, I feel like I am going into battle tomorrow with no ammo,” Meryn admitted.

“Trust me darlin', I can give you lots and *lots* of ammo.” He winked.

“Wonderful. I don't know if introducing the two of you was smart or not.” Aiden took the heavy shopping bag from Meryn and easily held it along with her new machine.

“Definitely not a good idea, but I have a feeling it will be entertaining.” Justice smiled.

“True. Okay, Menace, let's go.” Aiden steered her to the door. Meryn waved and laughed at Sydney who was holding his pinky and thumb up to his face in the universal 'Call Me' sign. She nodded.

Aiden took her all around the city, showing her his favorite hangout places and restaurants. She loved the childlike delight he displayed when they were at the bakery. She giggled when he ordered bear claws and he laughed with her. Then he amazed her by eating almost a dozen. She was enjoying the lemon shortbread cookies.

“You don't get to judge. You drink insane amounts of coffee and I love sweets.” Aiden poked a finger in her side, causing her to squeal.

"Bear claws for your bear claws. Grrrrr." Meryn held up her curled fingers in a mock growl. Aiden threw his head back and laughed openly. When his smiling face turned to her, she couldn't help it. She stood up from her chair and captured his lips. She saw his stunned expression before she closed her eyes as he took over. His hand cupped the back of her head and she felt his agile tongue trace the roof of her mouth. Her legs were shaking when they broke apart.

"You taste like lemons." He took a deep breath and shifted in his seat uncomfortably. He winced as he adjusted his pants. Dazed, she nodded and sat back down. Damn that man. His kisses made her stupid.

"Good work there, Commander," a male voice congratulated.

"Thanks, Darren. How's your mate?" Aiden stood and greeted the bakery owner, who had approached their table.

"She's fine. She'll kill me for saying anything, but I'm dying to share. She's expecting." Meryn thought the man would burst out of his apron with pride. Aiden's face lit up and he thrust his hand forward. The baker gripped Aiden's hand and shook it vigorously.

"She's hoping for a girl. I don't care as long as it's healthy. A boy or girl can always help out around here," Darren beamed.

"Darren, this is my mate, Meryn. Meryn, this is Darren Williams. He was third-in-command to the Gamma Unit a couple years ago. He retired to take over the family bakery here in the city. I think we are all thankful for that. His sweets are to die for," Aiden introduced the man. Meryn stood and found herself swept up in a hug. Darren released her and she moved closer to Aiden.

"Commander, I'm so glad the spell worked. I know from personal experience that you men need mates. I remember how bad some nights can get after a mission," Darren shuddered.

"It's been interesting so far." Aiden squeezed her hand.

"At first I was scared since I didn't even know any of this existed, but now..."--she looked up at Aiden--"I can't remember what my life was like before Aiden," she said shyly.

"We need to go," Aiden said abruptly. He picked up her espresso machine and shopping bag and pulled her from the store without even saying goodbye.

"Have fun, Commander!" Darren yelled as the door shut behind them.

"Rude!" Meryn snapped as Aiden, who, with her espresso machine tucked under one arm, dragged her through the crowd back to the parking garage.

"Aiden?" Meryn was confused. Had she said something wrong?

"Shush. Don't say anything else, my control is hanging by a thread," Aiden said, darting between people.

When they got to the car he popped the trunk and dropped her machine and bag inside. He opened the car door, got her seated, and practically ran back to the driver's side. He climbed in and slammed the door.

"If I said something I shouldn't have, just tell me," Meryn protested.

"Not another word."

Meryn fumed beside him. She hated being treated like a child. She gazed out of the window and the trees flew by. Before she realized it, they were back at the house. He parked right in front of the door. Not wanting to piss him off even further, she waited for him to come around open her car door. He jerked it open, grabbed her hand and pulled her out.

He surprised her when he headed to the back of the house instead of going to the front door. They walked past the manicured flower beds and koi ponds. She didn't have time to admire the gazebo or rose-covered trellis. He kept marching until they hit the woods, and still he walked. She could tell they were on an established path, but it was one created after years of being walked, instead of man-made with stone or brick.

He didn't stop until the trees cleared to reveal a small mountain brook. When she looked around, she felt like the city and the house were worlds away. This place felt so isolated and peaceful. Finally Aiden dropped her hand and went to stand by the brook looking down at the water.

"Aiden, whatever I did, I'm sorry. I didn't mean to embarrass you." Meryn hung her head.

"Is that what you think?" Aiden spun and closed the distance between them in two steps.

"I dragged you out of there before you said anything else that would have me claiming you on the tables of Darren's bakery for all of Lycaonia to see. Do you have any idea what your words did to me?" he demanded, seconds before his lips descended on hers.

One second, she was apologizing, the next she had forgotten what planet she was on. The more he suckled and traced her lips, the hotter her core became. Each pull felt like his lips were wrapped around her clit, shooting sparks of pleasure through her body. All from a kiss. She felt liquid pooling between her legs and she wanted him more than she had wanted anything else in her whole life.

She pulled away, breathing hard.

"Please," she whispered. He leaned forward and nipped at the tender skin behind her ear.

"Please, what?" His voice had deepened to a low growl and sent shivers down her spine.

"P-p-please," she stuttered. He had been right earlier. She wasn't sexy. She had no idea how to ask him for what she needed. When he looked down his face softened.

"It's okay, my sweet Meryn. I know. I know what you need. I'm your mate, I'll always provide for you. I'll always give you what you desire." Aiden spun her so that her back was flush against his body. Reaching around to the front of her he unsnapped her jeans and pulled them down to mid-thigh with a harsh jerk. She gasped as the cold autumn air hit her heated flesh. Seconds later his large, callused hand was caressing her. Gentle fingertips traced her mound and the crease between her sex and her legs. He dipped between her dripping folds and teased her opening. Without conscious thought, she thrust her hips upward, wanting more than he was providing.

"Shush. Trust me," he whispered and bit down gently on her shoulder as his fingers found the tiny nub that had been begging for attention. She cried out and bucked again. His fingers danced and her body drew tighter and tighter. Without warning, her body exploded. She screamed out her release and arched her back. Slowly his fingers stilled. Her knees gave out and she found herself being supported by one arm. With his other hand, Aiden ripped her panties from her body and used them to clean her up. Gently, he pulled her jeans back up and tucked the used fabric in his coat pocket. With both hands now free, he swept her up in his arms and carried her to sit in his lap under the large oak tree.

Meryn snuggled against his chest. No other man had ever been able to give her an orgasm before. It was as if he was the only one who could set her body ablaze. When she felt a hard bulge between them, she realized how selfish she had been. She sat back.

"What about you? I mean you didn't..." Meryn pointed at his crotch, and he smiled and pulled her head back down to his chest.

"I'm fine. This was for you. Your pleasure, your complete abandon was a gift. Thank you." Meryn frowned in confusion. *She got a mind-blowing orgasm, and he said thank you?*

"I meant what I said at the bakery. Life was good before I met you, but it's like every day since I met you, it just gets more and more perfect. I feel like I finally have a place where I belong." She looked up at him and saw emotion in his eyes.

"The things you say," he whispered harshly and kissed her again. When they parted, she rested her head on his chest and enjoyed the breeze coming off the water.

"I'll enjoy my visits to the house more now that you're here," he sighed contently. She nodded then realized what he said.

"What?" She lifted up to look at him.

"What?" he asked.

"What do you mean, when you visit?"

"I don't live here, Meryn. I live at the Alpha Unit estate."

"When do I move in with you?" She sat back on her knees.

"You don't." His brows knit together.

"What do you mean, I don't?"

"I mean, you will live here with my parents and learn how to run a household and I'll live with the Alpha Unit and command the men. I'll visit, of course." Meryn would have thought he was being deliberately cruel except for the absolutely confused expression on his face.

"Okay, you see, that's not going to work for me. Mated, married, dating, whatever you want to call it. I thought we would live together." She stood and he leaned back against the tree.

"That's not how things work, Meryn." His condescending tone was sending her blood pressure into the stratosphere.

"With me, that's how it works. You have two choices. Either you move back in with your parents and live with me, or I move into the Alpha Unit estate with you. That's it." She put her hands on her hips and scowled down at him.

"Quit acting like a child. We have reasons we do the things we do. I can't lead my men from my parents' estate and you would be a distraction if you moved in with me." Aiden closed his eyes. Meryn's mouth dropped. She fought the urge to kick him in the face, but the small rational part of her brain didn't want to seriously hurt him. So she did what she always did when she got truly angry. She shut down. She could feel her facial muscles relaxing and her body slumped forward. Without saying a word, she walked away. She made it all the way back to the house and to the back door before she heard his startled yell. She hurried through the back door and flipped the bolt. She looked up to see a surprised Ben frozen in place, biting into his sandwich. The door behind her shook in its frame as Aiden pounded.

"Dammit, Meryn, unlock the door this instant!"

"Go fuck yourself!" she screeched at the glass window panes. Behind her, Ben began to laugh then slightly choked on his sandwich. When his mouth was clear he gave her a salute.

"You tell him!" he cheered.

"Quit egging her on, Ben! Meryn, open the door now!"

Meryn shook her head.

"You do know he has a key, right?" Ben said nonchalantly.

She looked up at him, tears streaming down her face. "I don't want to see him right now." He sighed and put his plate down. He grabbed her hand and they ran. They ran up the stairs and through the halls. Just when she thought they couldn't go any further, he made them run in circles at the end of the hallway. She thought he was out of his mind until he reached up and tapped a tiny panel behind an antique mirror. A small opening appeared and he crouched down low and crawled inside. She followed him and he put the panel back. She was about to ask him how he knew about this when he placed a hand over her mouth. Barely breathing, they heard thundering footsteps in the hallway. In the darkness, Meryn waited.

"God dammit, Ben, this isn't funny!" Aiden roared.

"Aiden, whatever is the matter?" Meryn heard Adelaide ask.

"My stupid baby brother kidnapped my mate!" Aiden's voice was barely human.

"Calm down before I call your father. I'll be in the front drawing room waiting for you with a pot of tea. We'll drink a cup and you can explain why Meryn is upset enough with you to be hiding with Ben," Adelaide said reasonably.

"But!" Aiden roared.

"You have five seconds to get those canines retracted, young man, before I do it for you." Adelaide's voice was still level but had dropped an octave. It dawned on Meryn that, of course her voice could change; Adelaide was a shifter, too.

"Sorry, Mother," Aiden said sounding much calmer.

"Good. Now come downstairs with me and tell me all about it." Only when the sound of their footsteps disappeared entirely did Ben remove his hand. He groped in the darkness until he found her hand. He guided her through the small tunnel to a hidden room. It had a single small, round window that let in the fading afternoon sun.

"Man, I haven't heard Mom or Aiden that pissed in a long time. I haven't had to use this hiding place in the past two hundred years." Ben collapsed onto a long chaise lounge and a cloud of dust enveloped him. Meryn coughed and laughed as she tried to wipe off the dust from his clothes.

"Now you tell big brother Ben what Aiden did to make you so sad. Then we can plot a suitable revenge."

"You've done that a lot up here, haven't you?" She sat next to him on the lounge.

"You bet. My brothers were always bigger than me, but I was usually faster. I discovered this hidey-hole when I was a boy. My speed gave me enough time to run around to disperse my scent and duck in here. You can't move right away or they'll hear. I escaped many a beating that way."

"They didn't really beat you, did they?" Meryn, even though she was extremely pissed at him, couldn't imagine Aiden beating a younger brother.

"Beat may be a harsh word. Pound, maybe? Don't get me wrong, most of the time I totally deserved it, but that's just how brothers are. Now what did Aiden do? Maybe I can help." Ben's concerned brown eyes were her undoing. She was used to shouldering her pain and frustration alone. She wasn't used to having people worried about her or willing to anger their family members for her. She buried her face in her hands and cried. Ben wrapped an arm around her and held her close.

"Hey, nothing can be so bad that you and I can't take care of it. I know people who know people." Ben kissed her hair.

"Aiden doesn't want to live with me. Today was so wonderful, we went shopping and he showed me the city. He was perfect and charming and loving and passionate."

"Whoa on the passionate stuff sis, big bro doesn't need to hear that." She smiled timorously.

"Then Aiden says that we aren't to live together, that he has to live with his men and I have to learn how to keep house. That's not how I envisioned being together with someone. I'm anti-social, but that is too much space even for me." She wiped her nose on her sleeve.

"Aiden is in a tough spot. He's right. He can't live here. There's too much training and drills with the units for him to commute. Units live together because we can be called up at any time and have to organize and move out depending on the situation. We already arrive to scenes too late; there's no way Aiden can add twenty to forty minutes to that process for additional travel time and getting up to speed. You can't live there because living with a unit would be like living in a barracks."

"I don't want to live away from him. I'd miss his dumb ass."

"Sit down with him. Explain why you were upset. He's not like me. He doesn't understand the delicate workings of the female mind. You will literally have to spell it out for him."

"Maybe he doesn't really want me. He's called me a distraction a couple times already."

Ben laughed out loud.

"Of course you're a distraction; you wouldn't be his mate otherwise. Just your scent alone is a distraction to him. When you factor in your complete lack of knowledge about societal norms and your general wackiness, of course he's distracted. If he weren't, *then* you'd have to worry." Meryn looked at Ben as his words sunk in.

"He doesn't want me around because he wants me?" she asked and somehow that made sense.

"Pretty much. Now, let's go downstairs and have some tea. I bet Mom broke out the good stash to calm Aiden; it's delicious." Ben wagged his eyebrows at her.

"Thank you. Are you... will you be my friend?" Meryn held her breath.

"No."

Meryn's heart sank.

"But I will be your brother." Meryn tackled him and they landed on the floor.

"I've never had siblings before. Can I use your hiding spot if I need to escape Aiden again?"

"Of course, I live to drive my brothers crazy." Ben stood and helped her to her feet. They walked over to the wall and crouched back down again.

"Though I remember this being easier when I was younger." Ben squeezed through the small passage.

"Probably because you were smaller." Meryn giggled.

"Probably. One sec." He popped the panel off and helped her out before replacing it.

"Come on." He held out his hand and she took it, and they walked downstairs. She never had a brother before, but she liked the idea of someone being on her side for a change.

When they walked into the drawing room Aiden stood, his face full of remorse.

"Come along Benjamin, these two need to talk."

Ben's face fell, "But..."

"I'll make you your own pot in the kitchen." Adelaide winked at Meryn and pulled Ben out of the room before closing the door behind them.

"I'm sorry." Aiden said immediately.

"For what?"

"For talking down to you. For not realizing why you didn't want to be apart." Meryn couldn't forgive him just yet. She wanted to know how he felt.

"Why don't I want us to be apart?" she asked softly.

"Because you care about me." He watched her carefully.

"And how do you think I felt when it seemed like you were okay with being away from me?"

"Probably close to how I felt when you let my brother comfort you instead of me." She couldn't take the pain in his eyes anymore.

"You are such a big, freaking idiot." She threw her hands up. He watched her cautiously.

"But ... you're *my* big, freaking idiot and I don't want us to be apart." Aiden shoved the ottoman out of the way and pulled her into his arms.

"And you're my tiny menace. I don't want us to be apart either, but I'm not sure how we can get this to work," he admitted.

She shrugged. "There's no rush, right? We can figure something out."

"Yeah, we'll definitely work something out, because you're right. I don't think we should be apart either."

"Good. Now, can I have some of this amazing tea Ben told me about?"

Aiden laughed. "Come on, we'll have some fresh in the kitchen." Together they left the drawing room and walked into the kitchen.

"I'll share my tea with Meryn but not you, since you've already had some." Ben pouted.

"Little boys forever, I swear." Adelaide rolled her eyes.

"I'll just have a sip, I'm more of a coffee drinker anyway, unless I'm on my laptop, then I prefer Earl Grey, its better on my eyes." Meryn picked up Ben's cup and took a small sip. The tea was sweet, but not a heavy sweet.

"This is delicious. He likes his tea sweet like me!"

"Actually, there's no sweetener in it. It's naturally sweet," Adelaide explained.

"I love it! What is it?" Meryn took another healthy swig and passed the cup regretfully back to Ben.

"It's a hybridization of a rare Chinese Oolong and a fae blend. It's called Honeycup." Adelaide pulled out a small canister.

"The boys get it for me every year at Christmas." She smiled at her sons. Meryn turned and gave Aiden puppy dog eyes.

"Looks like we have to add Meryn to the list this year." Meryn danced around happily before she remembered that morning.

"Maybe you should save some for your dad," she suggested.

"Byron? Why?" Adelaide looked interested.

"I may or may not have called the vampire Elder guy a douchebag." Both Ben and Adelaide stared at her.

"It was an accident!" Meryn exclaimed. Adelaide stood.

"Marius! Marius!" she called and began to pull ingredients from the cabinets.

"My lady! What's happened?" Marius appeared in the doorway, a cleaning cloth in one hand.

"Can you reach out to your contact in the city to see if they have any fresh lobster delivered from Maine today? I'm afraid Byron may have had a rough afternoon with the council, and will need a special dinner," she grimaced.

"Of course. How bad?" he asked. Meryn looked anywhere but at Adelaide.

"I'm making a Honey Bun cake." was Adelaide's response. Marius paled.

"I'll go myself." Marius removed the apron and darted from the room.

"I'm so sorry!" Meryn wailed.

"Don't be, sweetheart, you haven't said anything we haven't all thought at one point or another. Plus, you're still so very young and new to our world." Adelaide pulled a dozen eggs from the refrigerator.

"She did earn an invitation from Elder Vi'Ailean to visit his prized gardens," Aiden said, grinning from ear to ear. Adelaide paused and she looked delighted when she turned to Meryn.

"High praise, indeed. Only a handful of people have ever been invited to the heart of a fae garden. I can't wait to drop that pretty little bomb on Daphne Bowers. Wonderful job, Meryn," she congratulated.

"But what about the vampire guy?"

"He's only popular with other vampires. It won't hurt your reputation one bit if that story leaks out; it might actually help." Adelaide giggled. "He is a pompous douchebag though," Adelaide said, breaking open eggs.

"Mother!" Aiden and Ben sounded shocked. Adelaide ignored them.

"Oh, Aiden, you might want to take Meryn to her apartment to fetch her things before dinner. She might like to put on some new underthings." Adelaide turned to the cabinet and reached for a bowl.

"How did you know he ripped them off? Are paranormals psychic?" Meryn demanded. Adelaide dropped a large stainless steel bowl. The deafening silence made the clanking of the metal bowl on the stone floor seem amplified.

"He did? Oh, dear. I only assumed that you would like fresh clothes." Adelaide blushed clear to her hairline. Beside her Aiden groaned and buried his face in his hands. Meryn turned to Ben, who was staring at them, his eyes wide.

"Right. Well, on that note, let's go!" Meryn grabbed Aiden's hand and pulled him out of the kitchen.

Just as they cleared the doorway, Ben exploded into laughter.

"I love having a sister!" she heard him shout. Meryn felt her heart swell. She had a feeling she was going to like having a brother too, if she could stop embarrassing herself around her new family.

CHAPTER FIVE

Aiden pulled up to a questionable-looking apartment building and stared in horror. When Meryn got out of the car and walked past a drug dealer to check her mail, he started having heart palpitations. She lived *here*?

He quickly got out and growled lowly at the man eyeing his mate. The man glanced up, startled, and kept moving down the street. The storm door was nothing but a sheet of cracked glass and rusted metal. When he stepped into the foyer, he noticed that the entryway light bulb had been removed. How convenient for a mugger. He was grateful that he wasn't able to see the state of the floor, but was concerned about the security risk the dim foyer presented. He followed her up a set of dark stairs, careful not to touch the railing. Meryn fished out her keys and went to unlock her door. The second her hand touched the knob, the door swung inward slightly. She jumped back as if she had been electrocuted. Her eyes were huge when she turned to him. Pushing her behind him, he violently kicked open the door, making it crash loudly into the wall. Meryn thumped his back.

"Shush, they may hear you," she whispered.

“Baby, if they're robbing the place, I want them to hear me so they leave,” he explained.

“Oh. Good idea.” She nodded.

“Stay here.”

“Yeah, *fuck* that. I'm sticking to you like glue. I've seen this horror movie, the person waiting in the hallway dies.” Meryn shook her head.

Aiden turned to stare at her.

“Later we're going to talk about your movie choices.” He edged through the open doorway and looked around the room.

“How many rooms?” he asked.

“Main room, kitchen and bedroom with attached bath. That's it.” Meryn grabbed his belt and he felt her small hand at his back.

He walked into the main room. There were no closets for anyone to be hiding in. He popped his head into the tiny, galley style kitchen. It was empty.

“Baby, stay here while I check the bedroom, okay?” She nodded. She closed the apartment door and her eyes darted around the room. He could tell she was trying to see if anything had been taken.

When he opened the bedroom door, he was immediately overwhelmed with the scent of another male. Someone had marked this room with urine and seed as his territory. Feeling sick, he pulled back the covers of the bed to find that the mattress had been slashed and semen decorated the pillows. His bear rose to the surface, roaring. He barely managed to keep from shifting. Breathing through his mouth to stay calm, he checked the bathroom and the closet.

“What's taking so long?” Meryn asked, about to walk in.

“Stay out!” he barked. She looked at him with a hurt expression, but then noticed his barely contained rage. She stared past him, her eyes noticing every small detail.

"Is that... is that semen?" she asked. He didn't answer; he didn't have to.

"I'm going to be sick." Meryn bolted down the hallway and he was right on her heels. She leaned over the kitchen sink and lost her latte. He rubbed her back. She rinsed her mouth out with tap water then stumbled to the fridge. She threw the door open and grabbed a container of orange juice. She swished the juice around her mouth before spitting that out in the sink. She took another drink and swallowed. Her hands were shaking when she put the juice back.

Aiden reached for his phone.

"What's up?" Colton asked.

"Have the Beta Unit fill in for you guys and bring Alpha to Meryn's apartment. I want the guys here five minutes ago," Aiden growled into the phone.

"Are you injured?" Colton demanded, in the background Aiden could hear Gavriel barking orders.

"I'm fine, so is Meryn. We're at the old apartment building on Ninth Street, apartment 3B. Just get here quick."

"On our way." Colton hung up.

"What if you hadn't found me yesterday and kidnapped me? What if I had come home to find this guy waiting for me?" Her body looked like it was trying to shake itself apart. Aiden scooped her up and sat down on the couch with her in his lap. He cuddled her close and kissed her hair.

"You were meant to be with me. It's why Fate had you climb that fence. He will never come near you, I promise you, Meryn. This guy is a walking dead man." He didn't have the heart to tell her that the semen was fresh. They had missed this creep by minutes.

"Let's get you packed up. The guys will be here soon." He stood and placed her on her feet.

"How will I know what he touched? I don't want anything he... touched." She made a face.

"I'll bring anything that carries just your scent out here for you to pack up. When that is done, you can walk through the bedroom to see if the things that he touched are things you're willing to part with. If you want to keep those items, I will clean them for you." He lifted her chin and kissed her softly. "How's that?" he asked gently.

Her eyes filled. "You're amazing. I might be sorry I hit you with your toilet after all." Though her eyes were filled with tears, she grinned.

"You're never going to let that go are you?"

"Nope."

"My little warrior." He ruffled her hair. "I'm going to get started; let the guys in or they'll break down the door when they get here.

Aiden had most of her things out in the family room for her to pack before the men arrived. When she walked through the bedroom to see what had been 'contaminated,' he noticed that her bottom lip quivered, but she took a deep breath and went over everything. His heart ached for the fear she was fighting, but he was proud of her spirit.

In the end, the items left over were things she could part with. Aiden was furious to see that nearly all of her underthings, lingerie, and nightgowns made up the pile on the bed. He would get her brand new things and make sure she had fun picking them out.

Gavriel hissed when he walked through the bedroom door.

"We need to find this guy; he needs to die." Aiden clenched and unclenched his fists.

"It will be done, brother. We will not let a threat to your mate exist." Gavriel laid a hand on his shoulder. Aiden was grateful for the unit's support. He knew, had they not been able to get there when they did, he might have lost control and gone after this guy alone. But knowing that his brothers were on their way helped him keep his bear under wraps until they arrived.

"Aiden, can you smell it?" Gavriel took another deep breath.

"The fact that this asshole jerked off all over the place? Yeah, I smell that."

"Then you missed the fact that it is a shifter." Gavriel took a step closer to the bed. "It is faint, so faint." He surprised Aiden by walking over to the closet and pulling out a hanger before returning to the bed. Using the plastic hanger, he shifted the bras and panties around.

"Found it." Gavriel lifted up a bra with the hanger.

Aiden shook his head. Whatever it was, even being a shifter, he couldn't smell it.

Gavriel laid the bra on the comforter and used the hanger to point to the bra clasp.

"Someone forgot about small metal hooks when they were using this to jerk off. There are faint traces of blood around each hook."

Aiden stepped closer and looked again. He could see smudges of red, but he would have missed them since the bra was a floral print.

"Good work. Bag it up and take it with us."

They walked out of her bedroom to the family room. Aiden snarled when he saw Darian packing the few pairs of panties that the psycho had missed into a small suitcase. Meryn laughed and walked over to him. She patted him on the chest and he quieted down.

"You're so cute." She smiled up at him. Aiden was glad to see that the traces of fear were gone. He frowned down at her.

"I am not cute. I am a ferocious killing machine. Paranormals everywhere tremble before me."

"My teddy bear." She pulled on his shirt until he bent down enough for her to reach his lips. She kissed him and went back to packing. He looked over to see Colton about to say something.

"Not a motherfucking word," he warned.

"Yes, Commander." Colton gave a salute, but his eyes danced with suppressed mirth. Aiden sighed. It was going to be a long day.

While they finished packing, Aiden called his mother and let her know what had happened. Meryn felt like part of the family when she promised to make dinner extra special for both her and Byron.

"What's next, Commander?" Colton asked.

"Call Lorcan, tell him I'm pulling Alpha out of rotation. Until we catch this fucker, you guys are assigned guard duty at my parents' house. I'm not letting Meryn out of my sight."

Meryn tried to hide her sigh of relief. It wasn't that she didn't think she'd be safe with Adelaide and Byron; she just felt better knowing that Aiden would be there, too.

"Roger that, be right back." Colton was pulling out his cell phone as he walked out the door.

Aiden turned to Meryn.

"Everything packed?"

"Yup, Darian and Keelan took the last of the boxes down and Gavriel volunteered to speak to my landlord about my lease."

Aiden smirked. "I bet he did. Come on; let's go make sure the guys aren't causing trouble."

Meryn didn't wait for him to take her hand; she latched on to his arm instead. She wasn't sorry to see the last of the apartment. She knew it wasn't in a good part of town, but it was the only place that didn't have a waiting list. When they passed the rental office, Meryn peeked inside and saw that Gavriel had the slimy-looking landlord up against the wall.

"And you will replace the front door and make sure that the foyer is well lit, will you not?" Gavriel's tone was pleasant, but the man in front of him was sweating bullets. Keelan watched, looking amused. Every time the landlord looked in his direction, Keelan would wave his hand and the trio of rats at his feet would hiss at the slumlord.

"Enough fun, guys, time to move out," Aiden barked. Gavriel and Keelan turned in unison and joined them. Outside, Colton and Darian had two men pinned against their SUV.

Aiden sighed. "I swear, I can't take them anywhere."

"When we got here, they had taken the tires off your car, Aiden, and I think Darian and Colton were just making sure that everything was good to go," Keelan said. Aiden's dark gaze turned to the two men. He stalked over and stood behind Colton.

"See, you didn't move quickly enough, our boss here has noticed what you've done. We tried to warn you, buddy." Colton spread his hands as if giving up.

"No, please! We're sorry! We put them back! We put them back!" the larger of the two men babbled.

"Run." Aiden's harsh tone made both men flinch. They stared at him in terror.

"I said, run! If you look back, I'll be the one right behind you!" Aiden growled. Both men screamed and took off.

Meryn walked over to stand beside the men.

"You're all little boys. Every single one of you." She nudged the back of Aiden's knee with her foot, laughing when his leg collapsed, causing him to wobble.

"Those men deserved worse. Maybe they will think twice before doing such wicked things again," Gavriel's tone was cordial.

"Move out!" Aiden barked and the men moved to their car. Aiden held the door open for her and she got in. Two days. Her life had been completely changed in just two short days. She shook her head and tried not to think about it. She was having more fun now than she had in years. She glanced over at Aiden. She had never been in love before, but so far it was a wonderful feeling. Growing up, she had learned to rely on herself. Having people take care of her was something new. Grudgingly, she was being forced to open her tiny bubble and let others in. That was more terrifying than falling in love.

"Whatever it is, quit thinking about it so hard. What will happen, will happen." Aiden's voice startled her out of her anxiety spiral.

"What if I'm scared about what will happen?" she whispered.

"Tell me what scares you, and I'll kill it," Aiden shrugged. Meryn shook her head; of course the arrogant bastard wouldn't dream that she was scared about her future with him.

“Why are you so confident about us? Do mates ever get divorced?” She watched his face carefully. She was beginning to like his frowny face. If that wasn't love, what was?

“No. Once we find our destined mates, we are with them for life.”

“How do you know that we're destined mates? Maybe you just like my perfume.” Meryn didn't know why she was fighting this so hard. Given what she had been told about paranormals, she knew Aiden was her mate. But, it was difficult to believe that he blindly accepted her because of Fate and not because he desired her.

“You don't wear perfume.” Aiden's simple reply made her want to beat her head against the dash. She turned and stared out the window, silent.

After a few minutes, she watched as the car Colton was driving turned to head toward Aiden's parents' house. Their car veered off to the right as Aiden pulled over to the side of the road. The tree branches overhead extended out over the road creating a fall-colored canopy in reds, oranges and yellows.

“Why did you stop here?”

“You don't wear perfume,” Aiden repeated. She went to turn away, but his hand cupped the back of her head so that she had to look at him.

“You don't wear perfume, so what I smell is the very essence of you. Every slight nuance, every chemical change your body makes, I can smell it. Every time you're angry, every time you're sad, every time you're aroused, there is a distinct smell. Today I smelled your fear, true terror, for the first time, and I nearly lost control. I know you're my mate because even though your scent is a physical manifestation, it's a true reflection of your soul, and that bright soul belongs to me.” His blue eyes seemed to radiate their own inner light. It was as if she could truly see into the depths of his being and what she saw brought tears to her eyes.

Deep in his heart, she saw herself.

“I'm weird and awkward! I don't like most people and I don't have one of those social mouth filters!” Meryn exclaimed, wiping her eyes. Aiden's smile was kind.

“I know.”

“I eat junk food and I don't know how, but I always find a way to get into trouble.” Meryn sniffed and wiped her nose on her sleeve. Aiden's mouth twitched.

“I know.”

“I can be violent, short-tempered and vindictive, and I don't know the first thing about being a lady.” Meryn looked into his face, saddened that she might not live up to expectations. He nodded.

“I know. I know all of that already, Meryn. You scaled a fence to trespass on private property because you were curious. You accused me of wanting to wear your skin and you knocked me unconscious with the back of my toilet. You called one of the oldest and most revered members of our society a douchebag, and threatened to castrate my best friend. That was roughly in the first twenty-four hours I've known you.” Meryn closed her eyes and dropped her head. Warm fingers under her chin guided her to look back up at him.

“Do you know what I thought about all of that?” Aiden asked softly. She shook her head, afraid to answer.

“I thought, 'This woman is completely unhinged. I don't know what the hell she's going to say or do next.' “ He paused. Meryn let her tears fall. She knew that there was no way he would want her! She twisted her face trying to escape his hand, but he refused to let go. Seconds later his lips were on hers. He nipped her lower lip until she opened her mouth. Then he began his assault. His tongue was relentless, twining and dominating hers. When he pulled away, she whimpered at the loss.

"I also thought, 'This woman is the most beautiful, brilliant and captivating person I have ever met. She will keep me on my toes for the rest of our lives. And I will love her until the day I die.' " Aiden's lips returned, this time to kiss her gently. When she looked up at him, there was no doubt left in her heart. She was meant to be his, for the rest of her life. Even though she was human, she felt the bonds that tied them together and she felt grateful for the man beside her. She felt the tears trickle down her cheeks.

"I didn't know what love was until you."

"The things you say to me, woman." Aiden sucked and teased her lips until they were both gasping. She pulled back and looked up at him.

"I will drive you out of your mind." She smiled through her tears. Aiden used his thumbs to wipe her cheeks.

"Gods, I hope so!" With a final quick kiss, he started the car and drove them back to her new home.

"I'm sorry someone broke into your place, Meryn, but can't help but appreciate the consequences. We get to crash here and eat Marius's food!" Colton shoveled another huge lobster tail into his mouth.

After returning to the house, Aiden had called the other unit leader, Lorcan, and arranged for him to interview the parents of the missing couples as requested by the council. He was serious about staying at her side.

"I can't imagine what a trying day it has been for you, my dear." Byron reached across the table and patted her hand.

"It wasn't so bad. I'm more sorry about any trouble I may have caused with that vampire Elder." Meryn grimaced at the memory. Gavriel's head turned in her direction.

"What is this about Elder Evreux?" He raised an eyebrow. Meryn felt her cheeks flush. Ben chortled at his mother's side. Now all of the men were looking at her, including Aiden's two older brothers, who happened to be home for dinner.

"It seems Meryn still has to learn that paranormals have exceptional hearing. She was trying to whisper something to Aiden and of course everyone in the room heard." Byron's face was stern.

"What'd she say?" Colton was on the edge of his seat.

"She asked if all vampires were douchebags, because Gavriel wasn't." Byron's cool composure collapsed and he began to laugh. He laughed so hard, he had tears streaming down his cheeks. The men around the table seemed to be in shock. Meryn couldn't tell if it was from her social gaffe or Byron's reaction to it.

"She called Elder Evreux a douchebag?" Gavriel whispered. *Shoot me now!* Meryn wanted to sink through the floor. Around the table, male laughter boomed. First Colton, then Darian, then Keelan, followed by Aiden's brothers. The one that shocked her the most was Gavriel's silent laughter. He simply covered his face with his hand and shook. She watched him closely.

“Is he breathing?” she asked Aiden, concerned. Aiden looked at his second-in-command and then raised a hand and slapped him on the back. Gavriel inhaled deeply and a contagious chuckle emerged. This, of course, set off the entire table again.

“I don't see how that's funny. I was so embarrassed.” Meryn frowned down at her lobster tail, determined to crack her own instead of having Aiden do hers again.

“We're not laughing at you, dear. It's just that so many of us have wanted to call him that and worse over the centuries, it feels good to finally see it happen.” Byron kissed her cheek.

“And it was my daughter who put that ass in his place. What an amazing day!” Byron easily snapped another lobster shell, handed Meryn the meat and wordlessly took the one she had been struggling with. Accepting that she was officially the weakest person in the room, no matter where she went, she decided to just enjoy the lobster.

“My mate is brutal in her honesty.” Aiden winked down at her.

“Only because I know my mate will keep me safe,” she said back to him flippantly. The laughter and chatter around the table quieted. Meryn glanced around to see what had happened. Aiden was staring down at her in wonder.

“What?” She frowned up at him.

“Say it again.”

“Say what?”

“What you just said.” Aiden's smile couldn't be wider.

“Because my mate will keep me safe?” Meryn looked up at him, confused.

Aiden let out a loud shout before he stood and scooped her up in his arms. Laughing, he swung her around in the air.

"Oh, that's just beautiful." Adelaide sniffed and dabbed her eyes with her napkin.

"Aiden, I'm gonna puke on you." Meryn's head was spinning. He immediately stopped and sat down, this time with her in his lap. She swayed, trying to get the room to stop spinning as he nuzzled the back of her neck.

"What in the hell has gotten into you?" she demanded.

"It's the first time you've called me your mate." He beamed at his parents.

"Oh. I kinda accepted that I'm stuck with you." Meryn picked up a breadstick to munch on until her stomach calmed down.

"Because I'm your destined mate?" Aiden teased.

"No, because I love you and I am horribly possessive. I'm never letting you go. So even if Fate made a mistake, she can kiss my ass." Meryn waved her breadstick around like a sword. Aiden stood, picking her up in his arms.

"Mother, Father, if you'll excuse us."

"Of course, son." Byron sounded choked up. All of the men at the table were grinning like idiots.

"I'm still hungry!" Meryn squirmed. Aiden ignored her and sprinted from the room, heading upstairs.

Once in his room, he set her down and closed the door.

"You must say these things on purpose." He stalked forward. She backed up.

"What do you mean?"

"You must know what they do to me." She backed up until the back of her legs hit the bed.

"Aiden..." He went to kiss her and she pushed him away. "We can't yet." Meryn felt lightheaded; all the blood in her body was boiling in her cheeks. He froze.

"What do you mean, we can't? We're mated. You just claimed me as your mate in front of my entire family. Give me one good reason why we can't!" he bellowed.

"Because I started my cycle this evening," she blurted out the words. When he didn't respond, she looked up. He blinked. Then blinked again.

"What does that mean?"

"What do you mean, 'what does that mean'?"

"It means I have no idea what you're saying. Again!" Aiden threw his arms up in the air.

Meryn thought about it. He had been raised by a warrior father and had three brothers. When he left his parents' house, he moved in with other men to train to be a warrior. She didn't really see Adelaide as the type of woman who would explain these things to her sons; those things were probably never discussed back then. It hit her like a ton of bricks: he really had no clue what she was talking about.

"Right. Do you remember when you told me that paranormals can only conceive one time during the year?"

Aiden nodded.

"Okay, for humans, we can conceive every month of the year. For a human woman, if we don't conceive, our wombs shed their lining in preparation for pregnancy for the upcoming month." She looked at him and he was staring at her, waiting for her to continue.

"So basically every month my womb contracts, rips the lining away from my uterus and I bleed and discharge that lining for about three to four days, all while in excruciating pain." In fact, all the bouncing around had kicked her cramps up in high gear, and she could tell this month was going to be a bad one for cramps. It figured.

"You mean to tell me that you are bleeding internally, right now?" Aiden's face drained of color. She nodded. He picked her up and placed her in the center of the bed.

"What do I do? Should I get a doctor, my mother?" Meryn almost felt bad at his level of panic, but her cramps were making her more evil than usual.

"I'm okay for now. But I noticed when we were packing that I only had one tampon left and I used that this evening. Can you run to the store and pick up some more?"

Meryn, you are going to hell!

Aiden nodded quickly, a shell-shocked expression on his face.

"Will they help? Should I leave you alone? Maybe I should have my brother examine you." Aiden paced beside the bed nervously.

"You want your brother to examine up inside me?" Meryn asked, amused. His head snapped to her and he growled.

"No! Of course not!"

"Aiden, this is a natural part of being a human woman. The pain should subside in a day or two, then I'll be just fine. Until then, I'll be very, very cranky." At least he couldn't say he hadn't been warned.

"Okay. Right. Okay. You stay right there in bed. I'll have Marius bring you up a snack. Do you need an extra blanket?" Aiden's concerned face hovered over her. She shook her head.

"No, Aiden, I'm fine." She smiled up at him.

"Okay. Be right back. Don't move!" Aiden was almost to the door; he paused and ran back to the bed. He kissed her gently as if she would break and then raced from the room. When the door shut, Meryn smiled to herself and curled up into a small ball as another wave of cramps started. Somehow, knowing that her badass mate was going tampon shopping made enduring her cramps a little easier than normal.

CHAPTER SIX

Aiden ran down the stairs, heart pounding. He skidded into the dining room and all eyes turned to him.

"That was quick, brother," Adam teased.

"Alpha Unit, move out. We have a mission," Aiden barked, and turned on his heel and left the room. Behind him, he could hear chairs being pushed back quickly and footsteps racing to catch up to him. He grabbed the keys to the SUV from the foyer table and went to the start the vehicle.

Minutes later, his men were in the car checking their sidearms and pooling their weapon stashes together.

"Aiden, what's the target? Did you get a call while you were upstairs?" Colton asked.

"No, I..." Aiden didn't know where to begin. The idea that his mate was upstairs in pain and bleeding internally made him feel ill. Whatever she asked for she would get. Clearing his throat, he continued, "Did you know that human women have the ability to conceive every month?" he asked. Around him the men shook their heads.

"Well evidently, when they don't conceive, their wombs turn inside out and shed their lining. It's extremely painful and causes internal bleeding." Aiden took a shuddering breath.

"Do you mean to say that Meryn is going through this now?" Colton looked shocked.

"I could barely tell she was in any pain; she's very brave." Aiden appreciated the level of admiration in Keelan's voice.

"Human females are truly mysterious beings," Gavriel added.

"They are. She does this every month. How does she survive? Wouldn't she die from blood loss?" Aiden gripped the steering wheel and turned the car onto the main highway. At their current speed they should be at the human city of Madison in a little under twenty minutes. He was sure he could find tampons there.

"Since it happens every month, I don't think she'll die from blood loss. What's the mission?" Darian asked.

"She needs tampons. Evidently it helps with this process. We have to secure the location of where they are being sold, acquire them and then get them back to my mate posthaste."

"You can rely on us, Aiden." Colton's hand appeared from the back seat to clap him on the shoulder. Suddenly he didn't feel quite so panicked. He wasn't about to let anything happen to his mate and he knew his unit had his back.

Not soon enough for his liking, they parked at the local grocery store, Duck In.

"Everyone ready?"

"Yes, sir!" The men sounded off. He nodded and they exited the vehicle. When they walked into the store, the cashier stopped what she was doing and stared. Aiden glanced behind him. Darian had walked in with a crossbow strapped to his back.

"Darian, maybe you could leave the crossbow in the car."

Darian shook his head. "No, sir, you're distracted with concern over your mate's health. We need to be hyper-vigilant."

Aiden thought about it for a second then nodded his approval. He clapped Darian on the shoulder.

"Good man."

Together, the five men walked up and down the aisles. Everywhere they went, eyes followed them.

"We're being watched," Colton whispered.

"I know. Just keep looking, maybe we'll get out of this without injury." Aiden's eyes scanned each shelf that contained medicine.

"Sir. Found them!" Keelan yelled. The other four men converged on his location. Together they started scanning boxes.

"Sir, I don't mean any disrespect to your mate, but the way these are shaped, do they go..." Keelan couldn't finish the sentence. Aiden understood what the young witch was saying.

"I think you're right, Keelan. It must help with the pain in some way."

Understanding filled Keelan's eyes. "Of course."

After a few minutes Aiden felt his head spinning with confusion.

"Sir, I don't know if these are safe. There is a warning about toxic shock syndrome. These things can kill!" Keelan dropped the box he held and wiped his hands on his pants. The other men immediately dropped the boxes they had been holding.

"This is what she asked for, so maybe she knows of a way to avoid that." Aiden didn't like the idea that these things could kill, but if she needed them he would take them to her.

"What do you think Super Plus means? She didn't say anything about pluses or minuses." Aiden held up two similar boxes except one said Plus and the other said Super Plus.

"Sir, I saw a chart on the side of this one, I believe that has to do with the absorbency capacity," Darian explained.

"Absorbency--you mean how much blood..." Aiden shuddered. His poor mate!

Darian paled, "Yes, sir."

Aiden felt panicked. Did it matter? What if he got one that didn't absorb as much as she needed, would it hurt her in the long run?

"Sir, I like this one. It says here it has an antigravity leak guard braid." Keelan held up a blue box.

"Antigravity, really? That has to be one of the best ones right? Is it a Super?"

Keelan checked. "Super Plus, sir."

"We'll take that one."

"How many boxes, do you think?" Keelan asked. Aiden looked around at the men. They all shrugged.

"How many are there?"

"About fifteen."

"Grab them all."

"Yes, sir!" Keelan and Darian grabbed every box on the shelf. Together, they made their way over to the registers. Instead of the young, pretty cashier, there was now a grizzled-looking older human. They placed their boxes on the belt and Aiden approached the register.

The older man took one look at the fifteen boxes on the conveyor belt and then eyed the five men in front of him.

"Son, your woman sent you out?" he asked in a lazy southern voice.

"Yes, sir." There was something about this old human that made Aiden want to salute.

"Newly married?"

"Yes, sir."

"Never been shopping for these before, I reckon."

"No, sir."

"You have no idea what you're doing, do ya, boy?" The old man regarded him with pity. Aiden slumped forward.

"No, sir."

"I heard your discussion about these things with your men here. Military?" he asked as he rang up each box slowly.

"Yes, sir."

"I ken tell. Anyway, y'all done good. These ones sell pretty well; most of the ladyfolk like 'em. Now, if'n you don't mind some advice from a man who has been married for forty-seven years and has raised six girls?" He paused.

"Of course not! Any advice you give will be welcome." Aiden heaved a sigh of relief. No wonder he felt the need to salute this man. He had lived around women all of his life and lived to tell the tale.

"Now, like I was sayin', these right here sell. But if you're just learning your lady's cycle I recommend the box that has all kinds in it. Some days women bleed lighter than others. With a box that has a mix, she'll have whatever she needs."

"Keelan!" Aiden barked. The old man jumped a bit as Keelan raced back to the aisle and returned with five boxes that held a variety of capacities.

"Another thing. My wife most days is as sweet as pie. But on the days when she was a'havin' her cycle, she got downright ornery. Threw an iron at me once."

"That doesn't sound too bad," Darian commented.

"She had just been ironing, so it was still hot," the older man clarified. Darian flinched.

"Sir, you say that under normal conditions, your wife was sweet and good natured?" Gavriel asked. The older man nodded. Gavriel turned to Aiden concern on his face.

"Meryn is violent and crazy under normal conditions." Gavriel looked as sick as Aiden felt.

"Dude, you're so fucked," Colton whispered.

"If that's the case, I was only going to suggest a chocolate cake, but if you have a feisty gal, you might want to grab some of the brownies, too. Chocolate eases their pain and makes them loving again. Well, most times," the old man explained.

"Darian, grab three chocolate cakes and five pans of brownies," Aiden ordered.

"Yes, sir!"

"Son, how violent is yer woman?" The older man asked sounding curious. Aiden leaned in and whispered.

"She knocked me unconscious once with the back of my toilet." The older man's eyes widened.

"Better get you some chocolate bars. You can throw those from a distance."

Aiden nodded. "I like the way you think." He grabbed the entire box of chocolate bars from the shelf next to the register as Darian returned with the sweets. The old man rang up his items and gave him a total. Aiden paid and the men grabbed the bags. They went to leave and Aiden paused. He went back to the register.

"Thank you very much for your insight. You are very brave and wise to have lived through so much." Aiden offered him his hand. The older man chuckled and shook Aiden's hand.

"Sounds like you have a firecracker on your hands, son."

Aiden grinned wide. "Yes sir, I do, and I wouldn't have it any other way."

"Good for you, son. Come back any time for advice."

"Thank you, sir."

Aiden knew that he had found an ally and a valuable source of information on how to take care of his human mate. Feeling better than he had since Meryn explained her condition, he got in the car and drove back to Lycaonia.

"So where is he now?" Sydney asked.

"Out getting me something from the store. I'm not sure how long it's going to take him so you'll have to talk fast." Meryn adjusted her cell phone on her ear. As soon as Aiden left, she remembered the café owner's offer. She decided that while Aiden was out, she would give him a call.

"Girl, I can talk fast. Now...most of the ladies, despite their paranormal selves, are sheep pure and simple, or should I say simpleton. I swear they share brain cells. There's a real mob mentality with that bunch. Imagine every single catty, hateful, backstabbing bitch you ever hated when you read a regency romance novel and put them in one room and you have the Daughters of Lycaonia Sewing Circle."

"How did you know I read regency romance?" Meryn interrupted.

"Hasn't everyone?" Sydney asked.

"Good point. Continue."

"Anyway. Most of the women are harmless little sheep, unless they are following someone's example. In most cases it's either mimicking Adelaide because she really is perfection, dah-ling, or they become backstabbing heifers when they are trying to stay on Daphne Bowers' good side to avoid retribution."

"So Daphne is the one to watch out for?"

"Yup. Rumor has it she practically had a meltdown when she heard that Adelaide convinced the council to do that spell to call the warrior's mates to them. She felt like Adelaide was upstaging her daughter-in-law who just popped pregnant."

"I heard that's like a real important thing," Meryn murmured.

"Girl, you don't know the half of it. In our society, it's a *huge* deal when a woman gets pregnant. The older crowd views each pregnancy as a blessing from the Gods, like, literally. There's no proof, but I would bet money that Daphne was the one that spread the rumors about Adelaide using black magic to get pregnant seven hundred years ago when she got pregnant with Aiden. Daphne's husband had just petitioned the council to say that Byron had held his council seat for too long and that they needed fresh ideas. They were leaning in his favor when Adelaide got pregnant. Everyone took that as a sign that the Gods were favoring House McKenzie and Byron was able to keep his council seat. Of course, that was reinforced later when Adelaide got pregnant again with Ben."

"Wow. Womb Wars."

"No lie. Makes me glad to be a gay man."

"So my being there is going to seem like Adelaide is trying to one-up Daphne?"

"Absolutely."

"They'll probably be really passive-aggressive and cruel to me, huh?" Meryn asked feeling depressed.

"You can count on that."

"So why am I going again?" she asked.

"Because if you don't, it will look bad for Adelaide." Sydney's voice sounded sympathetic.

"This is gonna suck."

"Sorry, hun. If you survive, swing by the café and I'll make you something special," Sydney offered.

"You're sweet. Thanks."

"Anytime. Listen, I gotta run, Justice is giving me bedroom eyes, if you know what I mean. Good luck tomorrow."

"Thanks again, Sydney, good night."

"Night." Sydney hung up and Meryn stared at her phone. A knock on the door had her jumping.

"Little miss, I've brought you some chamomile tea to help ease your cramps." Marius set the tea cup down on the nightstand. She stared up at him.

"How did you know?"

"I've been serving Lady Adelaide since she was your age and have a mate of my own. Plus..."--he cleared his throat--"a female smells different when she's begun her cycle." Marius's eyes twinkled.

"Just how old are you anyway?" Meryn sipped the tea and sighed. It was sweet, just how she liked it. She was starting to understand what Adelaide meant by needing a squire. Marius was comforting to have around.

"Older than I look. What did you tell Master Aiden? He ran out of here a bit wild-eyed." Marius raised a silver brow.

"I didn't lie," Meryn said quickly.

"Of course not. I think it will do him some good to think about the more practical things in life. He's a mated man now, and these things come with that responsibility."

Meryn felt her eyes grow heavy.

"You rock, did you know that?"

He smiled. "Yes."

When a yawn caught her off guard, she became suspicious.

"Did you put something in my tea?"

He nodded. "Yes, little miss. You've had a very exciting past couple of days, plus, you've started your cycle. You need a good night's rest." He pulled the covers up to her ears.

"Sneaky squire." Meryn yawned again.

"Of course. Good night, sweet Meryn."

"Good night, Marius, thank you." Meryn felt his warm hand push back her bangs in a fatherly gesture before she surrendered to the darkness.

When Meryn woke the next morning, she sat up and glanced around the room in shock. Boxes of tampons, cakes and brownies covered the surfaces of the nightstands and dresser. She hopped out of bed, grabbed a box, and headed to the shower. After washing up, she opened up a suitcase and almost danced in delight at being able to put on different clothes. Today was that sewing circle thing. She held up her t-shirts and sighed. She didn't have anything even remotely feminine. Nothing like the exquisite dresses Adelaide wore. She put a hand over her lower stomach as her cramps started back up. *Fuck it.* She was going to be comfortable. She pulled on her socks, jeans and boots. Instead of a pretty lace bra, she put on her favorite white cotton one. When she reached for her t-shirt, she hesitated. Thinking of how welcoming Adelaide had been, she chose the pink *Strawberry Shortcake* shirt. It was at least pink. She fixed her hair in a spike or two and used her pressed powder compact to take down the shine of her nose. She checked the mirror and shrugged. This was as good as it was going to get.

When she walked into the dining room for breakfast, everyone looked at her in horror.

"What are you doing out of bed?" Aiden jumped up.

"I was hungry and wanted breakfast. Can't I have breakfast?" she asked, confused.

"Of course you can. Come sit next to me, dear. I don't think Aiden fully appreciates how strong women can be." Meryn sat between Adelaide and Aiden. She noticed that Aiden watched her very carefully. Maybe she had laid it on too thick last night.

"I got you cake." Aiden leaned in and kissed her cheek.

"I saw. I totally plan on eating it later."

"Which one?"

"All of them."

"All?" Aiden asked.

"Yup, I don't know how you knew I was craving chocolate, but I swear last night I would have killed for some."

She saw Colton give Aiden a thumbs-up. What on earth had they gotten into last night?

"We can delay introducing you to the sewing circle if you're feeling unwell. As a shifter, I only get my cycle once a year; I can't imagine getting it every month." Adelaide shuddered.

"It's not so bad when you get used to it." Marius set a full plate of eggs, bacon, toast and fried potatoes in front of her, and she smiled her thanks.

"You can't have been getting it for very long. You're barely in your childbearing years." Adelaide sounded confused.

"I've been getting my cycle for about... twenty-two years now." Meryn took a huge bite of toast.

"Twenty-two years? How old are you, Meryn?" Adelaide asked.

"Thirty-four. Why?"

"That means you started your cycle at the age of twelve? Every month for the past twenty-two years." Adelaide looked ill.

"Yeah. So?"

"Do humans have babies that young? You're practically babies yourselves at that age," Adelaide asked.

Meryn shrugged. "Depends. Kids are having sex younger and younger these days. It's not unheard of to read about a twelve- or thirteen-year-old having kids." Meryn carefully lifted her egg onto her toast. Her favorite part was biting into the yolk.

"That's barbaric. These girls' fathers, do they seek retribution for their daughters?" Byron demanded.

"Sometimes, but sometimes the girls just get kicked out."

"Kicked out? What do you mean?" Keelan asked, getting pulled into the conversation.

"In some families, if a girl gets pregnant young or if a child comes out as homosexual, the parents kick them out of the house," Meryn explained. For all their paranormal worldly ways, she was discovering that Lycaonians were quite sheltered about the harsh truths outside their city.

"But that means they have nowhere to go, right?" Ben asked.

"Yup. If they're lucky, they have another relative that can take them in, but too many times they end up homeless, and subject to the predators on the streets. Most end up addicted to drugs or forced into prostitution."

"In Lycaonia, every child is cherished. I can't imagine abandoning your own child like that." Byron wrapped an arm around Adelaide. Meryn felt horrible for ruining everyone's breakfast. It was so commonplace to her, she didn't even think twice about discussing it.

“Those are extreme cases. It's not too bad out there. I survived and I lost both of my parents. There are good people out there, too.” Meryn set her fork down, suddenly wanting that chocolate cake.

Aiden, sensing her change in mood, lifted her onto his lap. It was starting to feel natural to her to be there.

“Would it hurt too much to discuss it?” Ben asked, sympathy in his eyes.

“There's not much to tell. Both of my parents died in a car crash when I was five. After that, I lived with my grandmother. She was strict, but pretty much left me alone. As long as there was food to eat, I was okay. She ended up passing away my senior year in high school. My guidance counselor let me move in with her for the last month of my senior year and the summer before I went to college. After that, I survived off of scholarships, part-time jobs, and grants. I graduated college and started working. It didn't take me long to figure out I didn't like working for other people, especially since most of them were dumber than me, so I started my own internet security business and I've been doing that ever since. The End.”

“You've been alone since you were a teenager?” Colton asked.

Meryn nodded, then thought about it. “Actually, since my parents died. My grandmother didn't really talk to me much. The only nice thing she ever did for me was get me my library card.”

“Humans are amazing creatures, are they not?” Gavriel said, his tone full of amazement. Everyone nodded. Meryn blushed.

Adelaide wiped her eyes, “You don't have to attend the sewing circle with me. I was thoughtless and never even considered your past.” Meryn pushed down her momentary sense of relief. She couldn't let Adelaide down.

“I don't mind. I'll just be real quiet in the corner. I'll meet everyone, that way no one can come back later and say I was being stuck up or thought I was better than them by not saying hello.”

“They *would* think that, too. Oh, dear, after the past couple days you've had, plus starting your cycle, I feel terrible about subjecting you to this.” Adelaide twisted her fingers together.

“Dear, if she says she can do it, she can, I think Meryn can do anything she sets her mind to.” Byron pulled his mate's hands apart so she didn't hurt herself.

“Damn, Skippy!” She paused and looked around. “I can bring my laptop, right?”

Meryn was in high school hell. Around her the ladies of Lycaonia tittered and giggled, each complimenting the other ever so sweetly. Meryn felt like gagging.

“I thought the dress you wore to Lady Rosethorn's fall tea was stunning. Did Laurel at Just Sew Sew do it up for you?”

Meryn had, of course, promptly forgotten everyone's names, but in her mind she was calling the blonde lady speaking Horseface. The poor thing had the unfortunate luck to be born with a long face and a bray-like laugh. Horseface was talking to a much stouter woman that Meryn had labeled Fruit

Loop. She was round, smelled like lemons, and was a bit loopy.

"How are you liking Lycaonia, dear? It must be hard keeping up with everything, being human and all." And there was Queen Bitch herself, Daphne Bowers. Ironically enough, the only one of the bunch that Meryn could stand was Daphne's sweet, unassuming mommy-to-be daughter-in-law, Elise.

"Nope, everything seems pretty easy to understand to me," Meryn shrugged. Daphne giggled. Meryn didn't know how old Daphne was, but where Adelaide could pull off a giggle, this woman could not. She should have stopped like two hundred years ago.

"Nonsense, of course you're confused, with only Adelaide here to guide you. You absolutely must come to us with any questions, my dear. After all, that's what the Daughters of Lycaonia Sewing Circle was created for--to help lesser, more unfortunate individuals." She said it so sweetly that Meryn simply blinked for a moment.

Did that heifer just refer to me as a lesser individual?

"How generous of you. But of all people, Adelaide is the perfect choice to help me learn about your world. She is, after all, the Councilman's mate and my mother-in-law-to-be. She has been so patient and wonderful explaining things to me about what it will be like to run one of the most powerful houses in Lycaonia."

She paused and sniffed dramatically. Meryn dabbed at her eyes with her tea napkin.

"Now I finally know what it's like to have a mother." *Sniffle again and someone cue the dramatic music.*

"You poor thing."

"Alone in the world, can you imagine?"

"Adelaide really is the sweetest, you couldn't ask for better, my dear." Meryn nodded and accepted their sympathy. Normally, she would have been sick to her stomach talking to so many unfamiliar people, but she was discovering she had a talent for acting. As long as she wasn't just plain old Meryn, she could do this social thing.

"Mothers really are special. I keep telling Elise that she will be a wonderful mother. We've been planning the nursery for weeks, haven't we Elise?"

Oh, oh, someone played the baby card early.

Meryn turned to Elise and in genuine sincerity congratulated her. "I'm so excited for you! I think you'll be an amazing mother. Do you decorate the nurseries using themes here in Lycaonia?" Meryn asked.

"Themes?" Elise's soft voice was barely heard.

"Yup. Like Hello Kitty if it's a girl, or a baseball theme if it's a boy."

"Oh, no. We don't have anything like that here. Just different colors. What would you recommend for a wolf shifter baby?" Elise asked, her eyes alight with curiosity.

"Hmm. Nothing too scary. Maybe cartoon wolf pups with different colored bandanas around their necks," Meryn suggested.

"That would be so adorable." Elise clasped her hands together.

"No one in Lycaonia has that, Elise; it would definitely be something new. Our announcement won't go out until later today, but my Eleanor is expecting. I bet she would like something like that too," the woman to Elise's right said, her voice bashful.

"I'm so excited for Ellie, Lady Canter! Tell her I'll call her later." Elise radiated goodwill. Meryn was taken aback at the completely different personalities between Daphne and Elise.

"Don't be ridiculous! Who has ever heard of decorating a nursery with cartoon characters? Preposterous. We're decorating in the traditional Lycaonian hues of blues and greens for boys. I'm positive she will have a son, a little boy just like my Donovan," Daphne interjected, her tone slightly stern. Elise shut down right before Meryn's eyes. Meryn began to seriously get pissed off; she hated bullies more than anything else.

"Elise, I think you should be able to decorate your nursery any way you want to. It's your baby, after all. I know you've probably been looking forward to this for a long time," Meryn guessed. Elise looked up, gratitude in her eyes.

"I would like something new and bright. I like the idea of cartoon pups. We could do bandanas in different colors so we could start right away. It wouldn't make a difference if I had a boy or a girl. I..."

"Elise, don't be silly. Look, you're getting too worked up. This is obviously upsetting for you." Daphne turned her gaze to Meryn. "Until you understand our customs a little better, it might be best for you not to interfere." Daphne's flinty gaze did not deter her. Meryn simply turned to Elise, ignoring Daphne and gave the woman her back.

"Or you could do wolf constellations racing across the ceiling. I've always thought that twinkly lights were soothing." Meryn turned her head so that only Elise saw her wink. Elise's eyes widened and she hid a smile behind her napkin.

"Really! Elise!" Daphne protested.

"Let the youngsters talk, Daphne. I like hearing about new ideas, very stimulating." Lady Fairfax, the old, cranky-looking woman spoke up for the first time. Meryn shied away from her at first, because she reminded her of her own grandmother, but she was rapidly becoming one of her favorites amongst the ladies.

"Yes, Daphne, Elise hasn't looked better in months," Horseface countered. Seeing that she was outnumbered, Daphne backed down. But Meryn could tell something else was brewing.

"So, Adelaide, how does it feel to have one of your children finally mated? I have to say I was rather shocked to hear you had to have the witch elder cast a spell in order for your son to find a mate, and a human at that." Daphne sipped her tea.

Bitch said what? Okay, gloves are coming off now.

"Isn't it miraculous?" Meryn gushed. She clutched her chest in a sensational fashion. The ladies leaned forward instinctively.

"Fate chose Adelaide to help so many warriors find mates. I mean, in *all* of the world, she trusted *her* to channel her purpose through. Because of Adelaide, so many good men will find their mates and fulfill Fate's design. Only Adelaide could have come up with such a practical, yet efficient, plan. It's almost like she became one with the Divine." Meryn closed her eyes and heaved a dreamy sigh. She opened her eyes a crack to take a peep. She prayed that she hadn't gone too over the top with it. To her delight, the women around her were weeping and staring at Adelaide in something close to reverence.

"I always knew she was meant for great things."

"Lady McKenzie, you simply have to come to my luncheon I have planned next week!'

"She was guided by the Divine!"

"I've always known that House McKenzie was blessed." The excited voices of the women around her had Meryn turning her head to hide her grin.

Check and mate, bitch.

"To think Fate herself worked through you, Adelaide. How exciting!" Horseface was practically vibrating in her chair.

Outside, the faint sound of bells ringing signaled the top of the hour. Adelaide stood and everyone quieted immediately. She looked somewhat surprised at that.

"Ladies, thank you so much for coming today to welcome my daughter to Lycaonia. Your presence here speaks volumes to your character. I hope that she has discovered as many friends amongst you as I have." The ladies all preened and clapped a round of applause.

"Until next time." Adelaide nodded and one by one each woman stopped to speak to her.

Elise made her way over to where Meryn was standing next to Adelaide and took both of her hands in hers.

"Thank you. I won't forget your help today. I would like to talk to you again," Elise said shyly.

"Sure. That'd be great, though I have to warn you, I'm really kind of awkward and have never really had a girlfriend before," Meryn confessed.

"Me either. Not a true friend. I have a feeling that you would be a true friend, Meryn McKenzie." Elise nodded and hurried to catch up to her mother-in-law, who had been one of the first to leave.

"Meryn McKenzie huh? Doesn't sound too bad," Meryn mused to herself. Adelaide walked the last woman out. When she returned to the drawing room, she was bubbling with laughter. She wrapped her arms around Meryn and practically tackled her to the sofa.

"Became one with the Divine? Oh, my goodness, Meryn, I thought you said you didn't know how society women were." Adelaide and Meryn sat up, breathing hard from all the laughter.

"I said I didn't like it, I never said I wouldn't be any good at it. It wasn't that hard. I just pretended I was in a regency book."

"You made an enemy today," Adelaide warned.

Meryn shrugged. "I can live with that. It's a good thing this thing wrapped at three; I was two seconds away from throat-punching that bitch. How can you stand her?" Meryn ground her teeth together.

"Because she does do a lot of good work in the community. Her motives may not always be pure, but the end result is the same." Adelaide shrugged.

"I liked Lady Fairfax; she seems like a cool old lady."

"I like her, too. She is very direct and honest. I think maybe she liked you, too. Her grandson owns a café in the city called The Jitterbug." Adelaide stood.

"Sydney is her grandson? No wonder I liked her," Meryn mused, putting two and two together. They both had Fairfax as a last name.

"Put your laptop away, dear. I can hear my son pacing in the kitchen. I can't wait to tell him how stupendous you were." Meryn blushed. She followed Adelaide to the kitchen. Aiden and his unit stood. They had been snacking on leftovers from the sewing circle's tea.

"So, how did it go?" Aiden held out a chair for her. For a second she felt disappointed he didn't scoop her up in his lap. She sat down and waved at Adelaide to fill them in.

"Your mate singlehandedly routed every attempt Daphne Bowers made to belittle her or me. In fact, she may have elevated me to a 'Divine' status." Adelaide smiled broadly.

"I've always thought you were divine," Byron said coming up behind his mate and kissing her neck.

"Oh, Byron, I wish you could have seen it. Meryn was absolutely perfect. When Daphne insinuated that the only way our son could find a mate was to cast a spell, Meryn turned it on her. She said that Fate chose me as a vessel to help so many warriors find their mates."

Byron looked at Meryn. "That's actually a very solid theory."

"Yup, it should also take the wind out of her sails in case she tries to revive that terrible rumor about Lady Adelaide using black magic to get pregnant." Meryn yawned. Adelaide and Byron looked at her in shock.

"Where did you hear that old story from?"

"I have my sources," Meryn boasted.

Byron rubbed his chin. "Very good move, Meryn. You're right. No one can resurrect that old tale to hurt Adelaide anymore. Excellent maneuvering." Byron's approval made her sit up straighter.

"My little politician. How is your condition?" Aiden asked softly.

"Oh. My cramps? Better. I found an old bottle of Aleve at the bottom of my backpack. I'm doing great." Meryn fought the urge to jump into his lap. What in the hell was wrong with her? She felt jittery, like she couldn't sit still.

"Aiden." Byron pointed to Meryn. Aiden's face broke out in a smile. Wordlessly, he lifted her out of her seat and into his lap. She let out a long sigh of relief and buried her face in his chest.

"I didn't think it would affect her, being human," Aiden murmured as he rubbed his cheek against her hair. Meryn felt like purring. When she realized what she was doing, she froze.

"What's going on?" She pulled back to look up at Aiden.

"That's the mating pull. It will get stronger and stronger the longer we're together." Aiden nuzzled her neck. Meryn turned to Adelaide and Byron.

"How in the hell do you function?" She knew they had been together for a long time. Byron just laughed.

"We're mated, Meryn. That feeling like you just have to touch your mate never goes away, but it does get easier after you've been claimed," Adelaide explained.

"Damn period!" Meryn snuggled down in Aiden's arms. Byron blushed and coughed.

"On that note, I'll be in my study until dinner." He leaned down and kissed Adelaide before making his way to his office.

"Why don't you take Meryn upstairs for a nap?" Adelaide suggested.

"We're going to patrol around the house," Colton announced as he, Darian, Gavriel, and Keelan stood.

"I'll check in with you later." Aiden also stood with Meryn nestled in his arms. They gave a smart salute and filed out the back door. Aiden smiled at his mother and walked upstairs.

"I could actually get used to being carried around like this."

"I could get used to having you in my arms all the time, too," Aiden said, and carried her into their room.

CHAPTER SEVEN

When Meryn woke from her nap completely cocooned in Aiden's arms, she had been surprised that she hadn't felt trapped or annoyed. With her previous boyfriends, she had often found herself praying at night that they would stop breathing so she could get to sleep, yet sleeping next to Aiden felt natural. The nap had done her wonders; she felt like a new person.

They were now downstairs in the dining room for dinner. The Alpha Unit and Aiden's brothers had joined them again. Meryn believed it was Marius's cooking that had them visiting, not her company.

When Aiden reached across the table for the basket of bread, she noticed something black on his upper arm. Curious, she started to lift up the sleeve of his t-shirt. Aiden, seeing what she was after, pulled the sleeve up to his shoulder. The tattoo was of a large shield, the inside quartered with different symbols in each quadrant. Strange letters made up the edge of the shield and Celtic knotwork tied everything together.

"It's gorgeous. What do the different symbols mean?" Meryn reached forward and traced the lines.

"The shield represents being a unit member. In the upper left hand corner, the crest with the griffin, that represents Lycaonia. The griffin has the body of a lion and the head and wings of an eagle. Since the lion is considered the King of Beasts and the eagle the King of Birds it was chosen to represent all shifters. In the upper right-hand corner, that is the Greek letter for 'A' or Alpha. It depicts I am in the Alpha Unit. Below that is a longsword representing my choice to do battle and defend our people. In the lower left-hand corner, the circle inside a square inside a triangle inside another circle, that's the symbol for transformation, indicating I am a shifter. At the top of the shield is my family crest and the star in the middle represents that I am the Unit Commander. The tattoos are spelled, so if a warrior changes units or status, the symbols update. If you had seen Darren's at the bakery, his tattoo has an outline; it means that he is retired. If he ever entered active duty again, the outline would disappear automatically." Aiden pointed to each symbol with reverence. Meryn looked over to Byron. Obligingly, he lifted his sleeve and he had an identical tattoo, since he had also been Unit Commander before Aiden. His tattoo had one more symbol than Aiden's, though. Byron pointed to the laurel wreath hanging from the top of the shield.

"This means that I am an Elder. Someday, Aiden will have this added to his tattoo as well."

"What are the squiggles along the edge?" Meryn asked.

Darian laughed. "Those aren't squiggles; that is the written language of the fae. They are spells to keep us safe, to help us heal, and to ask the Gods to watch over us." Darian lifted his sleeve. His family crest was different, but the symbols for Lycaonia, the Alpha Unit and the longsword were the same. She pointed to the intricate sun done in Celtic knotwork.

"Is that the symbol for the fae?"

Darian nodded.

"Since we're doing show and tell..." Keelan grinned and lifted his sleeve. Instead of a sun he had a crescent moon facing left, a full moon, and another crescent moon facing right.

"The witches' symbol represents the triple Goddess, it shows her three incarnations, Maiden, Mother and Crone."

Gavriel lifted his sleeve. He had a dragon twined around to make an infinity symbol with the head eating the tail. "It is the vampiric symbol for eternity, since we are immortal." He lowered his sleeve.

Meryn turned to Aiden. "I want a tattoo."

Aiden choked on his tea. "You don't get one."

"Why not? Don't they have mate tattoos? Is there a human symbol?" Meryn asked Adelaide since Aiden was being obstinate.

"I'm afraid not, my dear. Maybe you can design one," she suggested.

"Mother! I--" His words were cut off by his cell phone ringing. He immediately stopped what he was saying and answered.

"Aiden here. Yes sir, yes sir. I understand." Aiden stood and snapped his fingers to Gavriel. The men popped up.

"Right away." He hung up the phone.

"Colton, you stay here, I want you to guard Meryn. The rest of you, with me." Aiden leaned down and kissed her quickly.

"Take Colton with you, I'm fine here," Meryn protested.

"I wish I could leave more." She could tell Aiden was torn.

"What are we, chopped liver? Go, Aiden, we won't let anything happen to your mate." Adam stood and walked over to stand behind Meryn.

Adair nodded. "You may be Unit Commander, little brother, but don't forget that I'm Head Master at the training academy," he added. Ben also stood.

"And I'm a unit warrior too, Aiden. I'll call Sascha and tell him I'm crashing here." Meryn had never felt so protected.

"I don't need to remind you that I used to be Unit Commander do I, son?" Byron asked. Aiden shook his head.

"Okay, okay." He looked down at her.

"I'll be back as soon as I can. Colton will stay here with you." He turned to the men.

"Alpha, move out." The men sprinted out of the dining room. When Meryn heard the front door close, it hit her that he was leaving to go risk his life and she hadn't even said goodbye.

Adam ruffled her hair. "Hey, short stuff, he'll be back. Don't worry about him; he's very good at what he does." He took Aiden's seat and placed another slice of roast beef on her plate.

"Eat up. Red meat during your cycle will help restore the iron in your blood." Meryn nodded, but didn't think she could eat another bite. The food she had already eaten had turned to a brick in her stomach.

"Marius, maybe you could get Bronwyn to make Meryn a special cup of tea," Adelaide suggested.

Marius nodded. "I was just about to recommend that myself," Marius said.

"Who's Bronwyn?" Meryn looked at Marius.

"Bronwyn is my mate. She is painfully shy. I expect she will introduce herself in a few days. She makes the most calming and delicious teas in Lycaonia," he said proudly.

"Like the one from last night?"

He nodded, "Yes, that is one of her most popular blends." He gave a short bow and headed to the kitchen.

Meryn pushed her food around on her plate. Minutes later Marius returned with a cup of steaming tea and a large slice of chocolate cake. Meryn licked her lips.

"Thank you, Marius." Meryn pushed her food plate to one side and pulled the slice of chocolate cake toward her. Adam went to intercept and pull the roast beef back when she slapped his arm.

"It's chocolate. I'll cut you!"

Adam frowned down at her. "No need to get violent."

Colton chuckled, "She gave me a bloody nose. I've said it from the beginning, she's perfect for Aiden. She'll drive him nuts."

Meryn took another bite of cake, chewed and swallowed. "Aren't I supposed to?"

Byron nodded, "Yes, you are."

After finishing her tea and two slices of cake, Meryn yawned. Damn, that tea worked fast. She yawned again. Heedless of table manners, she crossed her arms on the table and laid her head down. She was just starting to doze when she heard Byron say.

"No, I'll take her." She was lifted gently. The swaying motion of being carried lulled her further before she gave up and fell asleep.

"Meryn, Meryn," a whispered voice pulled her out of her sleep.

"Aiden?" She blinked, barely making out a figure in the dark.

"No, it's Colton."

"What the hell time is it?" she muttered.

"Seven, just before dawn. I wanted to tell you Aiden made it back. He and the men are crashing at the Alpha estate; you'll see him later today." Colton sounded as relieved as she felt.

"Thank you for telling me." His figure started to walk away and suddenly she didn't want to be alone.

"Can't you stay, for a little bit?"

"Do you want Aiden to kill me?

"Please? I feel shaky, like I want to cry, but I don't know why. It's confusing," she admitted. She heard him sigh.

"It's because you're relieved that Aiden is okay and your body is craving his. Fine. But if you tell Aiden I did this, I'll deny it." She heard him rustle around in the darkness.

"Colton?" She got no response. Seconds later a heavy weight jumped up on the bed. In the pre-dawn light she watched as a giant wolf walked up the bed and curled up next to her. She was going to sleep next to a wolf! How cool was that?

"I've never had a dog before," she laughed when Colton growled.

"I think I like you better like this." Meryn gently rubbed the soft fur behind his ears. One leg started to kick.

"Do you like that, boy? Huh? Such a good boy!" She kissed his nose and wrapped an arm around him.

"Thank you Colton, I feel better now." She yawned and went back to sleep.

"One reason. Give me one fucking reason why I shouldn't kill him!" Meryn heard Aiden's angry voice and popped up in bed. He had Colton by the scruff and the wolf swayed from his grasp. Gavriel had a steadying hand on his arm.

"Because he is your best friend, because he is your third-in-command, and because he would never betray you, not that Meryn would," Gavriel explained in an even tone.

Meryn jumped out of bed, dressed in only in her *Voltron* sleep t-shirt and underwear. She pulled Colton out of his hand. Colton dropped down on all fours and sat passively. She wrapped her arms around his neck.

"Leave my puppy alone!" she yelled up at Aiden. He froze.

"Your what?" Gavriel asked as he and Aiden blinked down at her.

"My puppy. I've never had a dog before, so I'm adopting Colton." She rubbed the top of Colton's head. She had to swallow a smile when she saw that Colton was playing it up for all that it was worth. He rolled around on his back exposing his tummy for a belly rub. Grinning, she scratched his belly. She glared up at Aiden.

"Apologize to the both of us. Because Gavriel is right. Neither one of us would hurt you like that." She stood and put her hands on her hips. Colton stood, growling in a low rumble beside her.

"I am sorry, I didn't mean to imply that either one of you would betray me. But dammit! I walk in to see Colton's clothes on the floor and the two of you snuggled up together." Aiden threw his hands in the air. Meryn thought about it.

"Good point. Next time fold your clothes and put them on the dresser," she said, looking down at Colton.

"That's not the point!" Aiden yelled.

Gavriel pointed to the bathroom. "Colton, take your clothes into the bathroom, shift back and get dressed. Breakfast is almost ready. The sooner we go downstairs, the sooner Meryn can get dressed." Colton grabbed his clothes in his mouth and darted into the bathroom. Gavriel's eyes were laughing, yet he never broke a smile. Meryn looked up and saw the vein in Aiden's temple was throbbing. That couldn't be good, even for a shifter.

Aiden stared down at her. "You...you..." He pointed at her shirt.

"What? *Voltron* kicked ass!"

"I can't do this. I'm going downstairs. We'll start this morning over at breakfast." Aiden turned and slammed the door behind him. Seconds later, the bathroom door opened and Colton dashed out, not even looking in Meryn's direction. He swung the door open and bolted down the hall.

Gavriel stared down at her waist. Meryn pulled her shirt down. *Was he staring at her crotch?*

"What?"

"You are off by a day," he pointed out. It dawned on her that he was talking about her day-of-the-week panties.

"My OCD had a bit of an issue with that. When Aiden kidnapped me, my days of the week got off track. I was supposed to start a new week the day I was taken. I was relieved that the pervert who wrecked my apartment didn't mess with this set, it's my favorite. When we picked up my stuff I couldn't decide if I should still wear them in order or skip a few days and have them correctly correspond with the current day. If I skipped days, they would wear out at different times," Meryn explained.

Gavriel nodded seriously. "What did you decide to do?"

"I'm wearing this one until noon, then changing, I should be caught up and back on track later today."

"I cannot believe I understood that. See you at breakfast, Meryn." Gavriel gave a salute and closed the door behind him.

Meryn decided to take her time. She got her shower and reviewed her t-shirt selections carefully. Today she was definitely feeling like *Doctor Who*. She yanked on her TARDIS tee and dug around for her blue Converse in her suitcase. Her long multi-colored scarf completed her ensemble. She grabbed her hoodie and her MacBook Air, and headed for the door. Nodding in the mirror, she winked at herself as she walked by.

"*Allons-y*!"

She hopped down the stairs all the way down, eyeing the long wooden banister. Not today. But soon. She was going to try sliding down. The highly polished wood was practically begging for it. She walked into the dining room and sat down next to Aiden. She noticed that Keelan, Darian, and Aiden's brothers weren't there. She dropped her hoodie and laptop beside her chair on the floor.

"Where is everybody?"

"Adam is back at the clinic. Adair had early morning classes, and Darian and Keelan started morning drills with Ben's unit," Aiden answered before kissing her soundly on the lips. She kissed him back enthusiastically until she smelled something that had her mouth watering. Her nose twitched.

"What is that yummy smell?" She looked around.

"I remembered your espresso machine this morning. We both left it in the back of my car yesterday. Marius has been perfecting his espresso shots since I brought it in." Aiden took a bite of bacon.

"Speaking of cars. Where is mine?" she demanded. Aiden shuddered.

"You mean your death trap on wheels? At the Alpha Unit's estate."

"You be quiet about Serenity. She has served me well."

"You named your car?" Colton asked.

"You don't?" Meryn was surprised. She thought everyone did. The doors to the kitchen opened.

"I think I have it just right. If the strength isn't to your liking, please let me know." Marius brought over a small ivory cup capped in white foam. Meryn reached forward with eager hands and picked up the stylish cup before bringing it to her nose.

"Smells wonderful." She took a sip. The foam itself was sweet and the bitterness of the espresso shots was tempered by the milk. She looked up at Marius.

"I love you." Aiden froze. Marius didn't bat an eye.

"And I adore you, little miss. Crepes or french toast this morning?" he asked, holding an empty plate.

"What's in the crepes?"

Marius blinked. "Do you know, the boys have never asked me that. Not once."

"That's because they usually eat two servings of each. It doesn't matter what the filling is." Adelaide cut her crepe with ladylike precision.

"There are two different kinds of crepes this morning. Blueberry and cream cheese or cream cheese and almond," Marius answered Meryn, looking pleased.

"Could I have one of the almond ones, please?" Meryn tipped her cup and tried to suck the foam off of the inside wall. When she set it down, she sighed happily. She could already feel the caffeine working its magic.

"Could I also have another one of those cappuccinos?" Meryn held her empty cup up.

Aiden put his hand over the cup. "That depends, what are your plans for the day?" he asked.

"I was planning on taking her shopping, with Colton acting as an escort," Adelaide answered before Meryn had a chance to speak. She stared at the sweet woman in horror.

Aiden lifted his hand and shrugged. "Okay." He nodded.

Meryn eyed him. "What if I had planned on visiting with you today?"

Aiden looked at her. "As much as I would love to spend the day with you, I have to write up the report from last night's mission and go over some new concerns with the other unit leaders." Meryn just stared at him. He totally didn't answer her question.

"I wanted to go over those case details that Elder Airgead gave me some more," Meryn mumbled as Marius put a plate with a fresh crepe before her.

"You spent all yesterday afternoon in the sewing circle going over that laptop. Today, I am going to show you my favorite boutiques! We need to get your All Hallows' Eve costume. I'm hoping we can find something decent. At this late date, the best ones are bound to have been taken." Adelaide was nearly shaking with excitement at the thought of a shopping expedition. Meryn began to edge off her seat. She had done the sewing circle thing, but that and shopping in the same week was asking too much. Aiden's heavy arm wrapped around her shoulders, pulling her back on her chair.

"Mother has been looking forward to a daughter for a very, very, *very* long time, Meryn." He looked down at her, his eyes pleading.

"I guess." She thought about it for a second. "Can we go back to that café? I promised Sydney an update about how the sewing circle went." Meryn cut a huge bite of the crepe and stuffed it in her face. The cream cheese was smooth and sweet with a hint of almond. Marius set another cup in front of her.

"Of course," Adelaide agreed.

Meryn smiled at Marius. "Now I see why you said you needed him so much, Lady Adelaide." Meryn picked up her second cappuccino.

"I have arranged for your squire interview for the day after the ball. Marius has agreed to help with some of the qualification tests." Adelaide paused and Meryn glanced up. Adelaide hesitated before continuing.

"Meryn, Lady Adelaide is so formal. I'd like it if you called me Mother, or if you're not comfortable with that, just Adelaide." Meryn stared. She had never called anyone Mother for as long as she could remember.

"Mother." The word sounded funny to say.

"Muuuuuther."

"Maaaaa."

"Are you my mummy?" Meryn giggled, then turned to Adelaide, who was starting to look at her in concern.

"I've never used that word before. I like it. Mother. Does that mean I can call you Papa?" Meryn asked Byron shyly. She heard a sniffle and expected Adelaide to be the one who was emotional. She, however, was smiling at her mate. Meryn was surprised to see that it was Byron who rubbed at his eyes like a sleepy toddler. Manfully, he cleared his throat.

"I would love it if you called me Papa." Meryn smiled up at him; the man was just a huge marshmallow. He gazed lovingly at Adelaide.

"We have a little girl," he said in a voice filled with wonder. Adelaide nodded, then a lighting-quick flash of calculation crossed her face.

"Byron, I'm using your account to go shopping today." Byron nodded absently with a wide goofy grin on his face. Aiden leaned down and kissed her cheek.

"Thank you for making them happy."

"It's not like I'm not getting anything out of the deal. I've never had parents before." Meryn shrugged.

"I'm leaving Colton with you for the day. Tell him to keep his clothes on." Aiden kissed her temple and stood up.

"What's this?" Byron asked.

"I discovered I like Colton better as a dog." Meryn finished her crepe.

"I am not a dog! I am a *wolf*." Colton tried to sound haughty, but no one believed it.

"You should have seen him as a puppy! I think I have some sketches around here somewhere. Some of Aiden too," Adelaide offered.

"No photos?" Meryn asked.

"Cameras hadn't been invented then, dear," Adelaide explained gently.

"Oh." She looked up at Aiden. "Damn, you're old!"

He rolled his eyes. "Have fun shopping. Stay with Colton." He kissed her, went to walk away and returned. The second kiss lingered until her head began to swim. They broke apart reluctantly. Aiden kissed her forehead and stepped back.

"Be good." He grabbed a banana out of the fruit bowl and walked out with Gavriel.

"I'm always good." Adelaide, Byron and Colton stared at her.

"I am." They continued to stare. "Mostly."

“We're going to have a great time today.” Adelaide beamed.

“Yay!” Meryn cheered weakly. She hated shopping!

CHAPTER EIGHT

She had been lied to. Adelaide had promised her coffee; it was now after twelve o'clock and she hadn't gotten her mid-afternoon pick me up. They were now at the fourth boutique and the shop owner was giving Adelaide the same line as the other three. They didn't have anything that would suit her and had run out of fabric to commission a new piece. Adelaide's back was ramrod straight.

"I'm so sorry to hear that. Maybe next year." Adelaide wrapped an arm around her shoulders and steered her out.

"Maybe I shouldn't have shit in ole Lady Bowers' Wheaties," Meryn sighed. She was terrified of the prospect of going to a ball, being among so many strangers where she would be expected to make small talk and remember names. But she had to admit, she was looking forward to dressing up for a Halloween party in a paranormal city.

"Of all the juvenile things to do! I wish she would just let the past go." Adelaide shielded her eyes from the afternoon sun.

"Let's go get some of that caffeine you've been twitching for." Meryn perked up immediately at Adelaide's suggestion. Arm in arm, they walked to The Jitterbug. When they walked inside, Meryn inhaled deeply. The only thing that would make this place smell better was if it sold books.

"There she is! Sit and spill." Sydney pointed to the two empty barstools across the counter from where he manned the register. Meryn and Adelaide took their seats. Meryn ordered the Pumpkin Apple latte she had the last time and Adelaide surprised her when she ordered the same thing. Adelaide had a sheepish expression on her face.

"I love tea, but variety is the spice of life."

"Please tell me the rumor I heard about you ignoring Lady Bowers is true? You have been the talk of the city! No one can believe you stood up to her like that," Sydney shared as he made their drinks.

"I can confirm that happened. She was just being rude to her daughter-in-law."

Sydney snorted. "You've met the cow. Rude is just her nature."

"Aren't you afraid of saying bad things about her? Evidently she has already turned people against me. The shops in the city won't sell me a costume." Sydney waved a hand dismissing her concern.

"She and I had words when she said I was perverted and twisted. In her opinion, Fate only sanctions male-female matings. Everyone knows we have no say in our mates; that woman is just cracked." Sydney handed them their drinks.

"She must still believe I stole Byron from her. They were seeing each other when he and I met. She had grand illusions about becoming Lady McKenzie. But once you meet your mate, that's it. I thought she had moved past that, but seeing the shopkeepers' reactions to Meryn, I can't help but wonder." Adelaide shook her head. "I'll raid my closet and piece together a new costume by hand if I have to," she said vehemently.

"Don't worry about a costume. I can always just cut some holes in a sheet and go as a ghost." Meryn sighed happily as she sipped on her drink. The sweet, tangy brew warmed her from the inside out.

Sydney and Adelaide exchanged looks of concern.

"Meryn, you don't understand, this isn't just a costume party. It's one of the biggest social events of the year," Sydney explained.

"I say costume, but it's more like a ball gown with extraordinary accessories," Adelaide continued.

Meryn looked from one to the other. "So, no bobbing for apples or reaching into a bowl of peeled grapes pretending they are eyeballs?"

"Is that what humans do? That's disgusting." Sydney shuddered.

"Sweetheart, it's a grand ball. The meetings, discussions, introductions, social ladder climbing, and business arrangements made in this one night can determine the success for the major houses for the year." Adelaide's voice was kind. For Meryn the room started to spin.

"I can't go to something like that! Are you nuts? I'll humiliate Aiden!" Meryn gasped for breath. Adelaide pushed her head between her legs.

"Now you stop that. I've seen you in action during the sewing circle; you can hold your own. You do better than you give yourself credit for." Adelaide rubbed her back.

"Thought I might find you here. My grandson has been chomping at the bit to talk to you about yesterday's sewing circle."

Meryn glanced up, Lady Fairfax was standing in the doorway holding a satin bag. Her gray hair was pulled up in an elegant bun and her portly figure was fashionably clothed. She leaned heavily on an ebony walking cane. Though older, her eyes still sparkled with a mischievousness usually reserved for younger people.

"Grandmother, what are you doing here?"

"I heard rumors that Daphne Bowers had gone around to all the clothing shops this morning. What's interesting is that they were all the shops specializing in costume gowns. You haven't had a chance to get one yet, have you, Meryn?" The older woman plopped down at the table behind where Meryn sat on the barstool. Meryn sat up straighter and turned to face her.

"No, we've been looking all morning."

"You might as well stop wasting your time, Daphne Bowers doesn't do things in half measures. Sydney, can you be a dear and bring me a cup of tea?" She rested her walking cane against the table.

"Are you saying that Meryn shouldn't go?" Adelaide asked.

Lady Fairfax shook her head. "I think she should absolutely go."

"But she doesn't have a gown," Sydney pointed out, placing a cup of tea on the table.

"Sydney, be a good lad and hand her that bag." Lady Fairfax pointed to the medium-sized, white satin bag that she had set in the chair beside her. Sydney lifted it up and handed it to Meryn.

"Go ahead, I think you'll like it." Lady Fairfax indicated to the satin satchel. Meryn opened the bag and pulled out a large, white satin shift. It was completely shapeless, hanging all the way to the floor. The arms were so wide that Meryn was sure she could fit inside one of them.

"Um. Thanks?" Meryn frowned down at the material. When she looked up, she saw that Adelaide was staring at the shift in wonder. When her hand reached forward to touch the material, it was trembling.

"Is this what I think it is?" she asked breathlessly. Lady Fairfax nodded, smirking.

"I can't wait to see the expression on Daphne Bowers' face when Meryn walks in wearing that. Oh, oh that will make my year." Lady Fairfax hooted, her laughter startling the patrons around her. Meryn turned to Sydney as if to say 'Seriously?' He took pity on her.

"Meryn, this is a very special dress. It's been in our family for generations. It was a gift to my great-great-great-grandmother from the Queen of the Fae herself. This dress is the Gown of Éire Danu. You put it on and it changes into whatever dress you need; it morphs according to your thoughts and wishes. It hasn't been worn in a long time." Sydney's voice sounded sad. Lady Fairfax nodded.

"Since his mother, Gods rest her soul. I'm getting older, and as much as Sydney loves Justice, he was never one for cross-dressing. So I am gifting it to you. My only request is that if Sydney and Justice have a little girl, you hand it down to her."

"It changes into whatever I want?" Meryn looked at the dress dubiously.

"And it acts as your ladies-in-waiting. It will change your shoes, hair, makeup and accessories to match the dress. The only dress you will ever need."

"I can't wait to see her face." Adelaide was laughing so hard she covered her face. Lady Fairfax began to chuckle again.

"Lady Fairfax, I don't know how to thank you. Just the thought that I never have to go dress shopping again is a gift." To Meryn, that meant more than a dress that was made by the fae.

"Thought you might appreciate that. Tell me, girlie, how close were you to hitting Daphne yesterday?" Lady Fairfax's eyes danced with mirth.

"Oh, no, did it show?" Meryn reverently put the dress back in its special bag.

"I noticed, but I don't think the simpering twits that were there yesterday did. Really, child? 'Touched by the Divine'?" She raised an eyebrow.

"Hey! It worked, didn't it?" Meryn protested.

"I have a feeling things are about to get more interesting in Lycaonia." Lady Fairfax sipped her tea. Sydney watched his grandmother carefully before dropping his gossip bomb.

"Did you know that she called Elder Evreux a douchebag?" he said casually. Lady Fairfax sprayed her tea across the table and turned to stare at Meryn.

"It was an accident!"

"How do you call someone a douchebag by accident?" Sydney asked.

"He wasn't supposed to hear me," Meryn mumbled.

Lady Fairfax began to wheeze; concerned, Meryn hopped down and started patting her on the back.

"Are you okay?"

"Oh, I can't wait to tease him about that. Pompous ass. Oh, Meryn, you're good for my heart." Lady Fairfax laughed and pulled Meryn down to kiss her cheek. Meryn blushed furiously.

"Meryn, can you call Aiden? While we're out, I need to know if he wants me to pick up his dress whites out of storage at the tailors'." Adelaide was grinning from ear to ear. Grateful for a chance to escape being the center of attention, she went back and picked up her backpack to get her cell phone.

"You'll have to go outside; for some reason reception inside the café has been spotty lately," Sydney advised. She went to walk out and realized she didn't have his number. She turned back.

"Do you have his number?" she asked Adelaide. Adelaide wrote down the number on a napkin and handed it to her.

"Take your time, dear. I'm enjoying my latte." Adelaide winked.

"Thanks!" Meryn practically ran for the door. She stepped outside and took a deep breath. Fresh air. She got comfortable at one of the small bistro tables, pulled out her laptop and flipped it open. She fished around at the bottom of her bag for her phone. Once she found it, she dialed Aiden's number.

"Hello?" Aiden's deep voice sent shivers through her. He sounded out of breath.

"Why are you breathing hard?" she asked.

"We're doing drills. Are you okay?" As his breathing slowed, she imagined him sweaty and all of his muscles flexing. Damn hormones!

"Yup. I'm still out with your mother. She wanted me to ask you if you need us to pick up your dress whites."

"Thank the Gods for my mother! I completely forgot I had stored them at Seamless. The tailors in the city are witches and when they store your clothing, they cast a spell to keep it clean, pressed and ready to go. If I had waited until the last minute, there would have been a waiting period to get it out since they have to cast a reversal spell." Aiden's breathing sounded normal and his tone upbeat. She wished he were in front of her; she bet he was smiling.

"Okay, I'll let her know..." Out of nowhere she could have sworn she felt someone walk past her. She actually felt body heat. She looked around, the sidewalk where she sat, was empty.

"Meryn?" Aiden called her name. She shook her head.

"Sorry, got distracted there for a second. Will you be at the house for dinner?" She was starting to love eating. Before Aiden, eating meant choking down a Hot Pocket while on her laptop. Now it meant talking and laughing with friends and family.

"Yes, we'll be there. Marius let it slip that he was making his world famous meat loaf tonight. We'll have to fight the guys for a good slice."

"I bet Marius will save me some, he..." Meryn's throat constricted, someone had just breathed on the back of her neck. Goosebumps exploded across her skin and covered her body. A sinister chuckle had her gasping and spinning in her chair. No one was there.

"Meryn, what's wrong?" Aiden's frantic question barely registered.

"I think someone is here, but I don't see anything," she whispered.

"Where is Colton? Where is my mother?" he asked. In the background, he was calling out orders for the men to get into their SUV.

"I haven't seen Colton, and your mother is in the café." Meryn's eyes darted around.

"Get inside now!" Aiden yelled. Meryn stood only to have a heavy hand push her back down.

"Aiden, something pushed me! It won't let me go inside!" Her heart beat out of control.

"Scream. Scream as loud as you can. Ben's unit is patrolling the city today, someone will hear you," Aiden yelled. She opened her mouth to scream when something covered it. It wasn't until she felt the moist heat that she realized that someone was kissing her. A foreign tongue forced its way down her throat. She thrashed, and a strong hand gripped and twisted her breast. Flinging herself backward, she broke away from her attacker. When her mouth was free, she inhaled and screamed as loudly as she could. Seconds later, a figure appeared at her side. It was Colton.

"What happened?" he demanded, looking around. She couldn't answer. All she could do was shake and cry. The door to the café opened and Adelaide rushed out.

"Meryn, what's wrong?" She was pulled into Adelaide's arms, but she still couldn't speak.

"Colton, you worthless dog, pick up the fucking phone!" Aiden was yelling so loud even Meryn could hear him. Colton gently unwrapped her fingers from around her cell phone.

"Aiden, I swear I was watching her from across the street the whole time. No one approached her." Colton ran a hand through his hair.

Down the street, the sound of running footsteps heralded the arrival of the Gamma Unit. Ben ran over to kneel in front of Meryn.

"What are we looking for, kiddo?" he asked. She shook her head.

"A ghost," she whispered. Ben regarded her in confusion before turning to Colton.

"Colton, what are we after here?"

"I have no fucking clue, there wasn't anything there," Colton practically yelled. Ben remained kneeling in front of Meryn, holding her hands.

"You're safe now. Whatever it was will have to go through us to get to you." Meryn turned to Colton and they exchanged a look. Only Colton understood, because he hadn't seen anything, either. How could you fight something you couldn't see? Behind them, the Gamma Unit spread out and began to question the customers and shopkeepers that had come outside at the sound of her scream.

Twenty minutes later, Aiden and the Alpha Unit arrived. Gavriel immediately went to Sascha and

Ben for a status report, while Aiden went directly to her.

"Aiden," she whispered. He ran over to her and lifted her up in his arms. Under her hands she could feel that he was shaking. Pushing her own fear aside, she rubbed his chest.

"I'm okay. I'm okay," she kept repeating until he calmed down. Refusing to let her go, he sat down and kept her in his lap.

"What happened, Meryn? Take us through the sequence of events; don't leave anything out," Aiden asked. With his thumbs, he wiped her tears and kept his arm wrapped around her. Nodding, Meryn turned to the group.

"We were on the phone talking about the tailors and I felt heat, like body heat, move past me. But there wasn't anything there, so I ignored it. Then I felt a breath on the back of my neck and someone laughed. You told me to get inside, but when I stood up I was pushed back down. I went to scream and..." Meryn swallowed hard as tears filled her eyes. She took a deep breath before continuing.

"Something kissed me, he also twisted my breast. His breath was foul and he tried to choke me by forcing his tongue down my throat." Meryn felt tears spill from her eyes. Aiden cradled her close.

"I pushed backward and screamed. Then Colton was there." She wiped at her eyes.

"Colton, you had guard duty, how could you let this happen?" Aiden demanded.

Meryn shook her head. "What part of 'I didn't see anything' did you not understand? Whoever this jerk is had his tongue so far down my throat he was fondling my tonsils, and I didn't see anything. What could Colton possibly have done?" she questioned. Aiden continued to frown at his best friend.

"Aiden, I swear to you on my life I didn't see anything. I would never let anything happen to Meryn," Colton whispered harshly.

Aiden exhaled and took a deep breath. "I know you wouldn't, Colton. I'm sorry for snapping at you." Aiden turned to the Gamma leader.

"Report," he barked.

"Sir, we interviewed just about everyone on the street. No one saw anything, no one at the table or running away." Meryn eyed the white haired giant.

"Thanks, Sascha. I'll leave you and Gamma to finish up here. I'm taking my mate and my mother home. Alpha will remain assigned to House McKenzie until this guy is caught." Aiden stood.

"Yes, sir!" Sascha nodded and began ordering his men to finish up with interviews. When Aiden started down the street, Meryn squirmed to get down.

"I have to get my bag." Aiden set her down. She returned to the table only to realize, though her bag was still there, her laptop was gone.

"Motherfucking son of a fucking bitch!" she bellowed. The men around her froze.

"Meryn?" Aiden asked cautiously.

"He stole my laptop! I love my laptop--it's my baby. What am I going to do without it? It understands me and entertains me." She began to hyperventilate.

"We can get you a new one. Breathe, baby, breathe." Aiden was frantically trying to calm her. Her head felt like it was wrapped in cotton. She heard Adelaide ask Sydney for a glass of water. They didn't understand. Her laptop was her whole world; behind the keyboard of her laptop she was invincible.

"It had my favorite *Doctor Who* skin on it." she wheezed. She didn't want to face anyone anymore.

She didn't fight it when the small gray dots appeared. She let herself slip away.

"I don't understand; it's just a laptop. I'll buy her a hundred if it makes her feel better." Meryn woke to Aiden's whispering.

"It's not about the laptop, Aiden. Your mate, though she has done well with us, doesn't like interacting with people. Though she downplays it, she had a pretty isolated childhood. She never learned how to be around others. To her the laptop was like a security blanket. When that was suddenly and violently taken from her, it drove her anxiety level through the roof, triggering a panic attack."

Meryn kept her breathing even and her eyes closed. Aiden was talking to his older brother, Adam. The astringent smell led her to believe that she was at the clinic and not back at the house.

"I don't get it!" Aiden's voice was filled with frustration. She heard a heavy sigh.

"Okay. When someone hands you a gift that you don't necessarily like, what do you do?" Adam asked.

"What in the hell does this have to do with anything?" Aiden barked.

She heard a soft thud.

"Ow!"

"Just answer the question for your wiser, older brother."

"Fine! I say thank you, think of some way it could be used, and promise to tell them how it performs," Aiden answered.

"How did you know that?"

"I don't know."

"I do. Marius taught you, and all of us, how to accept gifts graciously. I specifically remember him teaching you before your sixth birthday party."

"What is your point?"

"What if you were never taught? What if someone handed you something and you had no idea what to do or what to say. What if you just froze, but then the act of freezing adds more stress. Now you're stressed because you're stressed, add in any potential negative reactions and the problem compounds." Adam's explanation was met with silence.

"Now imagine that is the reaction you have every time you have to speak to someone you don't know. Or are the center of attention?"

"Good Gods!" Aiden exclaimed softly.

"Like I said, she's done very well will us. It could be because you're her mate and any natural acceptance she has for you extended to your friends and family. But outside your social circle, she experiences true flashes of panic. I think she has learned to keep that at bay by using her laptop as a buffer. If she's in a situation where she may have to speak to others, I bet she has an open laptop in front of her so she can pretend to be busy or disinterested." Meryn sat up and both men turned to her.

"I do. If you look like you're working, people stay away and don't try to make small talk," she admitted. Aiden quickly moved to her side.

"Feeling better?" he asked. She shrugged. Her hands felt empty.

"Aiden, I recommend taking her home and tucking her in for the day. A good night's rest will do a lot of good," Adam advised. Meryn nodded, clutching Aiden's arm.

"Can we please go home?" She'd feel better if she was in a familiar location. She looked around.

"Why does this stuff look like overstock from the fifties?" she asked. The gurney she was on and the lime green metal cabinets around the room had seen better decades.

"Because it is," Adam answered.

"But why? Can't you buy newer stuff?" Meryn asked. Adam and Aiden shook their heads.

"Personal wealth cannot be used to fund a public establishment," Aiden explained.

"That sucks."

"We'll be doing another fundraiser at the end of the year, but most people don't think that the unit members need a clinic since we're paranormals and heal fast." Adam took a blanket out of the tall cabinet and wrapped it around her shoulders. "Take her straight home and put her to bed," he ordered.

"Come on, Menace, time to go." Aiden stood and picked her up gently.

"My legs will forget how to work if you keep this up."

"That's okay. I'll carry you if they do. Besides you're human, and short. This way is much faster."

Meryn stared at him for a second before flicking his ear.

"Ow! Stop that."

"I am not short. Or slow."

"Whatever you say, Menace." Aiden kissed her forehead and carried her to the car.

The trip to the house was quiet. Aiden held her hand the entire way, which she was grateful for. When they arrived at the house, Aiden lifted her from the car, still wrapped up in the clinic blanket, and carried her into the house. Marius and Adelaide hurried from the front drawing room.

"Is she okay?" Meryn could see the anxiousness on Adelaide's face.

"She's fine. We're going to spend the rest of the day upstairs relaxing. Marius, could you send up a light dinner later?" Aiden asked.

"Of course, sir." He bowed.

"We'll make you an extra special breakfast tomorrow, Meryn, you just rest now." Adelaide leaned forward and kissed her forehead.

"Thanks, Mom." Meryn was pleased at Adelaide's expression.

"Mom?" she whispered.

"Everyone calls you Mother, but I think Mom sounds better," Meryn explained.

"Of course it does." Adelaide's smile was wobbly.

"See you in the morning." Aiden said and carried her up the stairs.

Once their door closed behind them, Aiden began to laugh.

"I bet my mother ran to the office to call my father and to tell him that you called her Mom. Fully expect him to ask you to call him Dad." Aiden placed her on the bed.

"If it makes him happy, I will." Meryn curled up on her side. Aiden stared down at her and the love she saw in his eyes almost had her in tears again, but she was done crying. Aiden just continued to stand there. Meryn realized he didn't know what to do. She half turned and patted the empty space behind her. Without wasting any time he crawled in behind her and pulled her into the curve of his body. His strength and warmth were like a soothing balm. She turned just her head and lifted her face to his.

"Kiss me. I don't want to taste him anymore," she whispered. With a low growl, he lowered his head. His lips nibbled hers. When his tongue chased hers around, she had to pull away, laughing. He pressed his lips to the back of her neck and she could feel him smile. He was trying to make her feel better.

"Tell me about Christmas. I want to hear something nice to chase away the fear." She scooted backward until there was no mistake that their kiss had left him wanting. His hand stilled her backward retreat.

"Be careful or you'll be getting a present instead of hearing about them."

"My cycle will be over after tomorrow."

"Thank the Gods!" was Aiden's fervent prayer.

"Christmas story, please. We didn't really celebrate it much growing up. I would get two or three new outfits from the thrift store and a new pair of shoes, but that was it. We never even had a tree."

Aiden gasped. "No tree! That's my favorite part about Christmas. I love decorating the tree. We have accumulated so many different types of bulbs and ornaments over the centuries we had to start dividing them into different themes and rotating them. This year is the animal theme. It's one of my favorites, very rustic." Aiden's voice took on an excited cadence. "And the food! Gods, the food. Marius and my mother cook and bake every day. Turkey and ham and stuffed goose. Mincemeat pies and flaming pudding. Bronwyn's cookies make me want to cry every year, they are so good." Aiden sighed.

"The ball has to be the best though. There's no deal-making or business arrangements like at All Hallows' Eve. Just the joy of the season. There's dancing and caroling all night. The Elders make and serve a buttered rum that keeps everyone in high spirits. We light candles all through the night and stay up until dawn to greet the sun. From then on out, the days get longer." Meryn's eyes drooped as the day caught up with her. The picture that Aiden painted danced in her mind. She couldn't wait for Christmas, even if it meant another stupid ball.

CHAPTER NINE

"Your laptop sucks and you should be shot for owning it!" Meryn raged. The thing weighed about eight pounds and was running Windows 95. She had to sit close to his desk since it required a cable for internet; it was too ancient to connect wirelessly.

"I can't do anything with this! How in the hell do you get anything done?"

"Meryn, my job is to chase and shoot things. I need my gun, not a laptop," Aiden explained. He had taken his sidearm apart and was oiling it.

They were still sequestered in their room the following morning, for which Meryn was grateful. She hadn't had much time to herself to recharge her batteries. Surprisingly enough, she didn't even mind Aiden being in the room with her.

"I didn't think about it until now, but you lost everything you had compiled regarding the missing persons case, didn't you?"

"Who said I lost it? I always back up to my own personal online server. I just need to get to it. Ugh! For fuck's sake, it's trying to connect with AOL!" She wanted to scream. She was still cursing when there was a knock at the door. Aiden put his gun and oiling rag down and opened the door.

"I have brought you breakfast. Let me be the first to tell you that Miss Meryn was sorely missed at the table this morning." Marius wheeled in a cart.

"Coffee!" Meryn jumped up and skipped over to the cart. Marius had brought three cups of cappuccino and a pot of fresh coffee in a carafe. Aiden immediately went for the plate that had been piled high with bacon and sausage, grabbed it, and sat back down.

"Marius, would you be able to go shopping today? I'd like to get Meryn a new laptop to replace the one that was stolen. Evidently my laptop is useless," Aiden asked.

"Of course, sir. I believe that they just opened a new Apple store in Madison. I should be able to find her something there." Meryn glared at Aiden.

"*He* knows about Apple. Why don't you have a decent computer?" She sipped her cappuccino and fought the urge to kick his laptop. He held up an oiled gun barrel and continued eating.

"If little miss would write down everything that she needs, I should be able to go shopping today and be back this evening." Marius uncovered a plate with french toast triangles. He walked over to the small writing table she had been working on and proceeded to lay out her breakfast complete with her own tiny salt and pepper shakers. Meryn went to her backpack and ripped out a piece of paper from her notebook and scrounged around for a pen. After five minutes of searching and pulling out all the items in her bag, she found the pen clipped to the notebook she had at the beginning. Feeling frustrated, she started her list.

She'd show Aiden. Grinning, she wrote out a list and snuck it to Marius. He glanced at it and frowned. Maybe she wouldn't get away with it after all.

"Miss, this item, just two?" He raised an eyebrow. Meryn couldn't figure out what he meant. She shook her head, looking at him questioningly. He drew the letter 'A'. 'A?' Oh! Alpha! She should get enough for everyone.

"Twelve?"

He nodded. "That sounds about right. Enjoy your breakfast, little miss. I'll leave shortly to get you a working laptop." He bowed and left the room.

"He kicks so much ass!" Meryn fist pumped the air. She looked over and realized that Aiden was absorbed in his gun and missed her antics. Muttering to herself, she opened his laptop and waited for internet access.

Over the next twenty minutes, she finished her breakfast and her second and third cappuccinos. She was about to give up when she saw the familiar landing site to her server. It took her another ten minutes to open up the reports she had compiled the day prior. She was missing something obvious and it was eating her alive. She pulled up the information about the first couple that had gone missing, then the information for the second. What about these two couples linked them together? Why now?

"That's an impressive little growl you have." Aiden's voice startled her.

"I was growling?" she asked. Aiden nodded.

"It was very sexy."

"Dork."

"Now that's something I can honestly say I've never been called." Aiden laughed. Meryn rolled her eyes. She couldn't even insult him, his head was too big. She frowned down at the laptop.

"Why?" she thought out loud.

"What?" Aiden asked.

"Nothing, just talking to myself."

"Well, you have fun. I'm taking Gavriel back to the Alpha estate to meet with Sascha about yesterday. Colton, Darian, and Keelan will stay here." Aiden leaned down, kissed her on the lips and turned to walk away. Meryn felt her heart seize. She reached up and grabbed his shirt. It seemed like if he stayed with her, nothing bad would happen. He turned and knelt down in front of her.

"I'll be back before you know it. I have to check in with the men and feed Jaws."

"Jaws? What do you have, like a Rottweiler or something?"

Aiden blushed and shook his head. "I have a fish."

"A piranha?"

"No. A clownfish." She blinked and he scowled at her as if daring her to laugh.

"You have a clownfish named Jaws?" she asked and then it hit her. She began to giggle.

"You liked *Finding Nemo,* didn't you?" If anything, his face turned a deeper shade of red.

"That's too much!" She fell to her side giggling. Aiden continued to scowl at her.

"It's the ultimate story of survival! Nemo is taken by the enemy, but his father doesn't give up trying to retrieve him. He forms unlikely alliances and conquers his fears to get his son back. Nemo also refuses to remain a prisoner and follows the warrior's code to escape and return to his family unit." Aiden explained. Meryn sat up and wrapped her arms around his neck.

"You have to be the most adorable man I have ever met. I am so lucky Fate threw us together." She rested her cheek on his chest.

"I am not adorable. I am the Unit Commander, my enemies tremble..."

She looked up grinning. "Yeah, yeah, I know. You're über-scary."

He wrapped his strong arms around her and nuzzled her neck until she squealed. After a few quiet moments he spoke, his voice strained with emotion. "I love you, Meryn. And I will do whatever it takes to keep you safe." Her heart stuttered. She would never get tired of hearing him say that. She tightened her arms around him and he held her close.

He pulled back and she saw the determination and vulnerability in his eyes. Her heart melted; she had never loved anything more in her entire life than the man in front of her.

She closed her eyes and rested her head on his chest. "I love you, too. Yesterday I was surrounded by people, but I didn't feel safe until you were there."

He squeezed her tight.

She didn't want this moment to end, but knew he had things to get done. She stood back and pulled him down by his shirt to kiss him gently on the lips. "Go feed Jaws. I can't wait to meet your fierce little fish."

He straightened. "Be good." She just stared up at him.

"Try to be good?" She nodded.

"Aiden," she called as he walked through the door.

He turned. "Yes?"

"Thank you for coming for me." His smile was warm and kind, but his eyes scorched her with a promised heat. He closed the door behind him.

"Damn period!" She muttered and went back to Aiden's archaic laptop.

By noon, Meryn was ready to slit her wrists or beat Aiden with his own laptop, it was a toss-up. Finally completely disgusted, she slammed the lid down on the laptop and decided to get a shower. She let the antique drop to the floor and went to her suitcase. Should she claim a drawer? Was this her new room? She dug through her clothes and made a mental note to ask Aiden about their future. Feeling belligerent, she picked out one of her favorite black tees that read "I Hate Everybody!" and went to the bathroom. While getting ready, she realized that she was over her cycle. She did a little happy dance in the shower. As she shampooed her hair, she debated on the best way to let Aiden know.

"Come on, big boy--you, me, and Jaws." Meryn snort laughed, which was a mistake because she inhaled a nose full of water. Coughing and sputtering and feeling grumpier than ever, she finished her shower and got dressed. She left Aiden's laptop on the floor and walked out the door. She was just about to take the first step down the stairs when she looked at the banister.

And looked at it.

She glanced around to see if anyone was watching. Throwing caution to the wind, she climbed up on the wooden handrail, took a deep breath and shifted her weight.

Holy shit!

"Bad idea, bad idea, bad idea!" Meryn screeched all the way down. Still screaming she flew off the end of the banister and landed on her tailbone on the expensive marble foyer floor. With tears in her eyes, she rolled around on the ground clutching her butt.

"What on earth!?" Adelaide exclaimed as she and Byron rushed out of his office. They stared down at her as she wiggled around, moaning.

"You owe me five dollars," Byron said, holding out his hand.

Adelaide shook her head. "I may owe you five dollars because you bet she would go down the banister, but you owe me twenty because I told you she wouldn't think to put any pillows down like Ben did when he was little." Adelaide wagged a finger at her mate.

"Y'all are mean. I'm crippled!" Meryn got up on wobbly legs.

"Come sit down and keep us company in my office. The chairs are more comfortable there than in the drawing room." Byron helped her to hobble to his office and got her seated.

"Today sucks! Aiden's laptop sucks! And showers suck! And banisters suck!" Meryn knew she sounded childish, but she pouted anyway. Some days just needed a restart button.

"Poor dear. Here, have some tea, you'll feel better in no time." Adelaide passed her a cup of steaming tea.

Meryn inhaled and smiled at the light fragrance. "Jasmine?"

"Yes, it's one of Byron's favorites." Adelaide passed her a small plate filled with cookies. To their right, a large stone fireplace had a toasty fire that gave the room a warm glow. Meryn wiggled in her chair getting comfortable, ignoring the twangs of pain from her tailbone, and sighed. The day was looking much better.

In a comfortable silence, Adelaide wrote, *actually hand wrote,* letters, as Byron tapped away at his computer. Meryn was itching to see if his desktop was any better than Aiden's laptop. When she peeked over for the fourth time, Byron spoke up.

"Meryn, get over here before you sprain your neck." Byron stood and motioned to his chair.

Meryn quickly set her teacup down and practically ran over to his desk. Byron sat next to his mate and started to help her address the envelopes.

Meryn cracked her knuckles. It was a Mac. She logged in as a guest, and in seconds she was on the internet. She pulled up her online server and opened her database. In no time at all, she began pulling reports.

"Oh, rip that one up. We're not inviting the Bowers, not after what I found out this morning," Adelaide seethed. Byron regarded her in surprise.

"What did Ethan do?"

"Not Ethan, Daphne! Marius was almost ashamed to report that nearly all of the potential squire candidates that we had lined up for interviews after the ball have backed out. Evidently, Daphne is now interviewing for Elise on the exact same day and is saying that it's more prestigious to work for someone who is actually a paranormal in a smaller household than for a human in House McKenzie." Adelaide slammed her pen down.

Meryn shrugged. "If that's all it took for them to change their minds, then they might have done us a favor. Now we won't have to weed them out." She thumped her fingers on the polished wood of Byron's desk.

"That's a very positive way to look at it, Meryn." Byron sounded proud.

"That also means less interviews and talking to people." Meryn looked up grinning.

Adelaide laughed. "Of course, you would look at it that way."

"You're getting to know me all too well, Mom." Meryn went back to the notes that Elder Airgead had given her. A throat cleared.

"Ah, Meryn, I actually wanted to talk to you about something," Byron started. Meryn had a feeling she knew what he was going to say.

"Yeah, Dad?" The expression on his face was priceless. She had been right. He wanted to be called Dad. He swallowed hard.

"Um... how is the computer working for you?" He changed directions quickly.

"Better than Aiden's, that's for sure. Hey, can I ask you something? Are paranormals allowed on Facebook? Or is there some super-duper paranormal version?"

"No, we use the same version of Facebook as the rest of the world; we just have to be careful about what we share. All devices have Geo-tagging disabled." Byron explained.

"Hmm." She pulled up Facebook and went back to work.

"Well, as it stands, we have three interviews. A promising young man from London, one from Germany, and another young man from Japan. I've never heard his family name before so he may be new to serving. Honestly, all of this backstabbing and pettiness, because Daphne Bowers doesn't feel like everyone is paying enough attention to her future grandchild, is ridiculous. As if it weren't that time of the year for shifter birth announcements." Adelaide shook her head and Meryn froze.

"What did you say?" Meryn turned to Adelaide.

"About Daphne?"

"No, about shifter birth announcements."

"Didn't Aiden explain about our conception windows?" she asked.

Meryn nodded. "But why did you say what you did about birth announcements?"

"Meryn, shifters get pregnant around Summer Solstice. It's October. Most couples wait until after the first trimester to announce anything; it's bad luck. That's why there are always shifter birth announcements this time of the year," Adelaide explained.

"Oh, my God." Meryn felt the blood drain from her face.

"Please be wrong, please be wrong, please be wrong," she muttered to herself over and over again.

"Meryn?" Adelaide and Byron stood and walked over to her. Meryn quickly scanned the site she was on and sat back, feeling sick.

"I know how they were linked, the two missing couples. They both posted birth announcements on Facebook within a day of each other," she whispered.

Adelaide gasped and turned to her mate. "Byron!"

He was already moving. He grabbed his jacket and was heading to the door. "Good work, Meryn. Call Aiden and let him know what you've discovered. I'm convening an emergency council meeting. We need to send out a public warning to stop birth announcements." He ran through the door. Meryn was frozen in her chair.

"Meryn, call Aiden." Adelaide pushed the desk phone toward her. With a shaky hand, she dialed Aiden's cell.

"Father?" Aiden's voice sounded confused.

"No, it's me. Meryn, I mean."

"Why are you on my father's desk phone?"

"He let me use his computer. Listen, I found the link between the two couples--they were both pregnant. Both couples posted a birth announcement on Facebook, within a day of each other," she explained. He began cursing a blue streak.

"Your father is calling a council meeting to stop any new birth announcements."

"I've got to go. I need to update the unit leaders. Meryn, stay with my parents today. Don't go out on your own."

"I won't. I promise. Aiden?" Meryn hesitated.

"What is it, sweetheart?"

"Be careful, okay? I've kinda gotten used to you."

"I will. I promise. Love you," he whispered.

"Love you, too." She hung up the phone and stared at it. When she turned, she saw Adelaide standing near the doorway, staring out, a haunted look on her face. She went to her and wrapped her arms around her waist. Adelaide gave a low cry and hugged Meryn back tightly.

"This is why I've always wanted a daughter." Adelaide pulled back and wiped her eyes on the back of her hand. She smiled down at Meryn.

"Aiden would have promised to kill whatever was bothering me and then he would have left to go train to make sure he could. Sometimes you just need a hug."

Meryn laid her head on Adelaide's shoulder. She breathed in the older woman's perfume and buried her face in her dress. "Is this a mom hug?"

Adelaide laughed. "Yes, this is a mom hug, you darling girl. How about we take over the kitchen while Marius isn't here to chastise us, and make a huge mess making cookies?" Adelaide suggested. Meryn could definitely get used to having a mom.

"Only if I get to introduce you to the joys of eating cookie dough."

"Deal!"

They walked to the kitchen and Adelaide began pulling out ingredients.

"Adelaide, can I ask you something?" Meryn measured out the brown sugar; she poured some into the bowl and ate a teaspoon. A cup in the bowl, a teaspoon for her.

"Of course, dear." Adelaide was measuring the flour and chocolate chips.

"Was it hard living apart from Byron all those years?" Meryn sucked on her teaspoon. Adelaide paused for a moment and kept pouring.

"Yes. Yes, it was very hard. Some nights I would lie awake upstairs and wonder why we were so close but apart. I didn't like it, but there were nights where Byron left with his unit and they barely made it to the scene in time to save a life. Even the extra time to the Alpha estate would have cost lives. I understood why we had to live that way, but no, I didn't like it."

"Why didn't you move into the Alpha estate with him? From what I can remember, the place is like a small mansion, there had to have been room." Meryn snuck another teaspoon of sugar.

Adelaide blinked at her. "It just isn't done."

"Hmm." Meryn poured the brown sugar into the larger bowl with the flour and chocolate chips.

"You'll get used to it after a while and you'll have your squire to keep you company." Meryn watched in fascination as Adelaide easily stirred the wooden spoon through the chunky mixture. This was the part that she always had problems with; her scrawny arms could barely move the spoon. She kept forgetting that Adelaide was a shifter too, since she rarely exhibited signs of her bear like Aiden did. Adelaide was definitely less growly.

"Okay, it's mixed. Do you just eat it?" Adelaide looked down at the bowl.

"Nope. Let's put it in the fridge for a while. Then we should be able to eat it. Chilling the dough makes the cookies better, too." Meryn covered the bowl with a towel and placed it in the fridge.

"Let's have some tea while we wait." Adelaide put the kettle on the stove to boil.

Meryn sat down at the table and stacked the sugar cubes on a napkin. Without her laptop she felt exposed. She was working on the third row of her wall when Adelaide came over with two cups of tea. She sat down across from Meryn, added a single sugar cube to her cup, and began to sip her tea.

"What was Aiden like as a kid?" Meryn asked, seizing this opportunity to get to know more about her mate. Adelaide smiled.

"He was a very serious, conscientious child. He always defended Ben and took time to show him things. He always made sure that I was comfortable before leaving a room. And of course, he idolized his father. When he left the house to move into the academy as a trainee, I missed him terribly. Byron had already become an Elder when Aiden left for training, and Adam and Adair had already declined to inherit after Byron. I think that Aiden saw it as his duty to become a warrior and follow in Byron's footsteps. There are some days where I wonder if this is what Aiden really wanted, or if maybe deep down, he resents his brothers for choosing other paths, forcing him to become a warrior." Adelaide twisted her tea cup on its saucer.

Meryn thought about it for a moment and shook her head. "He's too damn stubborn. He may have felt obligated at first, but he wouldn't have stuck with it unless it was something he wanted to do. When Adam and Adair introduced themselves, I could see the pride in Aiden's eyes. I don't think he resents them doing what they want with their lives."

"It's nice to be able to talk about this with someone," Adelaide admitted.

"Don't worry, Adelaide, I'll help you keep those boys on their toes," Meryn promised.

Adelaide's tinkling laughter lifted Meryn's spirits.

"I think you're doing that already. Let's go into the front drawing room and I'll teach you how to sew." Adelaide stood and Meryn moaned.

"Why? I thought you liked me?" Meryn finished her tea and stood.

"You don't want to give Daphne Bowers a chance to look down her nose at you, do you?" Adelaide lifted an elegant brow.

"No! I give her enough ammo as it is." Meryn admitted.

"Good. I'll start with something easy. First lesson; threading the needle." Adelaide walked with her to the front of the house.

Kill me now.

For the rest of the afternoon, Meryn discovered how Sisyphus must have felt pushing that boulder up the hill, almost reaching the top, only to watch it roll back down again. After four hours she had yet to thread a needle. Every time she exhaled, she missed. Every time she inhaled, she missed. So she tried holding her breath and almost fainted. By the time Marius returned with her packages, Meryn was secretly planning to gather every needle in the house and melt them down in the backyard.

"I would think that you're playing a joke on me, but I can see how determined you are." Adelaide shook her head.

"I will thread this fucking needle if it kills me!" Meryn vowed, shaking her fist.

"Why don't you take a break? I think Marius has something for you." Adelaide pointed to the doorway. Meryn saw a large box with the universally recognized Apple logo, and let out a loud shout. She jumped up and danced from foot to foot in front of Marius.

Marius, with great flourish, opened the box and presented her with a brand-new laptop.

"Hello, baby, I'm going to take such good care of you. Come here, mama's boy." Meryn crooned at the small laptop and raced back over to her chair. In seconds it had booted up and was running her through the final set up. She installed a parallel Linux operating system and began installing her own programs from her flash drive. After a few minutes, she had established the wireless connection and was back on the internet.

"You treat that thing more gently than most people treat their pets." Aiden's voice pulled her out of her gleeful exploration of her new machine.

"You're back!" Meryn smiled at her mate.

"I'll help Marius organize dinner." Adelaide stood, kissed him on the cheek and headed toward the kitchen.

"I've been watching you fondle your new laptop. Should I be jealous?" he kidded.

"Absolutely." Meryn nodded and hugged her laptop close. She had opted for the 13-inch MacBook Pro. It was lighter than her old laptop and had more power. She had already gone online and located a new *Doctor Who* skin. She made a mental note to ask Marius about what address to use for shipping.

"What man can compete with a new laptop, huh? We ordered pizza to give Marius the night off, since he went shopping for us. After their showers, the rest of the guys will be here. Hope you like green peppers." He stretched his arms over his head and rotated his neck. She admired the way his muscles shifted under his tight cotton tee. She sighed and he raised an eyebrow.

“Maybe I can compete after all?” He closed the door behind him and stalked over to her. Meryn felt her heart begin to race. He plucked her laptop from her hands and placed it on the table beside her. With a move made possible by his shifter speed and strength, he pulled her from her chair and dipped her backward, scorching her with a passionate kiss. As the kiss deepened, they stood up straight. Meryn stepped into his body and felt the hard line of his erection against her stomach. She reached between their bodies and squeezed his bulge, causing him to moan deep in his throat.

“You can't do this to me, Meryn. You're still on your cycle and my mother would kick my ass if I took you in her drawing room.” His breathing became more ragged as she kept caressing him. Meryn let her hand fall away and Aiden's forehead dropped to her shoulder. She grinned evilly as she turned her lips to his ear.

“My cycle ended today.” His breathing stopped. He jerked back and his eyes were completely black. Just as his hands tightened on her arms to pull her closer, his mother opened the door.

“Pizza is here. Come get it while it's hot.” She walked away, leaving the door open.

“Yay! Pizza!” Meryn turned, grabbed her laptop, and headed toward the door. She glanced back at Aiden with an innocent expression.

“Not hungry?” His growl had her giggling as she sprinted from the room. His answering laughter and pinching fingers chased her all the way to the dining room.

When they got there, he kissed her quickly and then his attention was on the stacks of pizza boxes laid out on the large dining room table. Watching him grab a whole box, her heart felt light. She had to admit, even if it was just to herself, that she had missed him terribly today. Unlike Adelaide, she refused to be left behind while he lived at the Alpha estate. With a new item on her 'To Do' list, Meryn grabbed a plate and sat next to Aiden as the rest of the unit members joined them for dinner.

CHAPTER TEN

"What did the council decide?" Aiden asked as everyone got settled.

"Meryn, never, ever feel bad for calling René a douchebag. That man almost exceeded the limits of my patience today. He had the gall to imply that these couples deserved whatever happened to them since they chose to live outside Lycaonia," Byron growled under his breath.

"Will they stop the birth announcements?" Adelaide asked.

"We will be sending out a general public announcement tomorrow. We have to keep it vague to avoid mass panic, but I'm afraid most will ignore it. It's a part of our culture to celebrate our children and I know new parents-to-be will want to let the world know." Byron bit into a slice of pizza.

"Oh, that reminds me," Meryn turned to Aiden, "before I lost my mind with your laptop this morning, I came across a report filed by the county sheriff. They located a female body approximately five miles outside of Madison today. They won't be releasing that information anytime soon though." Meryn folded her slice in half and took a bite. Everyone stared at her.

"And how did you 'come across' it?" Aiden asked.

"You own a laptop still running Windows 95; I will not waste a perfectly good explanation on you, but rest assured it was completely illegal."

"Meryn!"

"What?"

"Won't you get caught?"

"No way! If the federal government can't track me, there's no way these small time sheriffs can." His face blanched.

"Federal government?"

"Yup, NSA is my bitch. They stopped trying to catch me years ago. They know that I don't cause trouble, sell secrets, or steal. In the end, they realized it was easier just to let me do what I want."

"So you just felt like hacking into the sheriff's email?" Darian asked.

"Uh, yeah. They don't realize they are dealing with paranormals and don't know to report stuff to you, so I set up a tiny little program that forwards all of the sheriff's email to my inbox."

Aiden's eyes narrowed. "What exactly can you do with that overpriced frisbee?"

"Take over the world." She took another bite of her pizza.

"No, seriously," he prodded.

She looked up at him and blinked. "No, *seriously*."

"Okay, I'm not thinking about this right now. Any other news?"

Meryn picked up the laptop from the floor and opened it up on her lap. She scanned her email before turning to Aiden.

"Did you want like a *Cliff Notes* version? It's kinda gory." She motioned to Adelaide.

"If those young women had to experience it, I at least owe it to them to listen. If I can help in any way I will," Adelaide insisted.

"Okay. A second body was found outside of Waynesburg, but because that is a different county, they haven't put two and two together that it's the missing person from Madison. Both bodies had been completely mutilated. The coroners are still trying to determine if they have all of the pieces. Oh..." Meryn paused to read.

"What?" Aiden asked leaning forward to look at her laptop.

"They are having a hard time identifying the bodies because, and I quote, 'It looks like something ate their faces off'. I wonder if they have pictures?" Meryn was about to check when Aiden closed her laptop.

"Excuse me." Adelaide put a trembling hand to her mouth and left the room, Byron and Marius on her heels.

"Sorry." Meryn felt like she really put her foot in it this time.

"It's okay. I think it's the fact that she knew that the women had been pregnant that got to her. We've discussed far worse at the dinner table before." Aiden rubbed Meryn's back.

Adelaide and Byron returned a few minutes later.

"I am so sorry," Meryn apologized.

"It's okay, dear. I hope no one minds if I skip the rest of dinner and go right to dessert. Cookies sound perfect right now." Adelaide pushed her pizza aside.

"Sounds perfect to me too!" Meryn agreed.

"First batch is out. Get them while they are hot. I have also taken the liberty of scooping out just the cookie dough for those who feel so inclined." Marius set a plate in the middle of the table. On one side, steaming fresh cookies--on the other, cookie dough balls. After Adelaide and Meryn got theirs, everyone else dug in. Meryn was just about to ask how their training went when the lights went out.

In the dark, Meryn heard a half dozen chairs scraping the floor as the men stood.

"Gavriel, take Colton and Keelan and check the back. Father, you, Darian, and I will check the front. Marius, stay with Meryn and my mother." Aiden immediately took charge.

"Of course, sir," Marius replied.

A hand appeared on her shoulder and she gasped.

"Just me." Aiden kissed her and moved away quickly.

"Meryn, feel around the table and make your way to me." Adelaide's voice sounded calm and sure. Meryn never would have guessed she had just chucked her dinner. She did as Adelaide advised and felt her way around the table until she grasped two warm hands.

"Now follow me. Byron has a panic room in his office. Hurry, dear." Adelaide easily navigated the hallway in the dark. They were just passing the front door when Meryn heard the sound of a canine whimper. She froze.

"Come on, Meryn." Adelaide gently tugged on her hand, but when a high pitched yelp was cut short, Meryn turned toward the door.

"That was Colton!" She tried to pull her hand free.

"No, Meryn! We have to stay inside." Adelaide began to pull her back toward the office.

"No! Please! We have to see if he's okay." Meryn tried to get away but couldn't. Then, as suddenly as the lights had gone out, they were back. Meryn took advantage of Adelaide's momentary distraction and tugged free. She ran and flung the door open. She had only taken two steps outside when everything began to move in slow motion. She couldn't seem to catch her breath. She was confused. Why couldn't she breathe? Panic set in when she realized that she was having a hard time breathing because she was screaming. Pictures flashed in her mind in bits and pieces. The door opening and then blood. So much blood. Arms wrapped around her from behind. A familiar perfume engulfed her as she was pulled back inside the house. The steady stream of screams from her own throat and the image that would forever be etched in her mind.

A gutted wolf, hanging by his intestines on the front porch.

And then as if someone pressed a resume button, the world was no longer moving in slow motion.

"No! God, no! Colton!" Her own screams echoed in the foyer. Men's angry shouts and pounding feet.

"Breathe, Meryn, just breathe," Adelaide's voice repeated in her ear. Meryn could feel Adelaide's hot tears on her neck. Meryn no longer screamed words, just long, anguished wails. Between one heartbeat and the next, her world went black.

Meryn struggled to wake up. When she tried to open her eyes, she realized that they were practically glued shut from sleep. Rubbing her eyes, she turned over. She was in her room.

"Aiden?" She felt movement behind her.

"I'm here." He pulled her close.

The events from the evening slammed into her and she began to sob.

"Sweetheart, it's okay."

"How can you say that? He was your best friend!"

"Colton is fine. Mother said you called out his name. Meryn, it was just a dog, some poor dog that this psycho used to scare us." He rubbed her arms.

"Colton's okay?"

"Yes, he's fine. When we die, even if we're shifted, we revert back to human form. He was very touched at your concern, though." Relief flooded her. She felt exhausted all over again.

"That poor dog. I heard it, Aiden, it was alive when he brought it here. I heard it crying on the porch." That was all it took for a new flood of tears to overtake her.

"I swear to you, I will find this guy, and he will pay for all he has done."

"Why would he hurt an innocent little dog?" Meryn blubbered. She could easily discuss hacked up bodies at the dinner table; it didn't bother her. She never really liked people, but animals? Animals had been her only friends growing up. She couldn't stand the fact that she had stood there and listened to this dog be murdered.

"Because he is a sick fuck and he's toying with us." Aiden pulled her in tight to his body and draped a heavy leg over hers.

"Get some sleep, sweetheart. Things won't seem so bad in the morning." Meryn just nodded. She closed her eyes, and found her solace being wrapped in Aiden's arms.

Meryn was on a mission. She was determined to find this asshole dog killer and bring him to justice. As soon as she woke up the following morning, she slipped from the bed and jumped into the shower. She managed to get dressed before Aiden woke and sat up in bed. He grinned at her t-shirt selection for the day. *She-Ra: Princess of Power* brandished a sword on her chest, making her feel like taking on the world.

"Be downstairs," she said, turning for the door.

"Get back here, woman." Aiden pointed to the empty space on the bed. She put her laptop down and walked back over to the bed. Before she could blink, his arm snaked out from under the covers and pulled her down beside him. Laughing, she turned and faced him. His slow kisses ignited a fire in her blood. He took his time and kissed his way down the side of her neck.

"We could always stay in bed today," he whispered, before his hand began to climb up the inside of her shirt.

"Have I told you lately that I think you're a genius?" she panted. He chuckled. His fingers had just slid inside her bra when a loud banging jerked them apart. Aiden snarled at the door. Meryn rolled onto her back, trying to catch her breath.

"What?" he yelled.

"A third couple was just reported missing, this time from inside Lycaonia," Gavriel reported urgently. And just like that, their passion evaporated. Aiden jumped up and began pulling on his uniform. Meryn hopped out of bed and waited for him to finish.

"Who?"

"Eleanor Canter," Gavriel replied.

Meryn frowned. She knew that name. How did she know that name? The conversation from the sewing circle popped into her head.

"Oh, no. Her mother will be worried sick. I met her at the sewing circle, Aiden. She was actually nice." Aiden's eyes met hers. She knew he was trying not to show it, but at the end of the day, they were both too much alike; she could see in his eyes that they both believed that Eleanor was already dead.

"I'm leaving Colton here. Call me if you need anything." Aiden leaned forward and rested their foreheads together.

"I wish I could stay. I want to show you how I feel," he whispered.

"I know. But we have time, Eleanor may not." She clutched the front of his shirt.

"I love you so much, Meryn. I need to claim you soon." She leaned back.

"Tonight," she promised.

"Tonight." He kissed her gently as if savoring the feel of her lips.

"Come on, Superman, your unit needs you." Meryn picked up her laptop and took his hand. Aiden opened the door.

"He is more like Yogi Bear than Superman," Gavriel informed her without cracking a smile.

"And you're more like..." Aiden began.

"Do not. Do not say it. Any comparisons made to certain sparkly vampires will be met with a slow death," Gavriel threatened. Aiden chuckled. Meryn rolled her eyes. They walked downstairs and said goodbye in the foyer.

"Until tonight," Aiden pledged.

"Until tonight." They left and Meryn made her way to the dining room alone. When she walked in, Adelaide and Byron were on their way out.

"Where are you two going?" she asked.

"Byron has another council meeting to discuss the new disappearance. I am heading to the Canters' to see if there is anything I can do. Then I'm off to the Council Manor to help set up for tomorrow's ball, though given everything that has happened, I'm not sure if people will feel like celebrating." Adelaide wiped her eyes. Byron kissed her hair.

"It's because of what is happening that we need to celebrate." Byron looked to Meryn. "Will you be okay by yourself today?"

"Like Aiden would leave her alone?" Colton said from behind Meryn. He walked up behind her and gave her a brotherly hug.

"I'll leave her in your hands." Byron's voice was pleasant but even Meryn could hear the unspoken, commanded order, 'Protect her or face me.'

"Yes, sir."

"Maybe I should stay with Meryn?" Adelaide wrung her hands.

Meryn shook her head. "No, Lady Canter will need you more than me. Tell her I am thinking about her and when we find Eleanor, I'll help with the nursery," Meryn promised.

"You're such an angel." Adelaide kissed her cheek and Byron the top of her head and they left.

Meryn looked at Colton, who stared back.

"So?" She asked.

"So?" He responded.

"Whatcha wanna do?"

"Can you show me the Sheriff's email? I'm not as good as Keelan with the tech stuff, but I'd like to help review some of the case information while I'm here."

"You mean while you're stuck babysitting me," she interpreted.

"That, too." His grin was completely unapologetic.

"On one condition."

"What?"

"You shift into a wolf later and play with me." She turned her face so he couldn't see her embarrassed expression. He just pulled her into a bear hug and swung her around. Laughing, she tried to get down.

"I knew you liked me!" Colton set her down and ruffled her hair.

"Maybe a little," Meryn admitted. She grabbed a muffin out of the basket from the small buffet-style breakfast set up on the sideboard. Colton got a napkin and filled it up. She grabbed a bottle of Diet Mt. Dew and he grabbed two bottles of water.

"Come on, Colton, I'll let you be my minion."

"Sweet!"

They ended up in Byron's office since he had the more comfortable chairs and the large fireplace.

She turned to him and opened her laptop.

"Let's get started."

"I'm bored!" Meryn closed her laptop. They had checked both of the Sheriffs' email and nothing new had come in. She showed him how she had hacked their passwords and set up the forwarding program.

"So what do you want to do?" Colton swung his feet down off of the sofa and sat up.

"Would you like some tea?" Marius asked from the doorway.

"No offense, Marius, but if I drink any more tea I'll float away. As it is I feel like I'm about to lose my mind." There wasn't much in the world she hated more than the feeling of being bored.

"Might I suggest a visit to Master Aiden? You do have that other package I bought. I left it in the pantry for safe keeping."

Meryn jumped to her feet and turned to Colton. "Can we go visit Aiden?"

"Sure. Keelan texted me a little while ago to let me know that they were back at the Alpha estate." Colton stood and stretched his legs.

"Aiden didn't text?" Meryn asked.

Colton laughed out loud. "Aiden doesn't text. I don't even think his phone *can* text."

Meryn stopped putting her laptop in her backpack and blinked at Colton.

"You're lying. Everyone texts!"

"Not Aiden, I think it's because of those manly fingers of his. It takes him forever to type anything. If any texting has to be done, either Keelan or I do it."

"He really is a Neanderthal." Meryn was going to have to pull Aiden into the twenty-first century whether he liked it or not. She walked over to the door where Marius was waiting for them. He had gone to the pantry and returned with a large box.

"Miss, your package." Marius set down a rather large box down in the hallway.

"Awesome. Thank you, Marius!" She jumped up and kissed his cheek.

He blushed. "You're welcome, little miss."

"Okay, Colton, that goes in the car."

He eyed the box curiously. "What is it?"

"I'll show you when we get there," she promised.

Meryn nearly wet herself watching Colton try to get the box into his trunk.

"Next time, you lift it. What in the hell is in that box, Meryn?" Colton rubbed his back.

"It wasn't that heavy, you big baby."

"Meryn, that box is almost as big as you are."

"And I know what is inside, so it shouldn't have been too heavy for a big ol' strong shifter like you."

"You're lucky the box is in the trunk, shortie." Meryn stuck her tongue out at him and got in the car.

It didn't take long before they were pulling up to the Alpha estate. Meryn stared. She had only seen it briefly the day she met Aiden, and that was while traveling panicked and flailing in his arms. She gawked up at the large mansion in front of her. It was smaller than the estate his parents lived in, but not by much.

"This place is huge!"

"All the unit estates are this big. Each warrior has his own suite, complete with a small kitchenette area. Downstairs we have shared spaces like the media room, kitchen, main dining room and offices," Colton explained.

"It's pretty." Meryn was taken aback by how homey it seemed.

"Adelaide has helped us make it more domestic." He pointed to the gorgeous landscaping by the door.

"Now will you tell me what's in the box?" He asked.

"You can see for yourself. Where do the men train?"

"Out back."

"Let's take the box to the back porch," Colton cursed under his breath as he manhandled the box out of the trunk and carried it to the back porch. It was a long way around the side of the house. He set the box down and, like a kid at Christmas, he started to tear into it. When he opened the flaps and peered inside, he started laughing.

"No way! Meryn, this is awesome!"

"Your job is to fill them up. I'm going to go challenge Aiden." Meryn lifted a super soaker from the box and looked around for a spigot. Colton grabbed two and showed her where the hose connected to the house near the back door. She filled hers up first and left him grinning like an idiot to go find Aiden.

She walked back toward the large obstacle course and stopped. Despite its being almost Halloween, most of the men had their shirts off and were doing drills. Each man was trying to attack his sparring partner, who was blindfolded. Quietly, she snuck up behind her mate and jumped out, screaming like a banshee. Aiden jumped nearly a foot in the air and turned around snarling. That was when she brought the gun to her shoulder, aimed...

"Meryn, don't!" Aiden warned.

... and fired. She shot him in the face, laughing as he sputtered. Behind Aiden, the men hooted and egged her on. When she stopped, Aiden's eyes took on a dangerous glint.

"Oh, shit!" she yelped.

"Heads up, Commander!" Colton called from behind Meryn and tossed Aiden a gun.

"Traitor!" Meryn yelled.

"Gamma versus Alpha. Meryn, you're on Gamma's team," Colton said and quickly began tossing guns to the men.

Ben ran over toting a gun of his own and grabbed her hand. "Come on!"

Meryn ran with Ben for all she was worth. Behind them, Gamma stood between her and Aiden, laughing and shooting each other. She and Ben took positions at the edge of the obstacle course. He scaled one of the many climbing obstacles and lay in wait on his belly like a sniper. Meryn knew if she tried something like that she would fall off, so she stood behind the rock-climbing wall.

Minutes later the men began running by in an effort to get to the woods. She jumped out and got Colton in the ear.

"Agghhh."

Laughing hysterically, she bolted for the woods. She could hardly run, she was laughing so hard. She ran until she couldn't go anymore. She looked around and took up a tactical position behind a tree. She listened to the men's laughter and cursing and congratulated herself. They had needed something to take their minds off the depressing case they were working.

As the minutes went by, she noticed how quiet it had gotten. Maybe she had run too far. She stepped out from behind the tree.

"Meryn!" She heard Aiden yell.

"Aiden, come and find me," she teased.

"Quit playing and come out," he yelled.

"Sourpuss!" She laughed and heard it echo through the trees.

"Come on now, no more playing," he called out. There was nothing but silence.

Meryn froze. She knew this scene. It was the scene she had been dreaming of for the past few weeks.

"That's not funny, come out!" Aiden's voice sounded frantic.

Out of nowhere a body slammed into hers.

"Aiden!" Her scream shattered the silence. She could feel someone on top of her but couldn't see anything.

"Almost time for you to die," a harsh voice whispered in her ear. A hand groped between her legs, and she began to fight.

"Do me a favor and drop dead, asshole!" She turned her head and bit down blindly. An angry roar emerged from above her. A heavy hand came down and clipped her cheekbone. Stars exploded and for a second she couldn't see, and then, as quickly as he attacked, the weight was gone. She lay on the forest floor, blinking up, trying to focus her eyes.

She could hear feet running and men shouting.

"Over here!" she yelled. Seconds later a familiar face appeared over her.

"Found!" he bellowed. He looked down. "Are you hurt?"

"Fucker punched me. I'm really starting to hate his invisible ass." She struggled to sit up. He offered her a hand and helped her lean against the tree. Aiden burst through the tree line and didn't stop until he was at her side.

"Has she been stabbed?" His hands pulled at her clothing, trying to inspect every inch of her.

"No, sir; she said that she was punched."

"Thank you, Sascha. Take Gamma and find this fucker," Aiden ordered.

"He's bleeding. I bit him." Meryn told the tall, Nordic-looking warrior with the white-blond hair. His icy blue eyes held admiration. He nodded.

"Good work--that will make it easier." He turned to the two men that had arrived after Aiden.

"Christoff, my vampire friend, you're up. He's bleeding; you're on point for tracking." The dark-haired man nodded. He walked over to Meryn and sniffed her jacket, which now sported blood splatter.

"Oron, you're with him. Report in every ten minutes," Sascha commanded.

"Yes, sir!" Both men took off.

"Aiden, let's get her back to Alpha." Sascha suggested. Aiden lifted her gently.

They ran back and Meryn wanted to groan. Each dip and jostle hurt her head. They ran past the obstacle course to where the other men had assembled by the house for orders.

"Ben, I'm assigning you to Alpha for today. Help them keep Meryn safe. Quinn, you're with me. We're going to ransack the archives. We're looking for an invisibility spell." Sascha and Quinn turned and started toward where the cars were parked.

"Sir, I'd like to assist Quinn and Sascha. I grew up helping my brother in the archives at Storm Keep. I know some of those volumes by heart." Keelan stepped forward. Aiden nodded.

"Go, do whatever it takes." Keelan nodded and ran to catch up with Quinn and Sascha.

"Aiden, we'll set up patrol around Alpha. Take Meryn upstairs and make sure she's okay." Ben gently pushed his older brother toward the door.

"Thank you, Ben. Gavriel, you're in charge," Aiden said.

"When you get hit, do you go blind for a second?" Meryn looked out at the men and closed one eye, then the other.

Colton smiled. "Sometimes. You took a punch, huh? I knew you were a tough little shortie."

"I bit him too; serves him right for groping me." Meryn shuddered. Aiden's grip tightened.

"We'll be upstairs." He turned and walked into the house.

"I remember these stairs." Meryn laid her head on his chest. "I must say this trip up is better than the last one."

"You had just bitten me, too, if I remember, right over my kidney."

"You had me over your shoulder; that shit hurts. I felt like I was gonna puke."

"Duly noted." Aiden turned down a long hallway.

"It didn't seem so big before." Meryn watched as Aiden turned down yet another long hallway.

"You were in a hurry last time. You had just brained me with my toilet. This is the Unit Commander wing." He stopped at a door and turned the handle.

"And this, as you may remember, is my room." He stepped inside and turned on the light, and she blinked. This room felt different than the room she was staying in at his parents' house. Everywhere she turned, Aiden's personality was reflected in the small mementos that decorated the room. She smiled when she noticed the small dent in the lamp on the nightstand.

"Put me down, I wanna see Jaws." Aiden put her down gently and took her hand. He led her over to a wall hidden by decorative screens and gently pushed them aside. He flipped a switch and the aquarium lit up. It took up most of one wall.

"No wonder I missed it before. Though to be honest, not many people have an aquarium for a wall."

"I had to reinforce the floor, but he's worth it." Aiden gently tapped the glass. Out of nowhere, a bright orange fish darted forward.

"Meryn, Jaws. Jaws, my mate, Meryn."

"He's adorable. He needs a girlfriend." Meryn watched the fish swim for a few more moments and tore her eyes away.

"The first thing I did when I assumed the position of Unit Commander was gut this suite and redecorate. Most of the unit estates are decorated in shades of green and wood grain. I hate it. So I changed it to blue." Aiden motioned to the walls. Each wall was painted in a different shade of blue to accent the calming waters of the aquarium. The decorative accents and furniture were black with splashes of silver.

"I love it. Your room at your parents' house is so bland." She ran and jumped on the impossibly high four-poster bed. She grimaced. *Note to self: Running and jumping is a bad idea after getting punched by psycho bad guy.*

"Meryn, I don't live there, remember?" Aiden reminded her gently.

"Oh, yeah." Wincing, she rubbed the side of her face. Aiden climbed on the bed and pulled her close.

"Did he touch you?" His voice sounded strained.

She nodded. "It's okay. I'm with you now--that's all that matters."

"Let me see your eyes." Aiden turned her to face him. With his large hand, he blocked the light, then let it shine back on her face.

"Your pupils are dilating, so I don't think you have a concussion." He ran a hand over her hair.

"No, but I sure did see stars."

"When you screamed I thought..." His voice cracked.

"I'm okay. In that dream, I had long hair. Things change." She snuggled up on his chest and yawned. "I didn't use to take so many naps before coming here."

"You probably weren't assaulted and traumatized on a daily basis before either," Aiden growled.

"No, but I'm having more fun now."

"Let me hold you for a while. You don't have to nap; I just need to feel you in my arms."

"I can do that." She closed her eyes and fell asleep listening to him breathe.

When she woke up, she was back at Aiden's parents' house. She must have been out cold not to have woken up in transit. She sat up and looked around. Aiden was sitting in the dark on his laptop in the chair in the corner.

"What are you doing on that thing?"

He closed it and stood up. "Playing Spider Solitaire."

"Why are we back here? I liked your room better." She lay back down.

"I had Adam check you out at the Alpha estate. He said you were okay, no visible signs of swelling. I was supposed to wake you in thirty minutes if you didn't wake on your own. After he checked you out, we woke you up around six to see if you wanted dinner and you said no. So I brought you back here to get settled for the night." Aiden lifted the covers and got in next to her.

"I don't remember any of that. What time is it?" She immediately rolled onto her side and he spooned in next to her.

"One a.m. Go back to sleep." There was something about his voice that had her turning to face him.

"What happened?"

He sighed. "Can I tell you in the morning? You've been through so much already."

"Nope. I'm a big girl. I can handle it."

"Body parts were delivered to the Alpha estate. We think they belong to Eleanor Canter. We brought you back here since this house is more easily defended." He sounded so defeated.

"Okay, let's pretend you didn't tell me that. Let's just go to sleep and pretend that there isn't a psycho out there hacking and slashing." Meryn buried her nose in his chest.

"Anything you want, sweetheart. Get some rest. We have the ball tomorrow."

"I'm kinda looking forward to it." She wrapped her arm around his waist and squeezed tight.

He rested his chin on her head and rubbed her back.

Tomorrow. Tomorrow will be a better day.

CHAPTER ELEVEN

"Meryn, you'll be with me today. I need to go to the Alpha estate to meet with the other units and make sure everyone knows where they are supposed to be for tonight's ball," Aiden said, pouring another cup of coffee.

"Sure. From what Lady Fairfax told me about this 'super dress' it won't take me very long to get ready." Meryn sipped her cappuccino. She looked down at the single muffin on her plate and swallowed hard. She wasn't hungry at all. Her stomach was doing cartwheels. Every time she thought about walking into a huge room full of people she didn't know, she felt like she was going to be sick.

"You need to eat." Aiden put a spoonful of greasy potatoes on her plate next to her muffin. She watched the steam rise off her plate. The second the smell hit her nose, she stood. Covering her mouth, she bolted from the room. She nearly knocked Marius over before she made it to the downstairs bathroom. Since she had only had coffee for breakfast, she was dry heaving by the time Aiden caught up with her.

"Oh, baby, it's okay." He got a washcloth out and wet it with warm water. When her stomach stopped trying to turn itself inside out, she sat back against the wall. Aiden handed her a tiny cup of water. She swished the cool, clean water around her mouth and spit it out in the toilet. She leaned back again and the warm cloth was placed over her eyes.

"I can't tell if you being sick is from your nerves or an aftereffect of getting hit yesterday."

"Nerves. Trust me--it's nerves." She removed the washcloth and got to her feet. Aiden helped steady her and they made their way back to the dining room. She was relieved that her plate had been replaced and the greasy potatoes were nowhere in sight. Marius placed a small plate of saltine crackers next to her tea.

"Thank you, Marius. I hope my squire is half as wonderful as you."

The older man smiled sadly. "I thought that more of my colleagues would show up for your interviews, but I am afraid they have been swayed by idle gossip."

"That's not your fault."

"I was hoping that my nephew would be able to come, but he has taken a position in Belgium."

"As long as you'll be there to help make the decision, I feel pretty confident about the interviews for tomorrow." Meryn snacked on a cracker.

"I will do everything I can to assist."

"What time will you have her back, Aiden? The ball starts at eight o'clock," Adelaide asked.

"Well before eight, Mother. Don't worry, you'll get your girl time," Aiden teased.

"Meryn, did you want anything else to eat?" Aiden asked, standing. Meryn shook her head.

"Little miss, I have taken the liberty of packing a few crackers in a bag for you. Just in case." Marius handed her a small Ziploc bag of crackers.

"Thank you, Marius. See y'all later." She grabbed her backpack and followed Aiden out of the room. She stepped outside and avoided looking at the recently repainted section of the porch. It was a gruesome reminder that they couldn't get all of the dog-blood stains out of the wood. She stepped off the porch and followed Aiden to his car. She took a deep breath. Aiden held the door open for her.

"I'll put the windows down for the trip. Looks like the fresh air is helping." He closed the door and seconds later he was climbing inside. He started the car and immediately lowered the windows. She sat back and closed her eyes without saying a word. She enjoyed the sound of the road flying by, the fresh air in her face and his warm hand around hers.

When they got to the Alpha estate, Colton met them as they were getting out of the car.

"Hey short stuff, feeling better?"

"I'm not seeing double anymore, if that's what you mean."

"Good to hear. Aiden, the men are out back awaiting orders. I'll keep an eye on Meryn since I already know where Alpha will be tonight."

"Thanks, Colton. Be back, baby." Aiden kissed her and walked around to the back of the house.

"He started drills with the men. We're practicing fighting while blindfolded, so we can attack and defend against what we can't see," Colton explained.

"I saw that yesterday. He's really good, isn't he?" she asked.

"The very best. Better than our last commander."

"I thought Aiden took over from his father?" Meryn asked, confused.

"Walk with me. I'll show you around and I'll tell you about how Aiden became Unit Commander." Colton took her hand and they walked toward the outbuildings.

"Byron was chosen to be an Elder right after Adair was born, about thirteen hundred years ago. He stepped down as Unit Commander and Edward Carthage was selected as the best warrior to become the new Unit Commander. For a while everything went on like normal, but after about fifty years, the men began getting disillusioned with their new commander. He would disappear during missions, come back drunk. Wouldn't organize training or keep an eye on the men. After centuries of Byron's fair and efficient leadership, the difference between the two was stark. Edward felt the pressure of filling Byron's enormous shoes and he resented him for it. Over time, being compared to Byron left him bitter and twisted." Colton pointed to the bench outside one of the buildings and they sat down.

"When Aiden and I were one hundred years old, we were training hard at the academy where Adair could keep an eye on us. Every so often, we would get sent out on patrols to get our feet wet. One night, Aiden was doing a standard night patrol, running the perimeter with the Alpha Unit, when a mission came in. Instead of sending Aiden back to the academy, like he should have done, Edward decided to use the mission to humiliate Aiden in place of Byron. The other Alpha Unit members argued, but Edward pulled rank. The men did the best they could to cover Aiden since he had never been out on a mission before, but they soon realized they didn't need to. He handled himself like he was born to it, and maybe he was," Colton paused. He leaned back and closed his eyes.

"The mission was worse than they were led to believe. The unit was up against eight ferals, them banding together was unheard of back then. Jean-Marc, Edward's second-in-command, put his foot down and insisted that Aiden stay behind and watch the horses; he didn't want Aiden getting hurt. Edward relented and took the position to keep their escape route open, only he didn't. As soon as the men left to go investigate, he abandoned his post. Later they found out that he had gone to the local brothel.

Aiden heard the men shouting, and, probably for the first and last time in his life, he ignored orders. He ran into the fray and covered the men as they tried to retreat, but what he didn't know was that it was already too late. The men were mortally wounded. Jean-Marc was the only one left standing, so Aiden pulled him out first and was able to get him to the horses and strap him down. He went back down that alley three more times, fighting against all odds to retrieve the bodies of the other Alpha Unit members. He managed to get the men onto their horses and led them to where the newly arrived Beta Unit was covering the perimeter of the town to ensure no ferals escaped. Aiden was so badly beaten and bleeding so heavily they didn't think he was going to make it. It would be a couple days before he woke up. I was at his side the entire time. Before Jean-Marc passed away, I heard him report what had happened to Byron. To this day I've never seen Byron get that furious again. When Edward walked into the infirmary where Aiden was being treated, Byron shifted into his third form and attacked. It took Beta, Delta and Gamma to pull Byron off of him."

"What's third form?" Meryn interrupted.

Colton opened his eyes and looked at her. "As a shifter, we normally have two forms. Man or animal. One or the other. But in rare instances when the man and the animal are completely in sync, when both want something with the exact same levels of intensity, we're able to shift into a third form, half man, half animal. It's only happened a dozen other times in our written history."

"And Byron was able to do that?"

"Yes, which practically cemented him as an Elder until the day he dies. At the hearing, Edward appealed to his men to testify on his behalf, and every single unit member turned his back to him. Edward was tried by the council and found guilty for the deaths of the entire Alpha Unit. He was executed and cremated so that his body would not be buried within the city. His ashes were given to his sister, one Daphne Bowers, formerly Carthage."

"Holy shit!" Meryn gasped.

"It gets better. Daphne pushed to get her son assigned as Unit Commander, Donovan Bowers. He's actually not a bad guy, but he never wanted to be a warrior. The men refused. They said they would only take orders from Aiden. The council didn't know what to do. Aiden was so young, barely out of his teens in shifter years, though Donovan wasn't that much older."

"What did they do?" Meryn asked.

"There was nothing they could do. It wasn't that Aiden went back and fought alongside the Alpha Unit, it wasn't that he cleared a path for escape despite the overwhelming odds. It was the fact that he went back for the fallen dead, that he risked his life to bring them home, that showed the men that he cared more for them than his own life. That is why his orders are never questioned and why every single active or retired unit member will always defer to him."

Meryn's heart ached for what Aiden had gone through, but more than that, she felt an overwhelming sense of pride. Even at a young age, his integrity had been written in stone.

"Not that I don't want to learn more about Aiden, I do. It's just..."

"Why did I tell you?"

"Hmm"

"Tonight you will see a different side of Aiden. I don't really know if I can put it into words." Colton grew silent and thought for a minute. "Aiden commands the respect of the most powerful men in the city, but more than that, he has their undying loyalty, love and trust. Nearly all of Lycaonia's unit members will be there, past, present and future, since trainees are allowed to attend in uniform. Even if he weren't Byron's heir, which is prestigious enough, their support alone makes him a voice to be heard."

"You mean in Lycaonia, right?"

Colton shook his head.

"Darling, when Aiden takes over from Byron he becomes the shifters' Elder."

"Right, in Lycaonia, since there are four cities and four council members per city," Meryn said. Colton stared at her for a second.

"You don't get it. Meryn, Lycaonia is the shifter capital of the world. Byron is the shifter Elder that represents all shifters. The other three shifter Elders report to him. In Noctem Falls, the vampire city, Magnus Rioux is the vampire Elder, all vampire Elders report to him. In the witch's city of Storm Keep, Caiden Ironwood is the witch Elder, all witch Elders report to him, and in the fae city of Éire Danu, Brennus Vi'Eirlea is the fae queen's consort and fae Elder, all fae Elders report to him."

"Oh, my God." The enormity of what Colton had just explained sunk in.

"Aiden commands every single unit warrior across all four cities. Right now, that plays a small part in our politics, but when he takes over from

Byron, he will literally be the most powerful man in our world. Did you really think that an average unit member's mate would get this much protection detail?" He bumped her shoulder with his. Meryn put a hand over her stomach. So tonight was actually going to be a million times worse than she had imagined.

"You okay?" Colton jumped to his feet.

"I need my crackers," Meryn gagged over the words. Colton dove into her backpack and practically threw the bag of crackers at her. Breathing through her nose, she slowly nibbled a cracker.

"You're really not a people person, are you?"

"Nope. You guys don't bother me, but tonight is going to be all these important people and now you tell me that Aiden is this super celebrity and I'll have to stand next to him all night and smile and nod and shit..." She took another deep breath.

"Listen, you concentrate on getting through the first half hour of introductions. Leave the rest to me."

She pinned him with her eyes. "You promise?"

"I swear. Just keep it together for thirty minutes."

Meryn grabbed one last cracker and put the bag away. "I can do thirty minutes."

"Good, you're getting some color back in your cheeks. For a second you went milk-white."

Meryn stood. "So, what now?"

Colton looked around and pointed to a smaller building off to one side.

"Wanna see the armory?"

Meryn brightened. "Guns?" she asked.

Colton hesitated. "Yes. Why do you look so excited all of a sudden?"

"I want a gun. After getting attacked twice, I want a gun."

Colton rubbed his chin. “That's actually not a bad idea. Can you shoot?”

“Yup. Just never got around to purchasing one. What do you have?”

“What *don't* we have?” Colton led the way to the small white building and reached for his keys. He unlocked the door and they stepped inside. Above them, the lights came on automatically. Meryn looked around. Weapons of all kinds and from every century were stacked from floor to ceiling.

“Are those nunchaku?”

“Don't touch.”

“But...”

“No.”

“Fine, then, do you have the Smith and Wesson Bodyguard?” Colton looked impressed.

“You do know something about guns. Let me check. I think we have the smaller guns in this chest.” Meryn followed him back to a tall steel cabinet. He unlocked the doors and started pulling out drawers. He handed her a small box. She opened it and inside was the gun of her dreams. It even had a box of ammo and a shoulder holster.

“Thank you! I've been dying to get one, but they are expensive.”

“I don't think Aiden will mind shelling out money for your self-defense.” She tucked the box in her backpack and zipped it closed before slipping it onto her back.

“Give me a second to lock up the cabinet and then we can find Aiden.”

“Sure.” Meryn walked around, peeking in boxes. Smiling, she pulled out a small hand grenade.

Colton walked up. “What do you have?”

Laughing, she held up the grenade and pulled the pin. His face dropped. Moving faster than she had ever seen anyone move in her life, he ripped the grenade from her hand, ran to the entrance, and threw the grenade into the woods.

"Grenade!" He yelled at the top of his lungs before knocking her down in a diving tackle. Seconds later, a deafening explosion rocked the small building they were in. When the smoke started to clear, Colton slowly got to his feet and looked down at her with an anxious expression. He helped her to her feet and began checking her over.

"Colton! Meryn!" There was no mistaking the fear in Aiden's voice. Meryn stepped out of the building and looked over to the new clearing that the small grenade had created. Coughing, she waved a hand in front of her face to try to clear the smoke.

"My bad! My bad!" She coughed again, trying to clear her airways.

Aiden and the other twenty-eight unit warriors formed a semi-circle around the doorway. Meryn fought the urge to go back inside and hide. Out of nowhere, hands grabbed her from behind, they turned her around. She looked up. Colton's expression was furious. His eyes were wild and his entire body was trembling. With his hands on her upper arms, he shook her.

"What. In. The. Hell. Is. Wrong. With. You?!" he shouted in her face. She opened her mouth but couldn't form any words. She'd never had anyone be this angry with her before.

"I'm so s-s-sorry! I thought it was like in the cartoons and you could put the pin back." She burst into tears.

Colton pulled her into a tight hug. "You crazy little idiot!"

"Give her to me." Aiden's voice was barely human. Colton pulled her away from his chest and kissed her forehead.

"Stop almost dying. I'm finally getting used to you." He gently pushed her into Aiden's waiting arms.

"No more. I can't take this anymore!" Aiden scooped her up and ran. Before she could stop wiping her eyes, he had her in the house, upstairs and in his room. He kicked the door shut and didn't stop walking until his legs hit the bed. He dropped her before stepping back. Wordlessly, he began to strip off his clothes.

"No more waiting, Meryn. I need to make you mine, body and soul." He pulled his black tee over his head. She licked her lips. He was just as beautiful as she remembered. There was no turning back; she wanted this man more than she wanted her next breath. She rose to her knees on the bed and lifted the hem of her shirt. She let it drop on the floor next to his. Grinning wickedly, she unsnapped her bra and dropped it on top of her shirt. She brought her hands up and cupped her breasts. His eyes never left her body as his hands moved to his belt. She heard the metal of the buckle and then the soft whisper of his zipper. When his pants dropped, she could see his erection straining against the material of his boxer briefs. She squeezed her legs together; she could already feel the wetness between her legs. He reached out and pulled her close by the top of her jeans. He unbuttoned them slowly and slid them over her hips and down to her knees. When she went to lay back to slide them off completely, he stopped her. He ran a finger down the front of her panties, slowly he traced his finger between her folds. The only thing separating them was the saturated material of her underwear. When he pushed a little harder and scraped her clit, she gasped. Slowly he tortured her, his finger teasing her nub, bringing her to the edge of ecstasy and then stopping. She dropped her head to his chest, her breathing ragged. His hand pushed her backward and he jerked her jeans off her legs. He removed his boxers and her mouth went dry. He palmed his heavy cock.

"Before you came into my life all I had was the unit, training drills, and missions. But now I wake up and I think of you, I go to bed with your soft body next to mine. I look forward to my meals because I know you'll be there to share them." He climbed onto the bed and crawled over her. He pulled her panties down and threw them across the room. She had never felt more alive or desired in her life. The possessiveness in his eyes sent an electric pulse to her core. She belonged to him--she had from the first day they met--she had just been too stubborn to admit it. He moved between her legs and spread them wide. He stared down at her, smiling. There was something erotic about being so exposed to him. The longer he stared, the wetter she became.

"I have been fighting all my life, protecting my people, keeping the city safe. Every single day a blur of routine. I didn't know that I was doing it for you." He eased a finger inside her and she moaned deep in her throat.

"I didn't know that one day it would all be worth it. That Fate would send me the most perplexing, complicated, and precious gift." He added a second finger to the first and began to stroke that elusive spot deep inside her.

"Aiden, I am no gift." He was. He was her protection, the rock she didn't even know that she craved.

"You are my treasure. I would relive those barren centuries a thousand times over without complaint, if I knew I had you waiting for me at the end." He slowly added a third finger, stretching her completely.

"I don't know what I would do without you now. You're my shield." She couldn't hold back the tears as he slowly brought her closer and closer to the edge. He removed his fingers and reached between them to guide his thick cock to her entrance. Slowly, he eased forward. She wanted him to go slow so that she could savor every second of feeling him stretch her for the first time, but she was also desperate to get him completely inside of her. She arched her back and wrapped her legs around his waist. His hands came up under her thighs to support her weight. Soon he was thrusting in rapid succession. He moved one of his hands from under her body and reached forward, capturing her breast and he teased her tightened nipple mercilessly.

"Aiden!" She could barely get his name out. Each time he ran his nail over her nipple, she felt a line of pleasure connect to her clit, which had her bearing down and convulsing around him. When he twisted, she threw her head back. He released her breast and grabbed her hips with both hands, thrusting inside her at a frenzied pace. She gave herself up to the sole sensation of his body filling hers. When he leaned over her, his eyes were jet black and she knew he was close. He thrust deep, his body stilled and he bit down savagely where her neck met her shoulder.

A wave a pain took her by surprise. It wasn't until he thrust again that the pain receded and her pleasure came roaring back magnified a thousand-fold. She felt as if she was lifting out of her body and then all at once the most perfect and overwhelming sense of peace and love expanded and embraced her. She slammed back down into her body as her orgasm exploded through her. She screamed and screamed. Above her, Aiden roared and she could feel hot jets of cum fill her. He pulled out of her and slumped to one side. Breathing hard, he barely had the strength to pull her close.

"Finally, our souls are one. I can feel you now. Your soul feels like a tiny hummingbird dancing around my heart. I swear I will love you for the rest of my life." Meryn realized that the warm, safe feeling she had was Aiden's soul protecting hers. She reached up and brushed the hair away from his eyes.

"And I will love you forever." Slowly their breathing returned to normal. Aiden got up, and on wobbly legs walked to the bathroom. He returned with a warm washcloth. Gently he cleaned her, kissing her inner thighs and biting down on her knees until she was laughing and squirming to get away. When he got back in bed, he frowned at her, his fingers tracing her side.

"What are these? They look like scars." Meryn glanced down and realized he was talking about her stretch marks. Had he never seen stretch marks before?

"Those are called stretch marks."

"Stretch marks? How did you get them?"

"Human females get them when we grow. If we grow too fast our skin rips apart and heals. It's a very painful process," Meryn lied through her teeth. There was no way she was going to discuss stretch marks after the most mind-blowing sex of her life. Nope. Wasn't going to happen. Aiden's expression became reverent.

"Human females are amazing creatures; you endure so much pain, yet are so fragile." He kissed each shiny line.

I'm going to hell.

Meryn smiled. She didn't care. He was worth it.

"Promise me something?" he asked.

"What?"

"Promise me you'll never touch another grenade for as long as we live."

"How about you teach me about grenades instead?"

Aiden buried his face in her stomach. "Gods help me."

"Someone better." She squealed when he pinched her butt. She retaliated by poking him in the side.

A couple hours and two orgasms later, they finally left their bed. They took a shower, washing each other lovingly before leaving to go back to his parents' house so that she could get ready for the ball.

They lingered saying goodbye, not wanting to give up their newborn intimacy.

"I'll meet you there. I'll be doing a security sweep before everyone arrives." He kissed her gently.

"See you in a couple of hours." She kissed him one last time and then went inside. She closed the front door and leaned against it. She fought the urge to chase after him. She placed her hand over her heart. She could still feel him, his strength guarding her soul. She missed him already.

CHAPTER TWELVE

"Meryn, is that you?" Adelaide called from upstairs.

"Yeah."

"Hurry, darling, the carriage will be here in less than an hour. I want to make sure that you are perfect."

"Yes, Mother!" she called out as she climbed the stairs. The sooner she got ready, the sooner she could see Aiden.

She walked into her room to see that Adelaide was already dressed. She looked like a queen with her long blonde hair in a braided coil on her head like a crown. The dress was done in brown silk with bright green embroidered vines and leaves. She wore a gold and green leaf headpiece that matched the theme, giving the dress a simple but elegant design. It was clear even to Meryn that she represented Mother Earth. The long white satin shift that Lady Fairfax had given her lay across the bed. When Adelaide turned, her mouth made a little 'O'. With a low cry she rushed forward and pulled her into a hug.

"You've mated!" she exclaimed.

"Okay, is this a freaky shifter smell thing? Because if it is, that's awkward and gross." Adelaide shook her head and pointed to her neck. “Oh. Yeah, I guess that's a pretty big clue.”

Meryn was about to set her backpack down when she heard a ding. She pulled out her laptop. The program had finished running a nationwide search and the results were ready. She looked over the numbers and fought not to gasp. She knew she had to tell Aiden, but seeing Adelaide's excitement, she decided to wait until after the ball.

“Is everything okay?” Adelaide asked.

Meryn nodded. “Yup, just nervous, I guess.” She put her laptop back in her backpack.

“Don't worry about a thing. With that mating mark, it's crystal clear that you are Aiden's mate. My son always had impeccable timing. Now all of Lycaonia will know that he is mated and claimed. I'm so happy, I could float away. Now let's see what your dress will be. I'm dying to see it in action. This dress is legendary.” Meryn stripped out of her clothing and hesitated at her undergarments.

“Do you think that thing provides underwear?”

“One way to find out.” Adelaide held up the shift. Meryn stripped completely nude and Adelaide slipped it on over her head. Meryn looked at Adelaide, who was beginning to panic.

“Do you think it's not working because I'm human?”

“It has to work! We don't have anything else for you to wear!”

“Maybe it...” Meryn felt something slide across her abdomen.

“Adelaide, I think something is happening.” Meryn watched in amazement as the material changed in texture and weight right before her eyes. One second the shift was long, white satin. The next it was a heavy brocade in a deep, royal blue. Meryn gasped.

"It's TARDIS blue!"

"What's Tardis, dear?" Adelaide asked.

"Nothing." Meryn ran to the mirror and couldn't believe her reflection. The dress had one strap over her left shoulder. The bodice hugged her tightly, pushing everything up and holding it in place. Her chest had never looked bigger or her waist smaller. Where the dress narrowed at her hips, the color faded to a lighter blue and kept fading until it ended up a foamy white at her feet. Meryn's mouth dropped. Covering nearly every single inch of the bodice were tiny blue and clear jewels. On her head was a delicate tiara woven in silver interspaced with pearls.

"Please tell me those aren't real. Please tell me those aren't sapphires and diamonds."

"As if the fae would use fake gems? Oh, Meryn, it's just perfect. Aiden loves the color blue. If only it had a wrap."

No sooner did she speak the words when a gossamer silver and white wrap appeared around Meryn's shoulders.

"It thinks of everything, doesn't it? Even your makeup is exquisite. Did it provide you with underthings?" Adelaide asked. Meryn shifted around a bit.

"Yup, it's like silk leggings. They are warm and comfortable. I could get used to these."

"Excellent. Let's go downstairs. Byron arranged for a horse-drawn carriage since, as an Elder, it's expected that he go through the streets waving to the people. I love the cobblestones in the city, but sometimes they can be a nightmare to work around." Adelaide picked up a small clutch off the bed.

They walked downstairs and met Marius and Byron in the foyer. Byron looked kingly in his Elder dress robes. She was dying to see what Aiden looked like in his dress whites.

"The loving earth and the gentle sea, the two of you take my breath away." Byron kissed each of them on the cheek. They were about to head toward the door when Marius cleared his throat.

"Is little miss wearing shoes?"

Meryn glanced down. "No, I..." Seconds later the world shifted as she was elevated four inches in the air. "Yes, I think I am now."

Marius smiled. "Have a wonderful time."

"You're not coming?" she asked.

He shook his head. "My mate Bronwyn has a terrible time around people. I will be celebrating with her in our quarters. She's the one who gave me the crackers for you earlier. She has really taken a liking to you." Meryn felt an odd sense of kinship with the woman she hadn't met yet. Those crackers had helped tremendously this morning.

"Tell her thank you, and when she's ready, I'd love to meet her."

"I'll do just that."

Meryn turned away from him and had only taken two steps when her ankle twisted and her entire body pitched forward. She landed on the marble floor.

"Motherfucker!" she yelled. Byron hurried forward and reached through yards of fabric to help her stand.

"I'll kill myself in these shoes!" Meryn wobbled unsteadily. She experienced a moment of vertigo and she was back on flat feet again; the dress had shortened itself to allow for flatter shoes. When she lifted the hem, she could see blue Converse peeking out.

"Kick ass!"

"Oh, dear," Adelaide sighed.

"I like it. Come along, my dears." Byron held up each arm and escorted them to the carriage. He helped them get in and shut the door.

"I feel like Cinderella."

"I hope you enjoy yourself tonight. If you start to feel unwell, come get me," Adelaide offered.

"I think I'll be okay." As apprehensive as she had been this morning about being among strangers, it didn't seem as bad now. She was just that eager to return to Aiden. The sound of the horse's hooves on the road beat a staccato that seemed to be in sync with her nerves. She realized she wasn't anxious, she was excited. The carriage wove around the narrow streets of Lycaonia as Byron and Adelaide waved to the people from the window. All too soon, they slowed, and she could see flashes of light up the road. They were in line to be dropped off.

"What are the flashes?"

"Cameras, dear, even Lycaonia has her own version of paparazzi. These pictures will appear in the paper tomorrow," Byron explained. And just like that, her anxiety returned.

"Just smile. If someone asks you something and you don't know the answer, direct them to me." Byron patted her hand.

All too soon, it was their turn. Byron got out first and the flashes increased. He helped Adelaide out of the carriage and reached up for Meryn. She took a deep breath and hesitated. He winked at her and she took his hand. When her feet hit the carpet, the lights exploded everywhere.

"Elder McKenzie, is this your new daughter?"

"Can you comment on the rumors that she started a fight with Elder Evreux?"

"Is that the Gown of Éire Danu?"

The questions were coming at her from all directions. Acting on a burst of inspiration she buried her face in Byron's sleeve and acted timid and scared. Byron played along with her act and comforted her loudly.

"It's okay, sweetheart, they won't hurt you, they are just asking some questions." He cooed at her, as Adelaide took up position on her other side. Byron turned to the crowd and in a booming voice began answering their questions.

"Yes, this is my beautiful daughter, Meryn, Aiden's mate. As you can see she is a gentle creature. I can't imagine where the rumor started that she picked a fight with Elder Evreux. And yes, this is the Gown of Éire Danu. Meryn made quite the impression on Lady Fairfax, and she has passed this gown on to Meryn." Several gasps and whispers detonated around them.

"Now if you'll excuse us, my son is waiting impatiently, no doubt, for his mate." Byron nodded and led them inside the building. Once behind closed doors, she saw his mouth begin to quiver.

"You? Meek and mild?" he guffawed to himself.

"Leave her alone, Byron, it was a brilliant move." Adelaide kissed her cheek.

"Meryn?" Meryn turned and saw Aiden looking awestruck.

"We leave you in good hands. Have fun tonight, dear." Adelaide and Byron walked arm in arm down the long hallway before stopping at a set of double doors. When the doors opened, a herald announced them and they walked inside.

"You... you." Aiden couldn't stop staring. Meryn took advantage of his speechlessness and marveled at the sight of him. He was every inch a prince. His dark hair brought out the blue of his eyes. The uniform he wore was bright white, accented in Lycaonian red. The black, polished belt fit snugly around his narrow waist, which emphasized his broad shoulders.

Feeling giddy she struck a pose. “Do you like it?” she asked then twirled round. When she stopped, he simply pulled her in for a long kiss. For the first time in hours, she felt calm. It was like she craved him, his very physical presence was needed for her survival. She pulled back and tried to catch her breath. His eyes shone bright.

“How long before this heat settles down?”

“A couple hundred years,” he teased and then offered her his arm. She laid her hand on his elbow as he escorted her toward the ballroom.

“Man, I'm going to stay pregnant,” Meryn muttered. Aiden stumbled but caught himself. His eyes had a wild look about them as they darted from her midsection to her face.

“Are you? Could you be?” he stuttered. She shook her head.

“No, well, I don't think so.” She shrugged.

“Don't *do* that.” His other hand clutched at his chest.

“Sorry.”

“Ready?” he asked when they arrived at the doors.

Meryn took a deep breath. “As I'll ever be.”

Aiden nodded to the herald and the doors swung open.

“I have the distinct honor to present Commander Aiden McKenzie, heir to the House McKenzie, Unit Commander to the four pillar cities and future Elder to all shifters, and his mate Meryn Evans, the new Lady of the Gown of Éire Danu.” The room quieted as Aiden walked them down the long carpet at a stately pace. Murmurs and whispers were everywhere. Meryn remembered Colton's words and just smiled and nodded at those who made eye contact.

At the end of the long carpet, the four Elders, two with mates and two without, stood to receive them. When Aiden stopped and bowed, Meryn inclined her head. She knew if she tried a curtsey, she would topple over. More whispers spread around them. Had she screwed up already? She swallowed hard and met the eyes of the fae Elder Celyn Vi'Ailean. He stepped forward and took her hand from Aiden's elbow. He kissed it and drew her forward.

"Darling, this is the sweet girl I told you about. Meryn this is my mate, Vivian Vi'Ailean. She has been very eager to meet you and is already planning a visit to our garden in your honor." A tall blonde woman stepped forward and took Meryn's hand from her mate's into both of hers and smiled. Like Adelaide, she didn't have to bedeck herself in jewels; she wore her dignity around her.

"She's been invited to the fae gardens?"

"Who is she?"

"She's just a human, why is she so special?"

Even with her human hearing she could hear the contempt in the voices around her. Vivian's eyes flashed.

"Lady Meryn, it's such a pleasure to meet you. My mate has had nothing but wonderful things to tell me about you and your ongoing assistance regarding the troubling disappearances of late. I know that you have squire interviews tomorrow, but maybe after that has concluded, you could come by for a visit? I would love to show you my garden." Her invitation started a buzz that spread like wildfire.

"I would love to visit tomorrow. The interviews should go quickly. We've had so many cancel unexpectedly. It's very curious how many had to back out at the last minute. Would it be acceptable if I brought my new squire with me tomorrow?" She kept her eyes wide and her voice sweet. Vivian looked down, her mouth twitching.

"Of course. I can't wait to talk with you tomorrow." Her words matched the admiration and sincerity in her eyes. Meryn just grinned up at her cheekily.

"I told you she was a darling," Adelaide boasted.

"And she is," Elder Vi'Ailean confirmed, then turned to Aiden.

"Commander, congratulations on your mating. She is an amazing woman."

"Thank you, sir. She has made me a happy man." When Aiden gazed down at her, there was no mistaking how he felt. His love was there for all to see.

"We won't hold you up any longer. Enjoy your first All Hallows' Eve ball, Meryn." Elder Vi'Ailean stepped back with his mate to receive other guests.

"I'm sure it will be an experience unlike anything I've ever known," Meryn said, and Elder Vi'Ailean coughed to cover his laugh.

"With your permission?" Aiden bowed and guided Meryn through the crowd that parted before them, making it easy to get to the refreshment table. He leaned down and nipped her earlobe.

"How are you feeling?" His eyes were dancing with laughter.

"Surprisingly well. The fae Elder is really nice. I like him." In the distance Vivian covered her mouth to hide her smile as her mate blushed. Aiden nipped her ear again. Right! He was trying to remind her that anything she said could be heard and, of course, held against her. She spun around and eyed the table. Everything looked amazing.

"Hungry?"

"Starved." She would keep her mouth full so her foot wouldn't have any room.

"Heads up," Aiden murmured.

"Darrrlllliiinng. So wonderful to see you again. I'm so surprised you could make it." Daphne Bowers stopped before her with two other women. Meryn couldn't help the mental image that popped in her head. They were like the evil stepmother and step sisters from *Cinderella*. With the regal atmosphere, her brain was stuck on Disney.

"You know, I almost wasn't able to come tonight. Most of the shops in Lycaonia were completely out of fabric and couldn't make me a costume. Imagine that, every single clothing shop in the city, running out of fabric at the exact same time. But I found out later that things happen for a reason. Due to my dire situation, Lady Fairfax was moved to give me this lovely gown. You could almost say it was meant to be," Meryn said sweetly. Behind them, Adelaide began to choke on an hors d'oeuvre. Vivian, laughing, pounded her on the back.

"I see. Well I hope nothing happens to the gown; that would be a shame." She sniffed and turned away, her twin toadies racing behind her.

Meryn opened her mouth and Aiden stuffed a bite-size brownie in it. She chewed and took a deep breath.

"The man at the grocery store said that chocolate helps make women more loving. I think he was right." Aiden held out another brownie.

"Especially chocolate sauce." She accepted the second brownie.

"How do you eat sauce?" Aiden asked frowning. Feeling wicked, she smiled.

"By licking it off of something."

"Licking it off of... Oh!" Aiden leered down at her. This time it was Byron who was choking, and

Elder Vi'Ailean hitting his back, laughing uproariously.

"It seems like you're doing just fine, short stuff." Colton walked up, also in his dress whites. Meryn sighed; men in uniform were always so yummy. Aiden nipped her neck.

"It's the uniform," Meryn explained. Colton preened.

"In that case, look your fill." Colton turned and pointed behind him. On the dance floor, the men of the different units were dancing with ladies of all ages. Each man wore a pressed white uniform and glided across the dance floor with his partner.

"Meryn, I hate to do this, but I'll be right back. Eleanor's grandmother is flagging me down. Colton will stay with you." Aiden kissed her hand. She nodded.

"Hurry back." She watched his broad back walk away. He greeted an older lady with a bow. She covered her face with a handkerchief and Aiden escorted her to a more private corner.

Meryn turned to Colton. "It's so sad."

"We do what we do so that other families won't know their heartache." Colton took a deep breath before pulling Meryn into his arms and dipping her. His boyish grin had her laughing.

"Come on, Meryn, let's dance." He stood them upright and tugged her toward the dance floor.

She started digging in her heels. "But I can't dance like that!"

"What kind of gentleman would I be if I couldn't lead a woman around on the dance floor?" Colton raised an eyebrow. Meryn looked around frantically. She grabbed a champagne flute off a passing tray and downed it then set the empty glass on the table.

"Okay, ready to go."

Colton swung her around and guided her onto the dance floor. Meryn realized that if she stopped thinking about where her feet were supposed to go and just kept up with Colton, it was a lot easier. Pretty soon she was getting the hang of the turns and bows.

"May I have the next dance?" Darian bowed at the waist. Colton handed her off to the fae.

"You didn't have to dance with me," Meryn blushed furiously.

"The pleasure is all mine. In fact, the Alpha Unit has dibs on the dances with you tonight. The other units were very upset with us. We all want to dance with our Commander's lady." He winked at her.

The dance with Darian was no less graceful or fun than with Colton. By the third time around, she was getting thirsty.

"I believe it is my turn," A silvery voice interrupted. Darian bowed in favor of Gavriel and twirled her over to the other Alpha member.

"I believe I will pass on my turn to dance. Let us find you something to drink." He guided her over to one of the festively decorated tables.

"Here you go, Meryn, mineral water." Gavriel handed her a wine goblet.

"Thank you." With little thought or care on how it would be perceived, she downed the whole glass. She smiled at Gavriel.

"Much better."

"I am so glad I could help." Meryn looked around the room. She watched as small groups of people merged to become larger groups, or how two or three people would leave a group to talk amongst themselves. It was then that she remembered that tonight was also about wheeling and dealing. She suddenly had a brilliant idea. She stood on tiptoe and didn't see a thing.

"Gavriel, do you see Adam anywhere?" Gavriel looked around.

"Yes, I believe he is talking to the Public Works Commissioner and a group of city businessmen."

Meryn paused, wondering if she could pull off what she had planned. "He must be trying to drum up support for the clinic."

"More than likely," Gavriel agreed.

"Can you escort me over there?"

Gavriel offered his arm. "You will be good, right?"

"Why does everyone keep asking me that?" By this time, they were already walking up to the small group.

"Hello, Adam," Meryn greeted her new brother. Adam's formidable frown disappeared when he saw Meryn.

"Hello, little sister. What do you think of your first ball?"

"I like the dancing," she said, honestly. Her gaze fell to the other men.

"Meryn, forgive me, let me introduce you." He turned to the group.

"Gentlemen, this is my new little sister, Meryn Evans. Meryn, this is Cecil Adams, our Public Works Commissioner, Peter Dawning and Jacob Lewiston. Peter and Jacob own two of Lycaonia's most successful import businesses," Adam completed the introductions.

Showtime. Feeling nervous, Meryn put on her most vapid expression and clapped her hands together enthusiastically.

"You gentleman must be talking about your support for Adam's clinic." Even Meryn thought her voice sounded young and innocent.

"Not exactly," Cecil admitted.

"Have you been to the clinic? I know that you as the Public Works Commissioner must be helping Adam raise the funds needed for upgrades. You look so important, no wonder Adam trusts you." She beamed up at him. A scarlet flush worked up the man's neck and ended up setting the tips of his ears ablaze.

"I have reviewed Adam's proposal. It's very well written," he conceded. Meryn turned to the two businessmen.

"And how much have the two of you donated?" she asked, practically bouncing on her feet. They regarded each other nervously. Peter took out a handkerchief and wiped his brow.

"We haven't really discussed it," Jacob informed her. Meryn covered her mouth with both of her hands and assumed a tragic expression.

"I haven't interrupted your numbers discussion, have I?" She let real tears fill her eyes. All three men fell over each other to assure her that she hadn't.

"Thank goodness. Adam had to treat me at the clinic, and I can tell you from firsthand experience that it does not represent the level of sophistication that I have seen elsewhere in the city. It desperately needs modernization."

"You were treated there?" Jacob asked stunned. Meryn swayed a little and felt Gavriel's hand on her back.

"It is okay, Meryn. You are safe now," he said. Meryn could have kissed him; he was playing along.

"I was brutally attacked by that monster that is out there stalking people. If it hadn't been for Adam, I don't know what would have happened to me." She turned her face into Gavriel's chest. He ran a hand over her hair.

"We never even considered that human mates might need to be treated there." Cecil ran a hand over his chin. Meryn turned to Jacob and Peter.

"You will donate, won't you?" She let her voice crack.

"Of course we will," both men agreed almost immediately.

"I'll let Adam continue this discussion. Talking about my ordeal has left me shaken. Maybe another dance or two will help me forget." She looked up pleadingly at Gavriel.

"Of course. Gentlemen, if you will excuse us?" Gavriel led her away from the group of men, and toward a group of unit members. Without slowing down he grabbed Keelan by the arm and kept marching until they were on the balcony.

"Keelan, a silencing spell," Gavriel choked the words out. Quickly Keelan cast the spell and turned to Gavriel, eyes wide. The second he was done, Gavriel threw his head back and laughed.

"What'd she do?" Keelan begged. Gavriel recounted the entire scene. By the end of it Keelan was slapping his leg and howling.

"I could get used to this stuff." Meryn felt proud of herself. It wasn't so hard to talk to people if she was acting.

"Let's go back inside. I still want my dance." Keelan reversed the silencing spell and offered up his arm.

"You're wearing underthings?" he whispered.

"Yes, legging things. Why? What kind of dance do you want to do?" Meryn asked confused.

"The kind only a witch can do." He whispered a long, low spell and seconds later they were floating. Keelan lifted her above the crowd and spun her around. Meryn had never had so much fun in her life. The other five witch unit members didn't want to be outdone and soon they, too, had lifted their partners in the air. At the end of the song, they all floated back down to the dance floor to a round of applause. Keelan winked at her and when he turned her one last time, she was spun into Aiden's waiting arms. He pulled her close as the lights dimmed.

"How is she?" Meryn asked.

"They are taking it very hard. DNA tests confirmed that the body parts that were delivered were Eleanor's. This is their first holiday without her." He rested his chin on the top of her head.

"Is there anything we can do?"

"We can find the one who took her from them."

"Then let's do that." Meryn rested her cheek against his chest.

"We will." He pulled back. "I heard you've been having fun." There was a slight smile on his lips, though his eyes stayed sad.

"I got to meet the Public Works Commissioner," she said simply.

"Meryn, you amaze me." He twirled her around and with more strength than Colton, more grace than Darian, more consideration than Gavriel, and more wonder than Keelan, and he spent the rest of the night treating her like a princess.

Meryn stripped out of her gown and hurried between the sheets. Though the house had central heating and cooling, it was close to one a.m. and it was cold. She snuggled up to Aiden's warm body. The sensation of his naked flesh next to hers tightened things low in her body. When he began to run his hand up and down her side in a leisurely fashion, she pushed him onto his back and straddled him. The surprised expression on his face was replaced by a look of pure ecstasy as she reached down and guided him into her. He had teased her all the way back to the house in the carriage. She was more than ready for him.

"Even if we are to live forever, I would never get enough of you." He closed his eyes and wrapped steadying hands around her waist. Slowly she rocked her body. She loved the feeling of him deep inside of her. She soon discovered that when she leaned forward slightly the flared head of his cock hit her g-spot perfectly. He held his arms up and supported her upper body. She quickened her pace as she chased after something she desperately wanted. She felt her entire body begin to burn with need.

"Take what you need, baby," he whispered. He let her have her way, let her set the pace.

Just when she thought that she couldn't take it anymore, her legs began to shake. It wasn't a huge detonation, but clusters of tiny explosions inside of her.

"Aiden, please. I need more," she begged.

He flipped her over and thrust inside of her with one deep thrust.

"Yes!" she screamed. That was what she had needed. "Just like that, Aiden, please!"

He took her at her word and began to pound into her mercilessly. She could feel him bumping her cervix. She was about to tell him to stop, that the pain was too much, when it changed into something else. His hand came down and he was teasing her clit every other stroke. It didn't take long before a second orgasm washed over her. Aiden cried out and collapsed next to her.

"You said that this heat dies down eventually, right?" Meryn asked. Aiden was breathing too hard to answer; he just nodded.

When they had both recovered and cleaned up, Meryn lay in his arms, staring up at the ceiling.

"I found something today," she whispered. They turned so that they were facing each other, lying on their sides.

"What?"

"I broadened the search parameters. I don't know if they are all paranormals, but eleven other couples between here and St. Louis have been reported missing. There may be more if paranormals aren't going to the police. Out of those eleven couples, only pieces of the women were found. What is he doing to the men?"

Aiden pulled her close.

"I don't know, but I'll find out. Email me the list; I'll go over it tomorrow with Colton and Gavriel to see how many are paranormals."

"Aiden, I think this is bigger than we realized."

"I'm afraid you may be right. Get some sleep, you have squire interviews tomorrow. You'll need your strength," he teased. She tilted her head up for a kiss. He didn't disappoint. When they broke apart, she snuggled close.

Fate, if you're listening, keep him safe.

Meryn closed her eyes and drifted off to sleep.

CHAPTER THIRTEEN

"Thank you for coming, gentlemen. Today's interview will be in the form of a practical. We would like for you to ask whatever questions you need to of Meryn, and then prepare a lunch and afternoon tea. We have reviewed all three of your credentials and are very satisfied that you are well trained for the position. Now, all that is left is to see how you respond to your future employer."

Adelaide continued to give instructions to the three men as Meryn observed them closely. The German applicant, Jungen, was on the short side, maybe five foot ten, with a receding hairline. She could see a fine sheen on his brow; he was sweating horribly. She felt like she was looking into the face of a serial killer. He had empty eyes; she supposed that was his version of a poker face, but she couldn't help the uneasy feeling he gave her. She turned her attention to the British applicant, Dennis. He was an even six feet tall and reminded her of Ben with his wavy blond hair and warm smile. He flirted horribly with Adelaide, but was pleasant. She knew she could get along well with him. Then there was the Japanese applicant, Ryuu. She had to remind herself that she was mated. Twice. He was the tallest of the three at six foot four. He exuded serenity and power, and it was a potent aphrodisiac. She had heard the term 'cool type' before, but didn't really get it until she saw Ryuu. He sat quietly, his posture perfect, and listened respectfully. She could tell that he was muscled under his traditional Japanese attire. The air around him even felt different, regal. She half expected Sakura blossoms to start blowing by at any moment.

"Okay, I'll open it up for you to ask Meryn any questions you need to, to better serve." Adelaide sat down.

Meryn squirmed in her seat as three sets of male eyes stared at her.

"What foods do you like to eat?" Ryuu asked, his voice surprisingly deep.

"I like pizza, sandwiches and Hot Pockets." He nodded.

"What is your favorite tea?" Dennis asked.

"I like strong teas, sweetened, no milk. Earl Grey, double-strength, preferably."

"I bet you would love my Yorkshire tea with milk." Dennis made a note on his sheet. Meryn smiled politely.

"Why do you drink it so strong?" Ryuu asked.

"I have a strong coffee first thing in the morning to get me going, and by the afternoon, I'm crashing and I need something to pick me up. It's why I usually like a light lunch and something sweet for tea. If I eat too much in the afternoon, I get tired," she explained. He nodded solemnly. They got quiet.

"Do you have any more questions for Meryn?" Adelaide asked, standing.

"Just one. What do you do in the afternoons?" Ryuu's handsome face turned to her.

"I'm on my laptop a lot."

"Thank you. I have no more questions, Lady McKenzie."

"Very well then, Marius will show you to the kitchen. We'll see you gentlemen at lunch." They stood and filed out behind Marius.

"Enjoy your laptop time; lunch will be ready soon enough." Adelaide picked up her knitting.

Two hours later Meryn had just finished writing a new program when Marius appeared at the door. His mouth was in a straight line. *Uh oh.*

"Lunch is ready."

"Oh, dear, I wonder what happened," Adelaide murmured. They stood and followed Marius to the dining room. As they passed the kitchen, she saw that one counter was littered with vegetable cuttings and food splatters. Meryn and Adelaide exchanged a look. Now they knew what was wrong with Marius. One of the men applying was a slob in the kitchen. Along three of the walls, each applicant had set up a lunch spread. Meryn noticed that only Ryuu bowed when they entered.

"Walk around, Meryn, and pick whatever you like. I would recommend trying something from each to see if you like his cooking," Adelaide suggested and picked up a plate for herself. Marius handed Meryn a plate and she began to walk around the room.

She went to Dennis's table first since it was the one on the left. He had made french onion soup and a tossed pasta dish. She skipped the soup and spooned a small helping of pasta on her plate. She smiled at Dennis and moved on. Jungen was along the middle wall. He had made a bratwurst sub with sauerkraut. For a side dish he had prepared a cabbage and red potato dish. She scooped out a helping of potatoes and moved on. Finally, she came to Ryuu. He had prepared simple-looking pastries shaped like fish.

"Taiyaki?" she asked. For the first time his expression changed to one of pleasant surprise.

"Yes."

"What did you use for a filling?"

"Pepperoni and cheese."

"Seriously?" Meryn asked, reaching for the tongs. She grabbed two and put them on her plate. She smiled at him in gratitude. He bowed. She walked over to the table and took a bite of the pasta. It was really good. She quickly finished what was on her plate. Second, she ate one of the potatoes, but couldn't eat more. It had been cooked in grease along with the cabbage. It was too heavy for her to eat. Eagerly she reached for the small fish. She took a bite and sighed. The crusty exterior gave way to melted cheese and slightly spicy pepperoni. After polishing off the second one, she was full. They thanked them and retired back to the drawing room.

A couple hours later, the men returned, each one pushing a service cart. Meryn rubbed her eyes. She had been staring at her laptop for hours and her vision was getting blurry. She needed a strong tea in the worst way.

"For this exercise, Meryn will review what each of you has prepared and pick the one which appeals to her. While we take our tea, Marius will serve you outside on the veranda while Meryn and I discuss your merits. Gentlemen, the floor is yours. Please tell us what you have prepared and why."

Dennis stepped forward quickly and removed the large dome lid, revealing his selections.

"I have prepared a double strength pot of Yorkshire tea with milk since Miss Meryn likes it strong. I opted to make cucumber sandwiches, since she advised that sandwiches were a favorite of hers," Meryn sighed. She really wanted her Earl Grey.

Jungen stepped forward and removed the lid on his cart. "I have also prepared sandwiches." He glared at Dennis. Now Meryn realized why Dennis stepped forward so quickly. He knew they had prepared the same thing.

"Instead of cucumber, I chose instead to use higher quality ingredients. On the left, we have egg and cress and on the right smoked salmon. For tea I have prepared a Darjeeling brew, no milk. I chose sandwiches as Meryn indicated they were a favorite and have prepared the tea without milk as she clearly stated she does not prefer it." Jungen looked pleased with himself. Meryn's eyes went to Ryuu. He had done so well at lunch, she couldn't wait to see what he had prepared for tea. *Please, let the man have made a pot of Earl Grey.*

Gracefully he stepped forward and bowed. With measured movements that reminded her of the ancient Japanese tea ceremony, he lifted the dome and presented his selections. The other two men snickered. With no pomp or pageantry the plate held small, ordinary-looking pastry balls stacked in the center of the plate.

"I have prepared *dango*, or dumplings coated in powdered sugar and green tea. I chose the dumplings since Lady Meryn advised she liked something sweet with her tea. They are small and easy to eat, allowing her to stay on her laptop. I chose green tea over her preferred Earl Grey since a single serving contains the same amount of caffeine as a doubly-strong brewed pot of black tea, yet also contains L-theanine, which improves brain function, helping her to concentrate later in the afternoon." He bowed again and stepped back.

"Thank you, gentlemen; everything looks delicious. If you would just follow Marius, he has prepared his own special version of tea as a thank you for applying." The men followed Marius out the door. Adelaide held up a hand when Meryn went to speak. A couple minutes later she turned to Meryn.

"So. What do you think?"

"I was hoping you would tell me what you thought."

"Your opinion is more important than mine; they will be serving you, not me," Adelaide reminded her.

"Jungen is a hell no."

"Can I ask why? I just want to hear your reasoning."

"He creeps me out. I would never feel comfortable around him."

"I agree. I would have dismissed him outright due to his slovenly appearance, but wanted to be fair."

"I bet that's what got Marius's dander up," Meryn giggled.

"I bet you're right. That man is fastidious. What about the golden boy Dennis?"

"He made me smile. He's very open and fun. I could see myself relaxing around him. But..." Meryn hesitated.

"What, dear?"

"He flirted with you, which I didn't like. He didn't listen. He acted on his own assumptions that he knew best. I could see Marius doing something like that, but he'd be right to do it and tell you why. Like; 'Meryn, wear your jacket, it's cold outside'," Meryn mimicked Marius's voice.

"The french onion soup was divine."

"I bet it was, but I don't like heavy meals at lunch time or milk in my tea."

"Go on. What about the dashing prince-like Ryuu, and don't bother denying you looked. I've been mated centuries longer than you have, and *I* looked."

"He makes me feel safe, like Aiden does. There's just something about him. I feel as though I know him from somewhere, as if he had been a childhood best friend or something. It's like I know I could depend on him for anything. He asked good questions about why I liked something and even though he didn't prepare what I preferred, he took into consideration why I liked it. If he were my squire, I wouldn't have to worry about a thing; I have a feeling he'd even think for me if I asked him to."

"I think you have your answer, dear one."

"Plus, he's dreamy."

"Yes, dear. But don't ever let Aiden hear you say that. I made the mistake of mentioning how handsome I thought Marius was when he first joined us. I didn't hear the end of that until after Ben was born."

"I'd never ever betray Aiden."

"And I would never betray Byron." They stared at each other before Adelaide gave her a knowing smile. "But that doesn't mean you can't appreciate a handsome face, especially one that will be taking care of you. I never once thought of Marius in that way, but there were days where I needed him more than I needed Byron. That creates a bond; it doesn't mean you don't love your mate, it just means that there is room in your heart for more." Adelaide poured a cup of Darjeeling.

"Do you love Marius?" Meryn asked.

"Yes, very much. But it's somewhere between brother and best friend."

"I think I know which one to choose."

"The men will be back soon. Eat your dumplings."

Meryn dug into the small sweet treats. She poured a cup of the green tea and sweetened it with a bit of sugar. When she took a sip with the dumpling, she sighed happily. They complimented each other perfectly.

"*Hana Yori Dango*." She popped another in her mouth.

"What's that dear?" Adelaide asked.

"Dumplings over flowers. Or, practical things over pretty things."

"Aren't you getting both?" Adelaide teased.

"Oh, hush, you," Meryn smiled. Adelaide just sipped her tea and let Meryn think.

An hour later the men returned. Meryn let Adelaide take over. She'd just stammer her way through and they wouldn't understand a word.

"Meryn and I have discussed things over with great deliberation. After taking all things into consideration, she would like to extend the offer to Ryuu Sei."

"What? Why?" Jungen demanded. He had turned an unhealthy shade of red and looked like he was about to blow.

"We feel that he will be a better fit in our household," Adelaide advised simply.

"I refuse to accept that this foreigner would be a better squire than someone of my caliber," Jungen ground out the words from behind clenched teeth.

"Dude, seriously, you never stood a chance. A little piece of advice. Shower before interviews. Okay?" Meryn couldn't help it. Jungen had no right to belittle Ryuu. She felt an irrational sense of loyalty to the man already.

"I should have listened to Daphne Bowers, there's no way a human mongrel like you would appreciate high-class service," Jungen spat.

"Marius, please escort this man from my home immediately," Adelaide ordered. Marius moved quicker than Meryn thought possible.

"Unhand me!" Jungen took a swing at Marius, who easily ducked before twisting the man's arm behind him.

"I'll get the door," Dennis said standing quickly. "I have nothing against humans; I think you're lovely, Meryn. Hopefully I'll see you again in another household." Dennis winked at Meryn and ran ahead to get the door for Marius.

"I liked your pasta!" Meryn yelled after him.

"Thanks!" was the reply. They heard a loud slam, the sound of a man's whimper, Dennis laughing, and then silence. Throughout the entire scene Ryuu hadn't said a word.

"I never even asked. Would you like to be my squire, Ryuu?" Meryn had a flash of fear that he would say no.

"Let me ask. Will it bother you that I am Japanese and not of European descent?"

"No, I never even saw that as being an issue," Meryn answered truthfully.

"I keep forgetting how very young and human you are," Ryuu answered with a gentle smile.

"Will it bother you that I'm human?" Meryn asked, feeling prickly, especially after Jungen's 'mongrel' comment.

"No. I meant that in a good way. You see things differently than we do. Paranormals live for long periods of time, and we tend to get trapped in the past. But you see things as fresh and new. Nothing is impossible and everything can be conquered."

"Do you think you'll be happy here? You'll be very far from home." Instead of answering, Ryuu looked toward the hallway.

"Would you like to go for a stroll outside?" Ryuu suggested.

"Stay close to the house. I'm not sure if Marius explained, but Meryn has been threatened. Her safety must always come first," Adelaide said in her mom voice.

"Of course." Ryuu stood and waited for Meryn by the door. She joined him and they walked side by side through the house and out the back door.

"I did not mean to be disrespectful to Lady Adelaide, but you will be the one I am serving. My story is for you to hear." Ryuu looked out at the trees and sighed. "You are right, Lady Meryn, I--"

"Just Meryn is fine."

Ryuu shook his head. "Your mate, when he inherits, will be the closest thing to a sovereign our people will ever know, I cannot speak to you in such a common way."

"I don't like the way Lady Meryn sounds. It makes you feel too far away."

Ryuu smiled. "I am a servant; our positions *are* very far apart."

"Listen, you're right. I am young and I am human, but more than that, I'm an American. To me everyone is equal. I don't need a servant. I need a friend. I need someone who will help me navigate this world without embarrassing myself or Aiden. I need someone that I can lean on when this world gets to be too strange. I need someone that I can rely on. Will you be my friend, Ryuu?" Meryn couldn't keep the emotion out of her voice. She wanted the level of comfort and trust she saw between Adelaide and Marius.

Ryuu cupped her cheek and for the first time, she saw the intensity of his feelings in his eyes. He took a deep breath and the veranda dropped away, a huge palace appearing behind him. Autumn disappeared, to be replaced by a balmy summer afternoon. In the distance she could hear a shrine's bell toll as a comforting breeze wove in and out of the bamboo trees. She didn't know how he did it, but she was standing in a royal palace in Japan and every breath and movement felt slow as if they were one step outside of time.

"When I lost my previous Master, I did not dare to hope that I would find another whom I could serve from the depths of my soul. But your sincere wish for a friend, not someone to subjugate, assures me that you are someone that I can serve. I have felt connected to you since the moment I entered the drawing room. It seems that Fate isn't quite finished with me, and in you I have a fresh start and a new purpose."

He stepped back and dropped to one knee, bringing her hand to his lips.

"I swear to you on my life that I will dedicate my existence to serving you. That my children will serve your children, until the day that one of our lines ceases to exist. I swear to put you above all others, save my mate and my children. Your health and happiness will be placed above my own. Do you accept me, Meryn Evans, as your guide, your sword, and your shield?" The words as they were spoken sounded as if he were speaking a ritual or a spell. Meryn hesitated only for a moment. Fate had brought her this far, she had to trust that Ryuu was brought to her for a reason, too.

"Yes, I accept you." No sooner had she spoken the words when a searing pain encircled her wrist. The vision cleared and they were back on Adelaide's veranda where the October sun provided just enough warmth to make the cool fall breeze enjoyable. Ryuu winked up at her and stood.

"We are bound together for all eternity. It feels good to be in service again." Meryn noticed that he seemed younger, happier, as if the burdens on him had lightened.

"Well, someone doesn't have commitment issues."

"We were meant to be, Meryn. Fate brought me here. Why would I have any problem dedicating myself to you?"

"I had the same thought about Fate before I said yes." Meryn pulled up her sleeve and stared. Around her wrist, like a sapphire bracelet, was a blue dragon tattoo.

"Wicked! I get a tattoo! Ha. Take that, Aiden!"

"It will allow me to monitor your health, track your location and interpret your feelings... amongst other things."

Meryn didn't know how she felt about that. "We're going to have to work on your communication skills."

"Oh, I don't know. I think I timed it perfectly," Ryuu said with a straight face.

"It's gorgeous. I love it." Meryn couldn't stop staring.

"*Denka*, it's getting colder, we should go inside."

"What's *Denka*?" Meryn asked heading toward the door.

"You don't like when I call you Lady Meryn. *Denka* is a formal mode of address in my language, equivalent to something akin to Royal Highness." Ryuu held the door open for her.

"I like it."

"Have you worked everything out?" Adelaide asked when they entered the drawing room.

"Yes. I think he and I will get along perfectly." Ryuu had taken a position behind her, standing feet spread, hands clasped behind his back.

"I'm glad. Meryn, I had Marius make you a cake to take over to Elder Vi'Ailean's for your visit. It's Vivian's favorite, a Lemon Crunch Cake. Please give it to her with my thanks. She made last night so pleasant." Adelaide sipped her tea.

"Sure, what time do I--" Meryn's question was cut off by a deafening roar. Aiden charged into the room and pinned Ryuu to the wall by the throat. Meryn's mouth dropped.

"What the hell, Aiden? Let him go!" Meryn yelled.

"I can smell him on you! He marked you! He put his mark on you. You! My mate!" Aiden roared. Ryuu, on the other hand, looked calm. He accepted Aiden's treatment. He simply turned his face to Meryn.

"What would you have me do, *Denka*? He is your mate and I don't wish to harm him." His voice was composed, even pleasant.

"Aiden, please!" There was no talking to her mate; Aiden had flipped his shit. She looked at Ryuu.

"Get away if you can, without permanently injuring him." She was so mad at Aiden, she was tempted to go get the toilet back from the downstairs bathroom and brain him with it.

"As you wish." Ryuu's dark eyes flashed as blue fire covered his body. With a yelp, Aiden dropped him and stood back, holding his arm.

"Did you electrocute me?" Aiden asked wincing.

"It can feel that way to some. You must be very strong; most are not able to remain conscious after receiving such a jolt." Ryuu complimented.

"Why did you mark my mate?" Aiden demanded.

"She accepted me as her squire. In my country this means the joining of our houses, it is a bond that will last until either my line or yours ends. The mark is simply a physical manifestation of the bond that will allow me to serve and protect my charge better," Ryuu explained.

"Look, Aiden, I got my own tattoo! It's not a sexy mark like your bite." Meryn held up her wrist and showed Aiden the mark. He brought her wrist up to his face and began to cover it with his scent.

"What do you mean, allow you to serve her better? I want to be crystal fucking clear about your serving duties," Aiden growled. Meryn rolled her eyes.

"I will watch over her, guide her, teach her. I will be her mentor and friend. I will guard her health and happiness and protect her with my life." Ryuu clarified.

"You touch her, if you even *look* at her like--" Aiden started.

Ryuu shook his head. "The bond I share with *Denka* is beyond the physical. You wouldn't understand, as you have never served." Ryuu crossed his arms over his chest.

"Master Aiden, maybe I can help explain." Marius stepped forward. Aiden gave a curt nod for him to continue.

"There was a time when your father and I stood across from one another much like you and Master Ryuu are doing now. Your father was afraid I desired his mate, and though I loved her, I would never hurt her by dishonoring her bond with Byron. To do so would have destroyed a piece of me. When you are a squire, a good squire, your whole world narrows and all you see is your charge. The bond is profound, but it is a platonic one, I assure you." Marius placed a hand on Aiden's shoulder.

"He will be to your children as I was to you. Please believe me when I say you could not ask for a better man." Marius nodded to Ryuu, who exhaled loudly.

"My story has reached even as far as here?" he asked. Marius nodded.

"Had I known who you were, we would have simply had you over for tea to see if you were compatible with little miss. You have my apologies for being subjected to such rudimentary tests." Marius bowed low.

"Umm. What did I miss?" Meryn asked.

"I must have missed something as well. Can you explain, Marius?" Adelaide demanded.

Marius turned to her apologetically. "I reached out to another squire I know in Japan to ask about Ryuu. There was a long delay in responding because they could not believe that Ryuu had left Japan and had to confirm if it were true. The reason why we assumed he was a new squire is because he has only served one family. That family lost their last surviving member last month and, in a drunken stupor, an extended family member accused Ryuu of murdering his uncle and exiled him from Japan. Everyone knew this to be a lie, but the damage had been done. Ryuu left Japan to come here. Ryuu epitomizes what it means to be a squire. He is used as an example of what to strive for when we are trained for service. I recognized the name, but thought that he had been named in honor of Ryuu, not that he was the man himself. He is legendary." Marius turned to Ryuu.

"I am sorry if I am over-sharing, but Adelaide is my charge and Meryn her daughter; they need to understand." Marius bowed again. Ryuu shook his head.

"It is better that this is discussed up front, that way we can put it behind us. I do not fault you for your loyalties."

"When you say he has only served one family, what does that mean?" Adelaide asked.

"I served my Master's family for a very long time. I protected his line, but in the end, I could not save them from old age. I came here to this new land to rest, to die. But it seems like Fate has something else in store for me. She is a hard taskmistress, but I think I will enjoy looking after Meryn."

Aiden cleared his throat. "I guess you'll do." he said begrudgingly.

"I am grateful for your words." Ryuu inclined his head.

"Shit! What time is it?" Meryn exclaimed as she realized that it was nearly time for her visit with Elder Vi'Ailean's mate.

"Time for you to be leaving. Marius, the cake," Adelaide reminded them.

Aiden turned to Ryuu. "She has someone after her..." He started.

Ryuu's answering smile was chilling. "I have heard of this monster. I hope that I get the chance to eradicate this filth from her life."

"If you keep her safe, we'll get along just fine." Aiden held out his hand. Ryuu clasped Aiden around the forearm and they shook.

Meryn rolled her eyes. "Men! I don't care how old you are, you're all toddlers."

Marius handed Ryuu a large, white square box. "I have arranged for a carriage. The easiest route to Elder Vi'Ailean's is to cut through the city," Marius explained.

Meryn turned to Aiden. "I'll be back after my visit." He nuzzled her neck repeatedly until she squealed in laughter.

"Stop it! I gotta go." She giggled and picked up her backpack.

"Take care of her, Ryuu," Aiden commanded.

"I intend to," Ryuu responded then followed Meryn out the door.

"Colton, looks like your vacation is over, buddy. You have drills to make up for, from when you were lounging around with my mate." Meryn heard Aiden tell Colton.

"Lounging? She almost blew me up!" Colton yelled.

Ryuu raised an eyebrow as he extended a hand to assist her up into the carriage.

"Long story, total accident." He nodded without saying a word and climbed up after her. Meryn waved until she couldn't see Aiden in the doorway anymore. Now she had two Neanderthals to order her around. Great.

CHAPTER FOURTEEN

When they arrived at Elder Vi'Ailean's estate, Meryn could only stare. The shifter council house where Byron and Adelaide lived was a huge, brick mansion. The fae estate looked like something out of *Lord of the Rings*. The heavy gates opened to reveal a sprawling elaborate house that was built right into the trees. Vines and carved staircases wound around the base of each tree invitingly.

"I swear if Legolas pops out from behind a tree, Aiden is gonna be in trouble," Meryn muttered as Ryuu opened the carriage door and stepped out. He held a hand up to help her down, then reached back in for the cake. The problem with being five foot three in a city built for paranormals was that everything was higher off the ground. She hopped down and turned to Ryuu. He waited patiently for her to walk up to the house. She stared and he stared back.

"*Denka,* I wasn't the one invited, they are waiting to see you," he reminded her gently.

She nodded. "I know, but dammit, look at that place and look at me." She pointed down at her worn sneakers, jeans and *Goonies* t-shirt then to the pristine manor in front of them.

Ryuu regarded her outfit. “Was there a dress code implied in the invitation for this visit?” he asked, brows knit together. She shook her head.

“Then I wouldn't worry about it. If it bothers you that much, I will make arrangements for a tailor to visit so you will have attire suitable for your station. Though I don't think you'll be as comfortable,” Ryuu offered.

“Maybe a dress or two, just for visits. I hate sticking out.” Meryn turned and walked toward the front entrance. Ryuu just nodded and followed behind her. Meryn was agonizing over the thought of fittings when she walked through what felt like a force field. She froze. The October afternoon was different, even the sun felt brighter.

“It's okay, *Denka*, it's a containment spell. It's how they are able to live in such open housing year round, without worrying about inclement weather,” Ryuu explained. Meryn turned and looked back at the carriage. It looked like a typical gray fall afternoon. But now that she was within the bubble the house shone brilliantly in the sun, giving it an almost unearthly appearance. She took a step back and it was gray and cool. She took a step forward and it was bright and warm. Laughing, she bounced in and out of the bubble, before straddling it.

“This is so cool!”

“So this is where you've been.” Elder Vi'Ailean walked forward with Vivian, both smiling.

Meryn popped back inside the bubble. “Your force field thing is neat.”

“We like it, especially during the winter. I am assuming this is your squire?” Vivian asked. Ryuu gave a half bow.

Meryn nodded. “Yes, this is Ryuu Sei. He is new to Lycaonia too.”

“A pleasure to meet you, Ryuu,” Vivian said.

Elder Vi'Ailean stared. “I didn't think your kind left Japan.”

“Normally, we do not. My situation is extremely rare and complicated. However, after meeting Meryn, I do believe that I was brought here for the single purpose of being her squire.” The fond expression on Ryuu's face was evident.

“What do you mean 'his kind'?” Meryn asked. Elder Vi'Ailean raised a brow to Ryuu, who shook his head.

The Elder turned to Meryn. “That will be a mystery you'll have to figure out later. Now, why don't I escort you two lovely ladies to our gardens? You're in for a treat, Meryn--the passionflowers bloomed this morning, and the entire place smells divine.” Elder Vi'Ailean held out both arms and escorted them to the garden.

When they walked through the entrance Meryn stopped and stared. Garden? The word implied a space set aside for pretty flowers and landscaping. This was no *garden.* This was a slice of paradise. Her head whipped around taking note of every detail. Slowly, she made her way over to the small table and chairs that had been set up for her visit. She sat down across from Vivian but continued to turn this way and that, trying to see everything. She felt one of her moments coming on. She sat still and waited for her brain to catch up.

Hibiscus rosa-sinensis, Lavandula, Jasminum, Passiflora

She blinked and turned to her hosts. They were watching her carefully.

“Sorry about that, I was taking everything in.”

“What do you think about our garden?” Vivian asked, looking relieved.

“It's amazing. I couldn't imagine a more perfect place.” She paused. “Do you get Wi-Fi out here?”

Elder Vi'Ailean laughed and shook his head.

Meryn sighed. “Okay, *almost* perfect.”

“I would take exception to that, but I know how helpful you and your laptop have been with the ongoing investigation,” Elder Vi'Ailean said, pouring her a cup of tea. Meryn looked at the cup and remembered the cake.

“Oh! Ryuu, can you put that down here?” Meryn pointed to an empty part of the table. Ryuu sat down the box and stepped back behind her chair. Meryn carefully opened it and lifted out the round, vanilla-frosted cake.

“Is that Marius's Lemon Crunch Cake?” Vivian asked, leaning forward.

“Yup. Adelaide said to thank you for last night, she said you made the evening pleasant.” Meryn set the cake down. Immediately, Vivian reached for a knife and cut it into slices. She lifted a piece onto a small plate and handed it to Meryn. Meryn lifted her fork and took a bite. This could easily become one of her favorite desserts. She turned around to Ryuu.

“Did you want some?”

He shook his head. “*Denka,* you have to pretend as if I wasn't here. A squire does not eat with his charge,” Ryuu explained.

“That's rude!” Meryn frowned. Maybe she hadn't thought this whole 'having a squire' thing through.

“She's so young. She makes me feel very old and jaded.” Elder Vi'Ailean sat back with his tea.

“I agree. We've had servants for so long, I've never even thought it might be considered rude.” Vivian took a bite of her cake. At that point, Meryn began to have serious doubts about her being able to fit into Aiden's world. A warm hand on her shoulder had her looking up. Ryuu's expression was kind.

“It does not bother me, *Denka.* It makes me very happy that you are concerned for my wellbeing, but you don't have to worry about me. Serving you and seeing the world through your eyes is reward enough for me."

"If it were me, I'd rather have cake."

Ryuu's mouth twitched, "Of course, *Denka.*"

Meryn took a sip of her tea and was pleasantly surprised.

"Honeycup!" She took another sip.

"I have such a sweet tooth. Celyn always keeps it in stock for me." Vivian took her mate's hand with a smile.

"I have to have my tea sweet, too." Meryn looked out at the garden and blinked. She rubbed her eyes. Just on the corners of her vision she was seeing darting specks of light. She turned back to Vivian.

"Thank you for supporting me last night. It really gave me the confidence I needed to face everyone."

"Don't get me wrong, my dear, I had already planned on inviting you over based on the glowing descriptions Celyn gave of you. But it was infinitely more satisfying to deliver the invitation in person at the ball instead of with a written card just so I could see the expressions on those nasty old harpies' faces."

"Vivian," Elder Vi'Ailean chided with a grin.

"Don't 'Vivian' me, Celyn. Those women have been a thorn in my side since I arrived here two hundred years ago. I won't stand by and see the same thing happen to Meryn," Vivian said, waving her fork in the air.

"So I'm not the only one who wants to stick them with a pin to see how loud they yell?" Meryn asked. She laughed when Vivian bobbed her head enthusiastically. Meryn squinted; the lights were getting brighter.

"I knew you and I would get along the second you chastised Daphne Bowers, indirectly of course, about the clothing shops in front of everyone."

"I didn't mind, but poor Adelaide nearly had a coronary shopping that day," Meryn shielded her eyes. "Okay, seriously! What in the hell are those little lights?!" she exclaimed.

Vivian gave her mate a triumphant look. "I knew she'd see them!"

"See what? Fireflies?" Meryn asked.

"No, dear, what you are seeing are the garden sprites. Not even all of the fae can see them. When I first mated Celyn, there were a lot of nasty insinuations that I wasn't his true mate since I was human. The fact that I can see the sprites quieted down those naysayers almost immediately. There's no doubt in my mind Meryn, you belong in Lycaonia."

Meryn turned to face the garden straight on. The more she focused the clearer they became. Soon she could discern tiny body outlines. After a few minutes, she could see them clearly. They laughed and played, dancing in the air and hiding behind flowers. Of all of the wondrous things she had seen since in arriving in Lycaonia, this had to be the best.

Meryn watched as one tiny male sprite made his way over to her. Unlike the others, he didn't dance or play, but stayed on the outskirts. Meryn scooped up a fingerful of icing and extended it to him. His eyes widened and he drifted down to the table. Hesitant, he reached out and took a handful of icing from her finger and began to eat.

"I know what it's like to not fit in. Everyone thinks you're strange because you like to be alone, when really you just don't know how to say hello," Meryn whispered to the tiny creature. He looked up, surprised, and nodded.

"Me too. Sometimes I get so nervous I throw up," she confessed. The tiny sprite nodded vigorously and pointed to his chest.

"You too, huh? Maybe we introverts should stick together," she joked. A huge smile broke out on his face. He gave a single nod and darted to the prickly holly bush. Meryn turned to Vivian.

"I thought your garden was amazing before, but the sprites make it magical."

"They were my only friends for a long time," Vivian said watching as one sprite pushed another into the birdbath.

"Well, now you have me," Meryn said without thinking, and took another bite of cake.

"Without guile, with no thought of gaining favor or station. A true offer of friendship. You couldn't ask for a more precious gift, darling," Elder Vi'Ailean said to his mate. She nodded, a look of wonder and gratitude on her face.

"I would love to be your friend, Meryn McKenzie. There's so much I can teach you about navigating the social waters here, especially how to avoid the sharks," Vivian said, happiness radiating from her.

Meryn shrugged. "Sharks don't bother me. I know they're just assholes. I just ignore them."

Elder Vi'Ailean chuckled. "I wish the reporters from the paper could have heard you say that. The article in this morning's paper reported you to be a shy and sweet girl, too timid to answer for herself."

"Yeah, I kind of panicked when those reporters started shouting questions at me, so I let Byron answer." Meryn sat back holding her teacup to her chest.

"Smart move," Vivian agreed.

"Adelaide thought so, too." Meryn was just reaching forward to put her cup down on the table when the small sprite from before emerged from the holly bush. He now carried a tiny cloth bundle. He flew over and landed on her shoulder.

"Um, Vivian?" Meryn turned to her host in confusion. Vivian was staring at them in shock.

"He wants to go with you," she whispered.

"What!" Meryn reached up and carefully lifted the tiny sprite in her hands.

"You don't want to come with me! I don't have a fancy house or garden, in fact I have no idea where I'll end up living." The sprite just nodded.

"I'm backwards and spend a lot of time alone on my laptop, I would be horribly boring." The sprite nodded enthusiastically.

"Are you sure?" Meryn asked. He gave one determined nod.

Meryn looked up at Vivian. "Is that okay?"

"I think maybe you two belong together. He hasn't been very happy here with the others and he seems to adore you. Just keep him warm as sprites are very susceptible to the cold," Vivian warned.

"I will." Meryn gazed down at the sprite. "Do you have a name?"

"If you still your mind, you will be able to hear him tell you," Elder Vi'Ailean told her.

Meryn looked at him, aghast. "My mind is never still!" Ryuu snorted.

She turned around. "Yes?"

He straightened. "Nothing, *Denka*."

"Just think about him, look at his face, his clothes. That will help," Vivian suggested.

Meryn lifted the little guy until he was eye level. He was staring up at her hopefully. She took a deep breath and tried to clear her mind of everything but him. In her mind's eyes she saw him standing there, in his brown trousers and dark green vest. He had shaggy red hair and bright green eyes that twinkled with mischief.

Felix. The whispered name floated through her mind.

"He said his name is Felix!" Meryn grinned down at her new friend, who nodded.

"Well, the two of you have a standing invitation to visit whenever you like," Vivian offered.

"Councilman! Councilman!" An extremely tall fae male came rushing from the house.

"You've been summoned, My Lord. There's been an attack on the outskirts of Lycaonia. It's ferals. They are reporting at least a dozen!" the man's voice shook.

"What? That's impossible!" Elder Vi'Ailean stood.

"Sire, they are calling a council meeting with the other pillar cities now. Units Alpha, Gamma and Epsilon have been sent to the border," the servant explained.

Meryn gasped. *Aiden!*

Vivian turned to her. "Are you okay returning on your own?"

Ryuu stepped forward. "No one will harm my mistress."

Meryn stood. She placed Felix on her shoulder.

"Hang on," she told him, and he grabbed a handful of hair above her ear. "Ryuu, let's go."

"I wish our visit could have ended on a happier note," Vivian fretted.

"Don't worry, I'll come again soon," Meryn promised.

"This way, *Denka*." Ryuu escorted her through the garden and back toward the carriage. Behind them, Vivian was already giving orders to the servants to prepare bandages and medicines to be sent to the clinic.

The entire trip back to the shifter council house, Meryn imagined the worst. She knew that Aiden had a job to do, but it was hard knowing he was in danger.

"*Denka,* we've arrived," Ryuu informed her. He helped her down and she practically ran for the front door. She flung it open.

"Mom!" she shouted.

"Oh, thank all the Gods you're safe! I was just about to send Marius to come get you." Adelaide emerged from the drawing room and rushed over to her. She pulled her into a tight hug.

"Aiden and Ben have been sent out and Byron has been called into an emergency council meeting." Adelaide wiped her tears.

"They'll be fine, you'll see." Meryn turned to Marius.

"Maybe a cup of that calming tea?"

Marius nodded and turned toward the kitchen. Meryn wrapped an arm around Adelaide's shoulders.

"Come on, Mom, let's go sit down. They'll contact us the second those feral things have been killed." Meryn steered the older woman back into the sitting room and sat her down. She couldn't stand the look of worry etched on Adelaide's face. Ryuu followed behind them and took a position standing by the doorway.

"I know. Let me introduce you to a new friend." Meryn pulled back her hair.

Adelaide looked up. "Meryn, why is your ear twinkling?"

"My ear isn't twinkling; it's my new friend, Felix. He's a sprite I met in Vivian's garden. He decided he wanted to come home with me." Meryn smiled as Felix flew down and sat on the edge of the coffee table.

“A sprite, here? Oh, Meryn, you have no idea the honor that has been given to you. Sprites are amongst the most elusive and magical beings in the fae world. For you to not only be able to see him, but also to befriend him... “ Adelaide stared down at the coffee table intently, from the way her eyes moved, Meryn could tell she couldn't see Felix.

“He's a loner like me. We understand each other,” Meryn said.

“We'll of course have to build him his own house, complete with furniture and bedding. Oh! We can get clothes too!” Meryn was glad to see her plan to distract Adelaide from her worry had worked. Felix began to dance around on the table in an exuberant fashion.

“I think he likes that idea. You're going to spoil him, aren't you?”

“Absolutely.” Adelaide reached over and took a cookie off her tea time tray and placed it on a napkin on the table.

“I heard that they love sweets.”

Meryn watched as Felix lifted the cookie and began eating. Meryn supposed from Adelaide's perspective the cookie lifted up on its own.

“Tea is ready,” Marius said coming through the door carrying a steaming teapot on a tray. He set the tea service down and poured a cup for Adelaide. When he went to pour one for Meryn she shook her head.

“I'm okay. Ironically enough I do extremely well under duress. It's the pleasant small talk that gets to me.” Marius nodded and set the pot down.

An hour later, Meryn was staring at Adelaide in wonder.

“How come when I drink one cup of that stuff it practically puts me in a coma, but you drink like four glasses and you just relax?” Meryn asked.

“I'm a shifter, dear. Our metabolisms are different.”

“Sneaky squire.” Meryn crossed her eyes and stuck her tongue out at Marius who turned his head away from them with a smile. Meryn was about to comment when they heard the front door slam open. Heavy footsteps sounded in the hall and a disheveled Ben appeared in the doorway, his face twisted in anguish.

“Aiden has been hurt. It's bad. They've taken him to the clinic.” Meryn was already moving. Felix flew up to her shoulder and Ryuu was already at the front door.

“I'll keep the light on for you all. Be safe,” Marius called after them.

Meryn heard Adelaide fall in behind her. Ben raced ahead of them and got back into the SUV he had driven over from the clinic as everyone climbed in. He started the car and turned onto the road toward the clinic.

“Go faster!” she snapped at Ben.

“I'm going as fast as I can and still be safe. Just a few minutes more, Meryn.” Ben gripped the steering wheel tightly. Against her cheek she felt a tiny hand pat her comfortingly. She brought her hand up and stroked her finger over Felix's shaggy curls.

To Meryn, the road to the clinic seemed to go on forever. When the car finally came to a stop, she jumped out and raced inside. Ben ran along beside her, guiding her down a long hallway. Meryn knew what room Aiden was in since as it had many of the unit warriors waiting outside in a show of solidarity. Adam stepped forward and pulled her into a hug.

“He's okay. He's going to be just fine. His body reacted beautifully to the stitches I put in. I estimate in another couple hours he'll be able to shift and be as good as new.”

Meryn's knees gave out and he easily lifted her into one of the chairs in the hallway.

"Ben said he was badly injured," she said as she took deep breaths. Now it was Adelaide that comforted her. The older woman sat down beside her and wrapped an arm around her.

"He was. From what I heard of the battle, half the ferals escaped and more were reported along the eastern border. He was lucky that the remaining ferals fled to regroup. I've never seen such a deep wound on a shifter heal well, so when Ben left earlier the prognosis wasn't good. I've never tried internal sutures on a shifter before and I didn't know how his body would react. It was touch and go for a while, but he's strong. He'll make it." Adam looked over his shoulder.

"Excuse me. Aiden wasn't the only one hurt." He turned and went back into the large treatment room.

"Lady McKenzie, maybe the waiting room will be a more comfortable place to rest," a deep voice recommended. Meryn looked up. It was the gorgeous white-haired man she had met before, the leader of the Gamma Unit. She took a deep breath and stood. She needed to know what happened.

"Sascha, report." She used the same crisp command she had heard Aiden use when her laptop was taken. Sascha snapped to attention in a knee-jerk reaction before looking down at Meryn with a frown.

"Maybe you should just go to the waiting area with Lady McKenzie." His tone wasn't quite condescending, but it was close. Without saying a word she lowered her backpack to the floor, unzipped it, and pulled out a small black box.

"Here we go," Colton muttered.

She smiled. He knew what the box was, because he had given it to her himself. She opened the box and pulled out her gun. Carefully she loaded it and put the shoulder holster on, and after a few adjustments it fit perfectly. She turned the gun over in her hands and looked up at Sascha, who swallowed hard.

"Listen up, all of you!" She raised her voice so that it carried down the hall.

"The few times I have met some of you I have either been crying due to an attack or laughing at the ball. Just so we are all clear, that isn't the real me. The real me is a cranky, introverted, psychopathic bitch who is extremely possessive of anything that I deem mine, Aiden being the most important thing that belongs to me. And since he isn't able to give you orders right now, you'll have to make do with me. I want the ferals responsible for hurting Aiden found and eliminated. They pose a threat to the city and the people I have actually come to like, and that's not acceptable." She glared at the men were staring at her in shock.

"Lady Meryn, we have trained professionals who can handle this situation..." Sascha started.

"Well, where in the fuck are they?" The men flinched. Meryn didn't know if it was because they weren't used to women cursing or from the question.

"Where is the Unit Commander? I demand to speak to him at once!" a voice echoed down the hall.

"Now what?" Meryn practically shouted. She turned to see the vampire Elder bearing down on them.

"I demand unit warriors be assigned to my home! It is ludicrous that the council members have been left unguarded." Meryn saw Byron coming up behind him, his face like a thundercloud.

"Elder, I'm afraid that isn't possible; all available warriors will be needed to set up a perimeter or patrol the city," Meryn said as she stepped forward.

Out of the corner of her eye, she saw Sascha give a slight nod of confirmation.

"Why are you even addressing this issue? Should you not be at home waiting for your mate to return with his tail between his legs? I heard he had been injured. What a disgrace! He is Lycaonia's Unit Commander!"

Meryn felt an evil smile form. The unit warriors around her stiffened at Elder Evreux's insult. Adair and Ben held Byron back as he snarled.

"Just what I thought--a useless human for a useless--" Elder Evreux started.

"Shut the fuck up, you slimy douchebag. Let me ask you something, jerk off: in all the long centuries you've been around, I'm assuming you learned how to use a sword?"

"Yes," the Elder hissed.

"Dagger? Rapier? Gun? Martial arts?" Meryn continued.

"Yes, of course! What does that have to do with anything?" he demanded.

"Because that makes you better able to handle a feral attack than most of the city. Now shut your fucking mouth and get out of my way before I assign you to a unit for patrol." Meryn's insides were shaking, she was so mad. How dare he insult Aiden!

The vampire Elder's mouth moved, but no words came out. Just when she thought his head would explode, he turned and stamped down the hallway. When the slamming door echoed through the hall Meryn, turned back to Sascha.

"Sascha, take Gamma and two units of your choosing and set up an outer perimeter. The other two units are to set up patrols in the city. Alpha stays here to guard Aiden. Check in with each other on your handhelds every ten minutes." When she finished, no one moved.

"*Today,* gentlemen, and someone find me a motherfucking map!"

Sascha, smirking, snapped his heels together and gave her a salute. The men followed his example, grinning from ear to ear. They dispersed. Meryn exhaled.

Byron pulled her into a hug. "That's my girl!"

"I think they were scared of my gun." Meryn held up the tiny revolver.

Byron nodded and, with a straight face, agreed. "I'm sure that's why."

Meryn put her gun in the holster and looked up at Ryuu. The pride shining from his eyes warmed Meryn. She rubbed her eyes and took a deep breath.

"I will definitely need another cup of coffee."

CHAPTER FIFTEEN

Aiden's recovery room set up as their command central. Colton handed her a map and she laid it out on a gurney.

"Mark where the attacks have been." She handed him a pen. He circled two locations almost directly across from each other. She picked up the handheld.

"Gamma Kitten One, Gamma Kitten One, come back, over." Meryn released the button.

"Is this really necessary?" Sascha replied.

"Yes, and you didn't say 'over'. When Aiden gets up, I'm going to go over how ridiculously lax your security is when it comes to technology. Anyway, assign a heavier concentration of men north and south of the city; they have already hit east and west. It looks like they are trying to keep the warriors on the outskirts of town. It's like they are trying to provide a distraction for something. Tell the two units in the city to keep their eyes open."

"Roger that, over and out."

"Normally, six units are more than enough to keep the city safe; now we're stretched so thin," Byron observed. Meryn looked up and realized if anyone, he should be in charge.

"Dad, I'm so sorry, you should be doing this," she indicated to the map.

He shook his head. “You're doing just fine. You've done everything exactly as I would have done. Have you studied battle strategy?” he asked.

“No, but I do play *World of Warcraft*.”

“Sounds useful, you'll have to show me later.”

Meryn smiled slyly. “Sure, I bet you would love it.”

Meryn looked up and saw Adair sitting with his mother, her eyes then went to Colton. She looked back to Adair then back to Colton again.

Colton pushed himself off the wall and stepped forward. “What?”

“Adair, the training academy is located in the city right?” she asked.

Adair looked up. “Yeah, why?”

“How many trainees do you have?”

He looked confused for a moment before answering. “Thirty. Five for each unit.”

“Maybe...” Meryn pulled her laptop out. She started accessing the city's wireless feeds. She looked around.

“Where are Darian and Gavriel?” She knew Keelan was assisting Adam in the infirmary with healing spells. In addition to Aiden, two members from Gamma had also been injured, one with a head injury and the other with a broken leg.

“Outside, I think,” Colton said.

Meryn put her laptop on the map. “Be right back.” She sprinted out the door. For her plan to work she would need Gavriel or Darian. She was about to open the door when she heard Darian's elevated voice. Not wanting to disturb them, she eased into the room beside the exit and stood next to the cracked window. Their voices were easily heard.

“Whatever you're doing, it's not working, Gavriel.”

“I've got it under control.”

"Bullshit! Aiden is in there hurt right now, because of you. You couldn't keep up and we had to double back for you and got caught between two groups," Darian's voice sounded more frustrated than angry.

"Do you think I don't know that?"

"Then do something about it! Vampiric transition is nothing to be ashamed of. So you're weaker than normal and need more blood--it's not like you slacked off on your training. How much longer do you have?" Meryn heard a heavy sigh.

"At least another month."

"A month? Gavriel, you've been in transition for nearly two weeks now."

"I know."

"The longer the transition, the older the vampire; I've never met a vampire who needed six weeks for transition. Just how old *are* you?" Darian's voice held a trace of fear.

"Old enough. I will get the additional blood I need, but it is taking a while. If I order all I need from one center, the Elders will get suspicious. I have to do a lot of smaller orders."

"Shit. Okay. Listen. You do what you need to do; I'll do whatever I can to help cover for you," Darian promised. Meryn tiptoed back to the exit door and banged it open.

"There you two are. I need your help. Darian, can you go see if Adam needs anything? He's been in with Aiden since I got here." Darian nodded and went inside. Gavriel looked at her, amused. She crossed her arms over her chest.

"Six weeks, my ass." Meryn watched him. She didn't know *how* she knew he was lying, but he was.

"Meryn, it is very important that the Elders do not find out how old I am."

"I don't care if you have to make one massive order and tell the Elders to kiss your ass. What happened tonight, Aiden getting hurt? Don't let it happen again."

"I promise."

Meryn felt like shit, he seemed so sad. "You're okay, right?"

He smiled, but his eyes were tired. "Yes, I am okay."

"Good. I have a job for you to do that may cover your ass until this transition thing is over."

"Do tell."

"Come on, I'll show you." They went back to command central. Darian had already checked in with Adam and was waiting on them. Meryn went to her laptop and started her program. Smiling, she picked up the handset.

"Gamma Kitten One, Gamma Kitten One, come back, over."

"Gamma Kitten One here, what's up, Menace?" Meryn was going to kill Aiden for giving her that nickname.

"Reassign the two units in the city to the perimeter, over."

"But, Menace, that will leave the city empty, over."

"Menace is good, Menace is wise. Trust the Menace, over."

"Aiden is right, you don't speak English, over."

Meryn stared down at the handheld then around the room. All she saw were blank expressions.

"Come on! That was *Twister*!" She stamped her foot. More blank stares. She pressed the button on the handheld.

"Just redeploy the men at the perimeter, over."

"Roger that, over and out."

"What in the hell do you think you're doing?" Aiden's voice growled from behind her. She spun around to see him looking pale and sweating as he slumped against the wall. Normally, Meryn would have been relieved to hear Aiden's voice if he wasn't yelling at her.

Meryn stepped towards him. "I'm helping, I..."

Aiden lurched sideways and, breathing heavily, caught himself with one hand braced against the wall. "I am the Unit Commander, not you. These men are my responsibility, and I won't allow them to be killed because you wanted to play around!"

"But I..." Meryn felt tears prick her eyes. Why wouldn't he listen?

"No! I've had enough of your antics, Meryn. Just go home and wait for me. At least then I'll know you're safe and not meddling." Aiden leaned against the wall.

She handed the laptop to Gavriel and pointed to what she had wanted to show him. His eyes widened. She picked up her backpack and walked toward the door. She stood in front of Aiden, feeling like he had stabbed her in the heart. He was supposed to be the one person who would never hurt her.

"And I was worried about you! Asshole!" She pulled her foot back and kicked him as hard as she could in the shin.

"Ow! Dammit, Meryn!" She walked away; she didn't want to hear him complain about her anymore. She made it to the end of the hallway before the tears started falling. She stopped mid-step and covered her eyes with her arm. Felix patted her cheek, trying to comfort her. Ryuu wrapped an arm around her shoulders and steered her into an examination room. He picked her up and sat her on the edge of the table. She rested her head on his shoulder. He let her cry and after a short while he finally spoke.

"He didn't mean it."

"Yes, he did!"

"No, he didn't, not really. He had just woken up after being critically injured, he doesn't know if his men survived or where they are, and he hears your voice. You're not at home safe behind locked doors, you're here with minimal guards. It was his fear talking, not his heart," Ryuu explained. Meryn buried her face in his chest.

"He hates me! I never used to care if people hated me, because I didn't like them, but Aiden can't hate me, because I love him." Ryuu held her close and kept drying her cheeks. A grunt at the door had them both turning. Aiden leaned heavily against the doorway before he walked into the room on unsteady feet.

"He's right, Meryn, I was scared to death when I realized you were here. I'm not completely healed and wasn't sure I could keep you safe." Aiden was holding his side tightly.

"I'll be right outside." Ryuu walked out, closing the door behind him. Aiden leaned against the back of the door.

"You're a fucking asshole." She wiped her eyes on her sleeve drying her face.

"I know."

"I had everything under control; your dad said that I was doing things the way he would have."

"I know." Aiden winced as he took a deep breath.

"You're a fucking asshole."

"You said that already."

"You were such a huge asshole I had to say it twice." She couldn't stay mad at him. He looked so damn pitiful. She hopped down and walked over until she stood in front of him.

"Does it hurt?" She pointed to his side.

"Not as much as my damn shin."

"You deserved that."

"I guess I did." Aiden cupped her face with both of his hands, pride shining in his eyes.

"Gavriel called me every type of idiot and told me to beg for forgiveness on my hands and knees if need be. He said that you had singlehandedly doubled our resources. He showed me what you did on your laptop. By hacking into the city's cameras, we can monitor the city streets and send reinforcements the moment one of the trainee units needs help. This allows us to put all seasoned warriors in the field without splitting our resources between the city and the perimeter." He kissed her gently. "Please forgive me. I love you and your antics. The thought of life without you scares the hell out of me." He placed small kisses all over her face. Careful of his injury, she wrapped her arms around him, and he held her close.

"Forgiven, though gifts of chocolate later won't go unappreciated."

"Duly noted." When he leaned forward and captured her lips, she felt it all the way to the center of her being. He made her soul sing. She squeezed him tight and he grunted.

"Oh, my gosh, sorry!" She stepped back as he fought to catch his breath.

Grimacing, he managed to smile at her. "Let's head back to the others." Aiden took her hand.

When they walked back into command central, Adelaide looked relieved.

"I am forgiven," Aiden announced to the room.

"Good, because we were about to kick you out of Alpha and put her in charge," Colton teased.

"Does this mean you'll show me how to use grenades?" Meryn asked.

Colton paled. "Maybe not."

Aiden laughed then groaned.

"You should be in bed," Adam admonished.

"I'm fine. Meryn has set it up so that I can keep track of everything from here." Aiden eased down next to Gavriel and watched the cameras.

"Your brother is an idiot." Gavriel pointed to the laptop. Meryn looked over Aiden's shoulder and saw that while she and Aiden had been making up, Adair had left to deploy the trainees in the city. He was now in front of one of the city cameras with a trainee unit. He was twerking against a light pole. Aiden laughed then moaned, caught his breath and kept laughing holding his side. Meryn was laughing when a huge yawn overtook her.

Aiden pushed her toward the door. "Head to the Alpha estate, get some rest, and feed Jaws. I'll be there soon."

Meryn hesitated. "Are you sure?"

He just looked at her.

Meryn pecked him on the cheek. "Okay, okay, I *guess* I'll let you be in charge for a while." He swatted her on the butt.

"Hey, not in front of your family! They don't need to know how much of a sexual deviant you really are." She rubbed her bottom. Aiden's mouth dropped and he began to blush. Darian and Colton started to crack up.

"Wait until I get you alone," Aiden muttered.

"Promises, promises." She winked and turned to the door.

Colton threw a set of keys at Ryuu. "Just follow the road, it's the huge house on the right. Can't miss it."

Ryuu bowed. "My thanks."

Once they were in the SUV, Meryn closed her eyes. It had been a draining day. She never wanted to get news that Aiden was injured again. A couple minutes later, they were pulling up to the Alpha estate. As she hopped out, she got the evil eye from Ryuu. He didn't like that she didn't wait for him to open the door either, just like Aiden. She stuck her tongue out at him. They walked up to the house. He took out the keys and unlocked the front door. He walked in and she was right behind him. All she wanted to do was feed Jaws and go to bed. Before she could close the door, Ryuu stopped so suddenly in front of her she almost ran into him.

"What?" She asked.

He held up a hand to silence her. He turned around to face her. His eyes widened and he quickly brought two fingers up to his lips to produce a high pitched whistle. Meryn watched in horror as a man-shaped object materialized behind Ryuu; she opened her mouth to warn him, but it was too late. He was struck from behind and slumped to the floor. A tiny light flew from her shoulder and out the door. She felt a spurt of hope when she realized that Felix had gone for help.

She turned for the door and was grabbed by the hair and thrown to the floor. "No!" She kicked at the slightly amorphous hands and managed to get to her feet as she unholstered the gun, gripping it tightly.

"What good is a gun if you can't see what you are trying to shoot?" a voice mocked. Meryn turned her head slightly so that she wasn't staring right at him. He didn't know that he was visible. She had to wait until he stopped circling her to get a good shot.

"Why are you doing this?" She knew the longer she kept him talking, the better the chances were that Ryuu would wake up or that Felix could send help.

"Just following orders," the voice teased.

"Whose orders?"

"Uh uh uh. No more talking. I've been looking forward to being alone with you for almost a week; you smell so delicious," the rusty voice taunted. He stopped his circling and stood in front of her. Smiling she brought the gun up and began shooting. She didn't stop until she ran out of bullets, but it didn't even slow him down. He grabbed her by the throat.

"Sticks and stones may break my bones, but bullets will never kill me," he cackled. He released her neck and backhanded her to the ground. She shook her head trying to clear her vision as she gasped for breath. Seconds later she felt his weight on top of her, pressing her into the floor. Gulping for air, she fought blindly.

"No one can save you. All the toy soldiers are along the perimeter and the baby soldiers are in the city. We're too far away for your mate to have heard your tiny gun." He leaned forward and ran his tongue between her breasts, up her chin, before forcing it between her lips. She gagged at the intrusion.

"Time for you to die." With one hand, he pinned her arms to the floor. He pulled back his other arm and she saw that he was holding a knife. She kicked and screamed. The silver blade descended and her heart stuttered; she closed her eyes and prepared for the pain.

But it never came. He paused and looked behind him.

She felt the floor vibrating from heavy footsteps before the sound of an ungodly roar shook her. Seconds later her attacker was lifted off her and thrown into the wall. He fell to the floor covered in splinters, drywall, and plaster. Meryn looked up and her eyes couldn't make sense of what she saw. It was a creature unlike anything she had ever seen before.

Rounded ears, brown fur, short snout, all on a humanoid-shaped head. It had an abnormally long torso and arms that extended nearly to the floor. It was wearing what used to be a pair of pants, which on this creature looked like frayed shorts. Even crouching low, shoulders hunched forward, it was nearly nine feet tall. If they weren't in the foyer with its cathedral ceilings, the creature's head would be scraping the ceiling. At the end of his multi-digit fingers, long claws were extended and swiping at the faintly glowing attacker. Each strike resulted in ripped flesh and broken bones.

She didn't know when it registered that what she was looking at was Aiden, but suddenly she knew. This creature was her mate and he was pissed! Only when the intruder stopped twitching did Aiden step back. All of the Alpha Unit and Aiden's family watched from the door. Aiden sniffed the air and walked over to her. When he nuzzled her hair, she yelped. When his tongue began to retrace the path that the attacker's had taken she pushed him away.

“Don't lick me! Eww!” She pushed at his hulking form. He snarled at her and she froze.

“I *know* you aren't snarling at me!” she yelled, reaching up to wag a finger in his face. The snarling stopped almost immediately. He lifted her up and nipped at her neck. She relaxed in his arms.

“She didn't even flinch,” Colton sounded impressed.

Meryn turned to him and noticed how high up she was. “This is great! Is this what you tall people see every day?”

Aiden gripped her as his body began to shift and shrink. After a few moments he was back to his normal human self.

“Thank the Gods you are okay!” He buried his face in her hair.

"Thanks to you."

He shook his head. "Thanks to a sprite named Felix. He made himself known to Darian and told us what happened."

Felix appeared hovering close to her head. She lifted her hair and he dove under for cover. Darian stared in amazement.

"When were you going to tell us you had a sprite?" he asked.

Meryn shrugged. "It's been a long day."

Gavriel and Colton walked over to what was left of the body of the attacker. It was still barely visible except for the faint glow.

"Keelan, is this a spell?" Gavriel asked.

Keelan shook his head. "None that I have ever seen."

"It is a *shikigami,* a servant of mine. It made the assailant visible." Ryuu sat up and rubbed the back of his head. He rolled to his knees before placing both hands on the floor in front of him and bowing low, touching his forehead to his fingers.

"*Denka*, I failed to keep you safe. Though it will cost me my life, you are free to sever the bond that ties us and proffer for a new squire."

"Oh Ryuu, get up, please. Your...whatever it was... made this guy visible so I could shoot him and Aiden could fight him. It's not your fault he attacked you from behind." Meryn couldn't stand to see such a proud man on his knees.

Ryuu stood and bowed fully at the waist. "I swear this won't happen again," he vowed.

"I'll forgive you even if it does. What's a *shikigami*?" she asked.

"They are trained spirits I have summoned," he explained. Meryn was impressed.

"They came in handy tonight. Could you make us some tea? I know I'll need a cup to calm down."

He bowed low again and immediately left for the kitchen.

"Good man there," Darian observed.

"He's the best." Meryn looked down at her would-be attacker.

"What's around his neck?"

The men looked down. Aiden set her down and walked over. "What do you see?"

Meryn pointed to the tiny sphere hanging from a cord around the dead man's neck.

"Meryn, I don't see anything." Aiden turned to her in confusion.

"It's right there!" she pointed again. This time Adelaide and Byron came over to look.

"Meryn, I don't see anything either," Byron told her.

Meryn walked over to the body and she was about to lean forward when Aiden grabbed her arm. She let out a screech and swatted at his hand.

"Don't *do* that! Are you trying to give me a heart attack? You don't just grab someone's arm when they are about to bend over a dead body!" Meryn clutched at her chest, trying to slow her breathing.

"I don't want you near him," Aiden bristled.

"Aiden, his brains are on the foyer floor, I'm pretty sure that is a universally accepted indicator that a person is dead."

"Fine, but be careful," he groused.

She knelt down and pulled on the cord until it snapped. Once the necklace was no longer around the body's neck it became completely visible and the faint green glow disappeared.

She held it out. "An invisibility spell?"

Keelan shook his head. "Not like any I have ever seen."

Meryn stood when the foulest odor she and ever smelled hit her in the face.

Gagging, she turned her head. “What in the hell is that smell?”

“That is what a feral normally smells like. It makes tracking them easy. The smell is a by-product of losing your soul. You begin to rot from the inside out. It's a bit unpleasant,” Aiden explained.

“A bit unpleasant? My eyes are watering. It smells like Cheetos. Cheetos and hot ass!” Meryn covered her nose with her hand. “Agggh! It's so strong I can taste it!” Meryn wiped her tongue on her sleeve.

Colton stared at her like she was a genius. “How come we never described it like that? It's perfect! Cheetos and hot ass, wait until Sascha hears this one.”

“Oh, Colton,” Adelaide sighed. Meryn noticed Adelaide was now standing on the front porch.

“I hate it when the enemy discovers something new,” Darian grumbled.

“Let me see it, baby.” Aiden held out his hand. When she went to hand it to him, she accidentally dropped it and it smashed on the foyer floor. Meryn turned to Aiden “I'm so sorry it...” She stopped mid-sentence when two small golden orbs floated upward through the ceiling.

Meryn watched them drift away. She turned to Aiden. “It's over, right?”

Aiden pulled her close. “Unfortunately, baby, I think it's just starting.”

“Are you sure you'll be okay living with the guys?” Aiden asked for the thousandth time.

“Yes. We need to be together and you need to be here. So that means *I* need to be here.” They were just finishing up moving her into the Alpha Unit estate from the main house.

"How did you get my mother to agree to it?" Aiden asked.

"I told her that her chances of becoming a grandmother would go up if we were sleeping together on a regular basis." She laughed at the lecherous look Aiden gave her.

"Plus we get Ryuu and his amazing cooking." Colton was practically skipping with excitement. The men from the other units groaned and started complaining that they didn't have a squire living with them. All six units had turned up to help her move. They started throwing empty boxes and packing paper at Colton, but he dodged them easily.

Meryn laughed when Sascha tripped Colton, sending him sprawling to the ground. She was about to join in the fun when she noticed two SUVs coming down the road. The men watched as they came to a stop. Elder Evreux climbed out of one SUV and Byron out of the other. The unit warriors formed a semi-circle around her and Aiden.

"There she is! I want her arrested! She illegally hacked into the city's mainframe and took command of the unit warriors, putting lives at risk!"

"For fuck's sake." Meryn rolled her eyes.

"She saved lives, René, and you know it. As it stands, of course she was forgiven for using our mainframe. But your complaint against Meryn commanding the unit warriors was overruled at council. You cannot bring a civil suit against her." Byron was nearly apoplectic.

"She is not the Unit Commander, Aiden is." Elder Evreux screeched.

Aiden rubbed his chin and nodded. "That is absolutely true, councilman. I am the Unit

Commander. I command every man standing here today and every unit warrior in the four pillar cities."

"See! See! He agrees with me," the Elder started.

Aiden held up a hand. "It is true that I am Unit Commander and command the men, but..." He paused and wrapped an arm around Meryn.

"But Meryn commands me. So if you follow true chain of command, she can rightfully give orders to the men," he explained.

Elder Evreux looked at the warriors. Sascha and a blond warrior that Meryn didn't recognize stepped forward.

"Men! Salute!" They barked. Moving as one solid entity the men stood to attention and saluted.

"Fine! Let the dignity of the unit warrior be degraded by this... this... *human*!" Elder Evreux turned on his heel and got back in his car. His wheels squealed as he peeled away.

"And good riddance! Jerk!" Meryn flipped the retreating car the bird.

Male laughter filled the air.

Meryn turned to Aiden. "Did you really mean it?" She clutched the front of his shirt and he pulled her close. She felt him breathe in the scent of her hair and kiss her neck gently. She would thank Fate every day for the gift of this man. He pulled back and kissed her senseless. When they broke apart he was smiling, a rare Aiden smile.

"Of course I did, you're *my* commander."

EPILOGUE

Oh, no, there she goes again. Why do you always take the stairs? Please, please! Watch where you are going. No! Do not turn around, you will...

Gavriel watched in horror as his mate tumbled down the stairs. Seconds later, she was back on her feet, grinning, and of course going back up the stairs again. When she got to the executive's office she was heading for, he watched her chat with the handsome man. Gavriel hissed. He couldn't hear what they were saying, but he didn't want any other man near her. The man indicated the filing cabinets near the window. Smiling and nodding, she carried the folders over to the cabinets. Unfortunately, she didn't see an extension cord, tripped, and went flying through the glass windowpane. The office she had been in was on the tenth floor.

Gasping, Gavriel woke from his dream and fought to breathe. Every night. Every, single, night he had to watch his mate reel from catastrophe to catastrophe like a drunken sailor at port. He could only pray that she would make it to Lycaonia alive, and in one piece.

Thank you for reading!

I hoped you enjoyed My Commander.

For a full listing of all my books please check out my website **http://alaneaalder.com**

I love to hear from readers so please feel free to follow me on Facebook , Twitter, Goodreads, AmazonCentral or Pinterest.

If you liked this book please let others know. Most people will trust a friend's opinion more than any ad. Also make sure to leave a review. I love to read what y'all have to say and find out what your favorite parts were. I always read your reviews.

Don't forget to sign up for my newsletters so you will receive regular updates concerning release information and promotions.

OTHER BOOKS BY ALANEA ALDER

Kindred of Arkadia Series

This series is about a shifter only town coming together as pack, pride, and sloth to defend the ones they love. Each book tells the story of a new couple or triad coming together and the hardships they face not only in their own Fated mating, but also in keeping their town safe against an unknown threat that looms just out of sight.

Book 1- Fate Knows Best
Book 2- Fated to Be Family
Book 3- Fated For Forever
Book 4- Fated Forgiveness
Book 5- Fated Healing
Book 6- Fated Surrender
Book 7- Gifts of Fate
Book 8- Fated Redemption

Bewitched and Bewildered Series

She's been Bewitched and he's Bewildered...

When the topic of grandchildren comes up during a weekly sewing circle, the matriarchs of the founding families seek out the witch Elder to scry to see if their sons' have mates. They are shocked to discover that many of their sons' mates are out in the world and are human!

Fearing that their future daughters-in-law will end up dead before being claimed and providing them with grandchildren to spoil, they convince their own mates that something must be done. After gathering all of the warriors together in a fake award ceremony, the witch Elder casts a spell to pull the warrior's mates to them, whether they want it or not.

Each book will revolve around a unit warrior member finding his destined mate, and the challenges and dangers they face in trying to uncover the reason why ferals are working together for the first time in their history to kill off members of the paranormal community.

Book 1- My Commander
Book 2- My Protector
Book 3- My Healer
Book 4- My Savior
Book 5- My Brother's Keeper